THE FRIENDS AND FOES OF ZENOBIA

CURATED BY DENISE TAPSCOTT

INDEPENDENTLY PUBLISHED

Contents

DEDICATION

I dedicate this collection to my mom.

Introduction

By Denise Tapscott

When creating characters for my first novel, Gypsy Kisses and Voodoo Wishes, I paid attention to certain details, such as the names of major characters. Each character had to have a name that meant something that relates to their personalities or represents something for the reader to gain insight about them.

When searching for a name for a voodoo priestess in New Orleans in the late 1800s, I first considered an old Southern belle name like Mama Adelaide or Miss Bessie. But they didn't seem to fit the regal, mysterious older woman I was trying to put together. When filtering through various websites for baby names, I somehow stumbled across the perfect answer for the woman I was constructing.

Zenobia.

It felt powerful every time I said it out loud. She was a real person who existed sometime between 240AD and 290 AD. There are many legends about Zenobia, queen of Palmyra (modern day Syria) who defeated Rome briefly, and was loved by her people. Thus, my character was transformed into a fantastic center piece for my novel.

After Gypsy Kisses and Voodoo Wishes was released, quite a few readers had lots of questions about Grandmother Zenobia. I was thrilled to share what I could about her without spoilers for future books. But then I began to think; How cool would it be to have short stories about Zenobia that I couldn't fit into the novels?

For example, why does she put out a sexy red shoe on a fence post when she's available to see clients? So, I excitedly wrote a handful of short stories about this immortal character, those who came across her path, and in some cases stories about what she does, and why.

Then I began to wonder what it would be like to see Zenobia through other people's perspectives. As a result, with the help of some absolutely phenomenal writers, I present to you, dear reader, The Friends and Foes of Zenobia. I hope you enjoy these amazing tales that span from ancient times to present day.

1

FRIENDS & FOES FOUND

BY LINDA D. ADDISON

Snake charmers & fire breathers,
the Djinn feeding off un-granted wishes,
terror in victim's eyes, reflecting a full moon,
warm blood flows, igniting spell
to draw demon to him, her one and only.

Tempestuous anger & sexy laughter,
the Djinn desiring, kissing the demon's
forehead, bodies wrapped in wings,
join to possess immortal Zenobia,
finding only loss & failure, snakes & dog bites.

Caribbean sea & bright yellow sun,
Zenobia's dog, Ahy, playing in sand
while loving *her* time in the ocean,
still remembering her stolen tribe,
leaving thieves screaming, bones cracked.

Sparkly indigo blue skin & iridescent scales,
Ahy petted by the mermaid pirate, Zenobia
recognized, honored, respected by Scarlette,
the day stranger, stranger by the moment,
few escape *The Reckoning*, she returns to the deep blue.

Deep booms of cannons & high-pitched screams,
the Negro infantry men fighting, hideous battle
endured. One house inherited, underlying stench
of decay, gunpowder, something's wrong. Bibles
don't clear the house, Zenobia & Ahy meet ghostly mists.

Making a lot of noise & a big mess to clean up,
Zenobia with a handful of shiny iron buttons,
3 buttons throw, one unruly ghost howls & sizzles,
spirits quarrel, not going into the light over a firearm,
choose peace over ton of iron, mound of salt on bones.

Steamed crawfish & southern deep-fried gator bites,
the Djinn returns hungry for revenge armed with
a rose barrette, Zenobia ruby red, high-heeled shoe
guarding, barrette offered to be blessed, wanting
her love. Vibrations filled barrette with joy, then darkness.

Sulfur & powdered snakeskin & graveyard dirt,
woke slumbering rose barrette, hungry for Zenobia,
gifting the woman with beauty, the man with darkness,

all return to the Purple door, un-welcomed, in agony,
she takes barrette, bathing all in holy water, healing love.

2

A Night Over Egypt

By Kirk A. Johnson

BEFORE BECOMING A WOMAN, she had dreamed of the joys of love—the discovery of warm touches and flirty smiles from wanton eyes; promises of a brave new world shared in the heat of the night. But when her menstrual flow came, those dreams had changed, and on the nights of her blood–cycle, her brave new world turned into visions of strange and dire things.

On some nights, she dreamed of Ahy, her dog, whimpering beside her, his nose inches from her head as lighting and smoke raced through the sky. Glooming grays and flashing whites shook overhead, and blood fell from the sky like rain during the flood season. On others, Ahy's ghostly coat glowed as he stood defiant to the yapping growls echoing from within the darkness.

And on others still, she heard the familiar sounds of the wild dogs or grim beasts ripping through their prey, tearing meat, or snapping bones. But no matter the night, she always heard a woman's voice bellow from a black sky with a sliver of madness flavoring her words.

"What are you?"
"What bore you?
"What loves you?"

ZENOBIA AWAKENED TO AHY'S wet nose, sniffing her face. His snout dug up into her cotton headwrap as she rubbed his solid, muscled neck. She had forgotten the details of her dream. However, she could still feel more so than see the images flash in and out of her mind's imagination like far-away lightning. She shuffled off of her pallet and offered a prayer to Sebiumeker, god of protection and fertility, while making her way over to a washbasin, and thanked her again for her uncle's servants replacing last night's water. She washed her face, clearing away the grogginess from her mind as Ahy hopped on her pallet and let out his characteristic basenji howl.

Zenobia quickly scolded him. She was having none of that. "Ahy! You know damn well you aren't allowed there!" Ahy immediately jumped off and scurried over to her. He nuzzled her feet and then stood on its hind legs. "What is the matter with you? Bad dream?"

Ahy huffed, dropped his rump to the ground, and then lowered his head with a frustrated sigh.

"What in the name of all that is holy are you pouting about?" Zenobia asked with her hands on her hips. As he did not answer, she shrugged and decided to take a walk to the river to pick the medicinal water herbs that only she could find. They'll come in handy for trade at the market. This early in the morning, crocodiles would be too far upriver to pose any threat to her, so it would be a relatively safe task. But that wasn't what worried her.

She had just had her fourth blood-cycle, and a year away from her twenties. As far as her family was concerned, it was well past time she entered society as wife and mother. A prospect she wasn't excited for. She had already seen from her aunts and uncles that it was a burden she wasn't keen on participating in.

After a warm bath, she replaced her blooded papyrus roll with a new one, and readied herself for the day. Flinging her shawl over her shoulders and linen wrap dress, she grabbed her basket and opened the door. Ahy, protective as always, dashed through and alertly scanned the trail leading to the river. Zenobia grinned. She doubted if any man could ever sneak up on Ahy. And she was grateful for that, if she was being honest with herself.

FROM A HILL CLOSE to the river, he watched her. A chill bristled up his back as he smelled her scent drift along the morning breeze. It was this strange, sweet fragrance that alerted him to her in the first place. It filled his nostrils with an aroma that aroused the promise of a mystic fulfillment that wrinkled his nose in wet delight. Drooling, he watched her gather reeds by the Nile's shoreline, wondering how delicious her blood would taste.

He sat in awe of the luster of her black-brown skin shining in the sun while her braided hair, tied up in a wrap, revealed the smooth, unearthly perfection of her round nose, full lips, and bright smile. He then noticed her little white dog. Its ears perked up. It sniffed in his direction, and he ducked further into the brush. He watched it back into her legs with a low chortle, and he ducked further past the bushes and down the other side of the dune as she turned and looked intently in his direction.

He held his breath for several heartbeats before peeking over the sandy ridge. He watched her soothe the beast before bending over to pluck a stubborn batch of reeds from the shallows. Soon after, she left.

Damn clan law, he thought to himself. *I must have her. She will be mine alone.* He would hunt for this one by himself. And within the city of Thebes, he knew he would find her. And feed.

FOR THE THIRD TIME, Zenobia glanced out the corner of her eye. And again, there he was, the handsome man with skin as dark as fertile soil that she had noticed entering the market behind her, and who was now only three stalls away. She wasn't sure if the man with an unpicked crown of hair was truly following her or just inspecting the fruits and vegetables from the produce booths along the market thoroughfare.

Pharaoh Ramses was known to hire spies to secretly scrutinize and report on the produce sold under his reign. His warring ways had made him suspicious of all within his domain. Especially when it came to those who weren't true-born Egyptians. It didn't help matters that many of the merchants glared at her or ignored her when she approached their wares. They just couldn't hide their jealousy of a foreign-born merchant finding favor with the ruling dynasty.

She wouldn't be surprised at the possibility of someone falsely reporting her to the Pharoah with the accusations of sorcery, and the possibility of this man being a royal spy was sent out to investigate her. She looked around, wondering where Ahy was until she recalled she had left him home. He would have been helpful if not for being banned from the market. That's what he gets for misbehaving around the meat stalls. He'd probably be a better thief if not for his pure white coat.

"Pardon. My dear. Are you still interested?"

Zenobia faced forward, remembering she had come to this stall out of curiosity. Awasi, a mature woman with a dark complexion and scarifications along her cheeks, smiled, presenting her with something in both hands. Awasi was a foreign merchant from the far west and known throughout the market to always be in possession of foreign trinkets and knick-knacks, curiosities that always titillated her customers. Its ashy-black pitted surface was as crude as a rock, but for its concave edge, which was smooth and flint sharp. Its wooden handle was well-crafted, but plain.

"What is this?" she asked as she gently ran her hand over the surface.

"This, my dear Zenobia, is a sickle made of a special metal." Awasi whispered this last part. "A merchant from the west brought me a few pieces. He called it iron. Yes, yes. I know it is an ugly thing, but he swears it's more durable and keeps a sharper edge than bronze.

"It doesn't look like much. Truly an ugly thing." Zenobia lifted it and found it to be lighter than she expected. Its coarse surface underscored its crude smelting.

"Oh no, my dear," the tool merchant said, gingerly pointing to the edge. "The blade is keener and harder than copper or even bronze. This will last longer... with some needed maintenance, of course."

"Of course." Zenobia said with a cocked eyebrow. Then something like a breeze blew past her ears. A whisper. As if a message on the wind, coming from the gods. "How much?" Zenobia finally asked.

"A twelfth deben of silver."

"Awasi! For this?" Zenobia turned it over again, and once more, as the urge to have it tickled her imagination. Her neck hairs stood on end, chilled by the mystery of what it could mean for her future. Reluctantly, Zenobia drew a piece of parchment from her leather gathering sack and gave it to the merchant. It was marked by her family's promissory insignia. Zenobia then took a quill from Awasi's table, dipped it into a bowl of ink, and drew the price in hieroglyphs with her name as signatory.

"Come to the Merchant Quarter and present this to the magistrate. There, you will be paid in full."

"Oh, thank you, my dear. The Diop name is certified throughout the quarter."

After Awasi placed the parchment in her pocket, she wrapped the iron sickle in camel leather and handed it back to Zenobia. As Zenobia turned away, she saw that the mysterious man hadn't left his post. He was still inspecting the dates a few stalls behind her when he made the mistake of slightly turning his head towards her and briefly caught her watching him before quickly turning away. Zenobia smiled to herself before deciding to try something mischievous.

Feigning to have forgotten something, she doubled back while he wasn't looking and slid up beside him as he picked through some dates. She noticed a strong, musky scent with hints of leather and cinnamon lingering in the air around him. But there was something else. Something she didn't recognize. He smelled of something seductive… delicious. She could feel it run from her nose through her chest, down into her belly, and nest warmly between her legs.

Her hand intentionally brushed up against his. He quickly turned and their eyes met. It felt like they were caught on a string, connecting the black pearls of their pupils pulled taunt, drawing each other in. He was about to speak until the tumultuous sounds of chariot wheels and howling shattered the moment.

"Zenobia! Zenobia!"

She turned towards a crowd of shoppers scattering to the side and into stalls, creating a wide berth for a chariot entering the marketplace thoroughfare. Ahy led the way like a messenger spirit announcing the coming of the Ra. And that's when she saw them. Two princely warriors with wild laughter standing tall in their chariot.

One wore a shiny blue robe, while the younger one wore a simple bronze breastplate covered in the dust of the road and the splendor of youth. Both wore perfectly styled afros and matching gold earrings. Her eyes brightened at the sight of one of the handsome young warriors waving to her.

"Memnon!" she cried. "By the gods of Nubia!"

The robed warrior gracefully sprang from the chariot and sprinted into her wide-opened arms like a child in summer. They embraced, crushing each other with grateful hugs and joyful kisses, paying no heed to the sweat and dust of the road.

"Zenobia, light of a thousand suns. Daughter of a hundred moons.

"I see your tongue is still not as agile as your limbs."

"I hoped you'd still be here."

"Of course," Zenobia sneered. "Just because His Majesty wages war in Canaan doesn't mean life must hold its breath."

"Is your uncle still here? I imagine he will make more than enough coin to supply Pharoah's military caravan."

"He is not. He travels with the army as an honored member of the logistics council. This season has been both lucrative for him and bothersome to me. Some locals have complained that we foreigners are taking all the best contracts. They claim we use sorcery for our unfair advantages."

Memnon gave her a suspicious look. "And have you?" he whispered.

Zenobia let out an exaggerated gasp as Ahy sniffed her hand. "But of course not! I swear it. You know I have no talent for such mysteries and mystics."

Ahy scoffed, turned his head, and growled, sensing something unnatural in the air. But Memnon, mistaking Ahy's reaction as a response to Zenobia's answer, bent down to one knee and smiled as he rubbed behind his ears. "Smart boy. You know more about her than she knows of herself. A coy smile with fluttering eyes is magic of a intimate sort."

Then the bronze-armored charioteer stepped out behind Memnon. He was as tall as Memnon, with broad shoulders and almost as thick armed as the prince. But to Zenobia's delight, she found him much more handsome.

"It is unseemly to accost children in the market, my prince." His voice was a deep bass string plucked from an oud—the voice of someone far older than his appearance.

"Zenobia. This barbarian from the Sudd is my comrade and great friend, Juba. He is as a brother to me as I am to you." Memnon slapped Juba on his shoulder. "More by affection than by womb."

Juba sucked his teeth at Memnon's playful jest before turning to Zenobia.

Zenobia caught the wariness in his eyes—an aloofness at odds with the smoothness of his deep blue-black skin. It stirred something in her that brightened her heart and lips. "From the Sudd. A dangerous land." She felt her mouth widen in a smile that was too broad.

"You have been there?" His vibrating bass melted through her skin.

"No. But many travelers have told me of their trials there. Those who have returned, of course." She felt stupid for stating the obvious with that goofy grin still in play.

Until a knowing smile cracked Juba's stoic demeanor, and her heart lifted again.

"The Sudd is not for fools or children."

"And which one am I?"

"Are you planning a trip to the Sudd?"

"No. But who knows where our paths may lead?"

Her heart sank when he glared at her. She quietly admonished herself for being too clever. Trying to hide her blush, Zenobia quickly turned back to Memnon, whose cocked eyebrow indicated that he saw right through her playful questions.

"So, where are you staying?" She finally asked.

"We found lodging amongst my countrymen within the Nubian Quarter. Luckily, I found enough room and board for my retinue until we leave. I assemble with the rest of my army in Memphis before we head to Pi-Ramesses."

"So many warriors outside of Ta-seti. Aren't you afraid it will raise alarm?"

"We carry a guarantee of passage by Pharoah Ramses himself. I convinced him that King Priam would be a valuable ally in Mesopotamia. And that my family still has strong ties with him. Pharoah thought it best to honor their request for aid. So, we both agreed that if he cannot aid Troy, I should. And keep their goodwill. Especially after he regains dominance over the Canaanites once again."

"I stand corrected. It seems your tongue has matured. At least enough to convince a pharaoh. So once again, you're off to play at war?"

Memnon let out a hardy laugh. "With the Achaeans this time."

Zenobia felt a chill shiver up her spine at the mention of the Achaeans. She had heard about the ferocity of the Myceneans and their allies, and she chose to put on a brave face for her friend. "They will surely piss themselves at your arrival."

"Yes. But before I depart, I had to see my little sister." His smile was slight.

"I would curse you to the high heavens and beyond if you didn't. Let me organize a proper celebration. In honor of your expedition and to implore the gods to show you favor."

Memnon looked at Juba and smiled. "Brilliant suggestion."

"Good." She began to shoo them away. "Now off you go. Gather your warriors and I shall make the arrangements. Seek out Ka-matef's estate. In the Nubian Quarter."

"I have coin—

"You have nothing to offer but your tales and presence. Now go."

As they spoke, the man with the smell of leather and cinnamon disappeared into the crowd to hide along the edges of the market, downwind from Ahy's nose. He watched her, following her supple curves as he ran his tongue across his pointed canines. He sniffed the air, delighting in her scent as all the other smells of the market gave way to her hidden sweetness. The two man-boys who had arrived in the chariot looked weak to him, but still dangerous.

He recognized them to be warriors of an ancient bloodline, bowmen of blessed talent. But it was her dog that gave him the most worry. There was an alertness about the beast that troubled him. He watched as it snuffled about the ground, its white coat glowing like a bringer of doom. That dog would need to be dealt with. As he schemed, he scratched at the furry bristles itching just under his skin.

LEAVING THE MARKET WITH Ahy, Zenobia quickly made her way to the Nubian Quarter to prepare for Memnon's send-off. Through her uncle's fellow merchant, Ka-matef, and delicate negotiations, she secured a private two-storied villa for Memnon and Juba on the outskirts of the Nubian Quarter. The proprietor provided her the most opulent chambers, with servants, fresh meats, and exquisite wine from Byblos, with just one stipulation: Ahy was kept outside the villa's walls.

Zenobia couldn't besmirch her uncle's good name, so her friend and protector had to stay outside. She had no time to go home and change, so the proprietor offered her a private room with clothes and perfumes she would need to fashion herself for the evening. Ahy, as clever as ever, found a way to sneak in without anyone noticing until he jumped on Zenobia's palette and inspected the leather-wrapped bundle Zenobia had tossed on the bed.

Ahy sniffed and pawed at it until he found the release string. He pulled at it until its tautness turned slack, and it unfurled before him. He stood on the bed and inspected this crude thing. To Ahy, it looked like a great, big claw with a concave edge. That's when Zenobia turned and caught him jumping up and down in excitement over her iron sickle.

"What? How did you get in here?" Zenobia cried.

Ahy stopped and stared at Zenobia before taking one good whiff and dashing out of her chamber.

"You are acting so strange as of late," she said to herself. She was about to chase after him until a flash of a dream image chilled her to the bone, and she forgot about Ahy and the sickle. All that was on her mind now was getting ready for tonight's festivity. *What better way to occupy my mind,* she thought to herself.

Before they arrived, Zenobia, with the aid of servants, bathed and perfumed, and slipped into her beaded kalasiris sheath dress, which hugged her curves and thighs like a second skin. That was for her. Over this, she donned a silk shawl of Tyrian purple, an expensive luxury she specifically requested. That bit of indulgence was to showoff for others.

The proprietor explained that he had purchased it from a Phoenician trader a season ago and was all too happy for Zenobia to wear it. She imagined she would wear it again soon as suitors became more abundant. It was her favorite color, and it made her feel like a freeborn woman with joy in her heart. And she finished off her look with a gold septum ring cause she knew it looked alluring.

THAT NIGHT, MEMNON AND Juba entered with all their warriors from the lodging houses within the neighborhood. It wasn't as many as Zenobia thought, but enough for a rowdy event. Nubian men and women lounged about from courtyard garden to the second-floor chamber: on cushions within the courtyard, in recess by the altars, and in alcove nooks, while musicians played oud lutes, camel skin tambourines, barrel-shaped drums, and tablas.

Music, laughter, and wine spilled into the moonlit night as platters of meat and fruit adorned tables and spaces on the floor. Zenobia even got the temple brothels of Bes, Beset, Taweret, Hathor, and Min to send their most delicious of acolytes. She was told by one of the older handmaids that these "entertainers" were a good mix of both the shy and the bold when it came to offering of sexual distractions—for all manner of appetites. After a long journey from Kerma to Thebes, Memnon had confided in her that they earned a night of boisterous comforts.

Outside, lonely Ahy rested on his forelimbs, huffing miserably to himself. He had just completed his third patrol around the mansion, and luckily for him, everyone was too busy laughing, drinking, and fucking to have seen him. After a few minutes of relaxing to the sounds of rowdy foreplay lulling him to sleep, he caught a whiff of a familiar scent. Immediately, his ears perked up, and a low growl vibrated from his throat.

It was the same smell from early this morning, and again in the market, filling the air around him. But it was stronger this time. Thicker. He left his post at the front of the entrance and sprinted out into the dimming dusk towards an outcropping of bushes crowning a small hill. The sky was turning blue, with its amber strip of light falling into the horizon by the time he surmounted its summit. And as the moon revealed itself in the sky, an incredibly large hyena sat there waiting for him. It glared at him and grinned with long dagger-like fangs shining wet with drool. Ahy's back bristled as he growled and bared his own sharp-as-death teeth.

Ahy charged. His heart raced with the wind, and the smell of violence filled his snout. But the beast did nothing. It sat there as still as a rock. Ahy, jaws opened wide, was a whisker away from its throat before the hyena moved. It was faster than Ahy could ever guess to react. It was a blur of speed and pain that slammed into Ahy's side. A weight like never before clamped down on the dog's neck as his fur became warm and wet. The air immediately grew thin, and night descended too fast over his eyes. *Where was the sunset? Where'd the moon go?*

OCCUPYING THE MAIN CHAMBER not far from the festivities, Zenobia, Juba, and Memnon reclined lazily on wool-covered lounge chairs with plush cushions stuffed with down. Servants brought sweetmeats and wine from the kitchen while the surrounding sounds of hot gasps, passionate moans, pounding flesh, and tambourines filled the air. Zenobia sat across from her two guests, trying to remain as composed and coy as possible. Except for the flirtatious glances she stole at Juba, as he playfully challenged Memnon's heroic tales to the soft beating of a drum.

"...three arrows struck the man in the same place, right where his armor missed covering his skin."

"Why do you keep adding arrows to that tale!!!" Juba laughed. "Two of those were mine. You were still stringing your bow when I cast my first shot!"

Zenobia noticed the wine had softened his scowl, and to her delight, his smile was just as bright as she had imagined.

"Scandalous liar! Your arrows were never so quick!" Memnon cried as his cup tipped this way and that, spilling some wine onto Juba's lap.

It was then that Zenobia freely gave in to her delight and erupted in a series of deep, full-throated belly laughs. She had missed Memnon's antics when it came to telling his battle tales: running around the room, arms flying, mimicking a man being chased by an overgrown hippo or his arrows, which was unbelievably ridiculous already. It was a joy to see a man of violent vigor, unbothered by the future, and clown about like a child filled with honey. Until she caught a whiff of something both strong and alluring, like the sweat of the heated arousal that surrounded her.

She wondered if there was a couple fucking too close to them until she recognized its faintly tinged scent from earlier in the day. It had hints of oud, leather... and cinnamon. She turned to find the man from the market standing before her with two chalices in hand. His kilt was tied at the waist with a piece of hide. He wore no sandals, but his physique was toned and youthful like Memnon and Juba. She blushed at his scent.

"Greetings, Lady Zenobia." The stranger's voice was like syrup pouring over her. "It is a pleasure to finally meet you."

"You know me?" For a stranger to reveal knowledge of her while she knew nothing of him would have alerted her to action, but Memnon and Juba suddenly went quiet. That assured her they were at full attention, just in case she required quick action.

"Who doesn't know the niece of one of Egypt's most successful foreign merchants? Possessed of both wealth and beauty—

"What? No mention of my wit?"

"But of course. All know the name of Zenobia Jalio." He offered her one of his chalices, and she gracefully accepted it with a slight nod.

"Come join us," Memnon invited, intentionally making space for the stranger between himself and Juba. The thought of two men she found "interesting" began to titillate her fantasies, filling her mind with kisses under the moon. But her auntie's words began to echo over in her mind. "A woman must remain demure. Be mindful of your actions when men are involved."

Zenobia noticed that the stranger instead sat cross-legged on the floor between herself and Memnon.

"Accepting gifts from strangers without a name is taboo in my land," Juba said as he placed his hand over the rim of Zenobia's cup.

"I am not so well-off to have a proper name," the stranger said. "But I am called Heru by my friends... and family."

"And what do your enemies call you?" Juba asked with a slight grin.

"I don't have enemies," Heru grinned back with a glint in his eye. "They don't live long enough to know it."

"Ha!" Memnon laughed. "Neither do mine! We make sure of that. Well, I do." He then nodded his head over at Juba. "This one shoots with his eyes closed."

As Juba turned to glare at Memnon's taunt, Zenobia flirtatiously moved her cup away from Juba's palm and raised it to Heru. "Praise and welcome to you for your kindness, Heru." She made sure to smile and flutter her eyelashes.

As they raised their cups in good cheer, Juba eyed Heru carefully. He noted the man's black stained fingernails and the ease with which he sat amongst them. He was too comfortable for his liking. And he was taking up too much time with Zenobia. To his surprise, that's what annoyed him the most.

Zenobia made sure to sip her wine slowly. Her uncle—and Memnon—had warned her to always keep her wits about when the wine flowed too freely as the night lengthened, especially when men were present. Men, especially warriors, lose themselves in such conditions, allowing their desires to rule their actions.

Sooner than expected, she was left alone with Juba and Heru. A man and woman, acolytes of Beset, had taken Memnon by the arms and eagerly took him to one of the second-floor rooms reserved just for him. He refused to put up a fight as they escorted him by his phallus.

"Lady Zenobia," Heru sidled up closer to her. "You are of marrying age, are you not? Where is your husband?"

"Husband? My uncle and I both agreed I am too valuable to be married off just yet. And I prefer to marry the man I choose." Zenobia noticed a slight parting of his lips as a woman's grunt of pleasure punctuated her words.

"That is good to know," Juba replied before catching himself. "I mean... I...

"He means if you were, we would have been bereft of your presence this evening." Heru winked. "Are you not married, Juba? A man of your prowess and skill."

The question took Juba by surprise. And he momentarily lost his composure once he noticed Zenobia lean in closer to him for his response. "I...I haven't had the time to court." Someone groaned in ecstasy from a nearby window.

"Is it time or courage that holds you at bay?" asked Heru as he took a sip.

Again, Juba found himself unable to respond. But to his surprise, Zenobia answered for him.

"Or perhaps you haven't met one who can turn your heart to more pleasing pursuits," Zenobia said, turning to her cup. She felt another chill run up her back—like when Memnon mentioned the Achaeans. The wine did little to ease the feeling that Memnon and Juba were destined for some ill-fated adventure.

AS THE NIGHT TURNED late, snores and dimming torches now filled the villa. Zenobia retired to her chambers, and Juba was left to sleep where he lounged. And in the stillness of the estate, Heru's primal instincts alerted him to act. He focused his mind, tamping down his desires and honing his senses to begin his hunt. A fight with any of these warriors would lead to too much bloodshed and awakening them to his existence would anger his clan. He had to stay a mystery to them.

Heru was extra cautious when passing Juba, sensing the warrior was a light sleeper. Careful not to awaken any of the young, sleeping revelers to his movements, he crept through the dark corridors. He stepped over outstretched arms and legs, gingerly placing his feet in spaces uncovered by relaxing muscles. Silently climbing the stairs, he picked up on Zenobia's scent and prowled to her second-floor room. Quietly, he slid open the door and found her still modestly dressed, to his surprise.

She was in her evening gown, laid out quietly on her palette of fleece and cotton. Compared to his strength, she weighed nothing, as light as a dove and he breathed a sigh of relief. The drug he mixed into her wine was the perfect dosage. He figured she'd be asleep long enough to take her far into the desert, away from human interference. Far enough away for him to have privacy or for anyone to hear her cries.

Binding her limbs, he hauled her over his shoulder and sprang straight out the window into the courtyard. He landed in between a two drunken bodies laid out under the stars, but the heavy snoring of the inebriated warriors put him at ease. Making his way to the front gates, he heard whimpering. Ahy limped out from the bushes and hissed at him. The dog was much stronger than he should be. He realized the beast was god-blessed, but he had no time to find out which god protected him or finish the job; so, he continued into the night with Zenobia in his arms.

ZENOBIA DREAMED DEEPLY THAT night, unbothered by the jostling of Heru's rush through the desert. She dreamed of darkness and thunder. Lightning branched across the sky with flashes of crimson bolts, shattering her vision with concussive blasts. In the distance, Zenobia saw a great box of fathomless black onyx. She had never seen so deep a blackness. It was like looking into a square void. And every time the sky flashed, she saw its immenseness silhouetted along a horizon that rolled beyond her vision.

"Finally. Your presence has been anticipated."

The voice was like a deep rumble of earth with the vibrating surge of godly power.

"Come and address me properly, child."

Zenobia's body stood still as the structure rushed towards her at a blinding speed, billowing her gown from its gust of wind. Then the world spun around and around as the structure abruptly stopped an arm's length from her unbending frame. She wrinkled her nose at the smell of sulfur and rot. And the hairs on the back of her neck stood erect.

"You have been watched. And desired."

Zenobia could hear herself say, "Desired?"

And with a flush of red lightning, she saw a shadow fall over her as quick as a thought. A shadow with great ears rose to the black heavens as glowing red eyes peered down at her, searching—caressing her soul—with an ethereal touch that forced her to quiver with an unknown sensation. A warm yet unfamiliar coziness that caused a sensual moan to escape her full lips.

"Oh, wicked mortal, I see your womanhood has come full blossom. But still, you are not ready to experience what I have to offer."

"You offer...," she gasped. Her heart thumped with a heavy pounding that threatened to burst from her chest.

The scent of musk and juniper filled her mind, but no one could smell in a dream.

"I will not abandon you, my love. We have a future together that must be...consummated."

ZENOBIA SUDDENLY AWAKENED, STARTLING Heru, who was caressing her face. Bright eyed and aware, she saw Heru eyes glow from the new moon's reflection. He was as beautiful as when they first met, even more so with those eyes, and the small fangs peeking out from under his full lips.

"Heru?"

A low guttural sound vibrated from his throat as he crept away from Zenobia, while admonishing himself for untying her too soon. "You rise earlier than expected. The drug was meant to keep you asleep, but alive."

"For what purpose?" She smelled the sweat from his skin and noted a brutal tension in his movements. So much like a stalking beast searching for a place to sink his teeth into. Again, Zenobia was drawn to his eyes, and she felt his hunger beam from that amber-bright stare.

"I've stalked you for what seems like an eternity." A string of saliva glistened in the moonlight. "Your skin and hair revealed the lush juice of your body in the wind. A want brought me to you."

Slowly, Zenobia sat up, bringing her knees up to her chest. She felt the ground with her feet, taking note of the dead, cold grass. She noticed the brush and shrubbery that surrounded her. She was in a hiding place. A secret little clearing encircled by thorn brush, hiding them from the cold open savannah; a killing place. That's when she saw how bright the moon shined. She felt Heru move closer and turned quickly to stop him.

"Heru! What do you plan? If my brother finds you, he will show no mercy."

"Mercy? The strength of mortals is more hubris than truth. Out here, only I can grant mercy." Heru dropped to his hands and knees, grunting in pain and pleasure as bones cracked underneath his muscular skin. He arched the full length of his torso as spotted fur sprouted from his pores. Bloody claws replaced his dirty nails, and paws replaced fondling fingers. And with a snarl, he spat blood from his mouth, before revealing teeth growing long and sharp with each passing moment. Finally, a boldly spotted great hyena stood in place of Heru under shafts of blue moonlight.

Zenobia wanted to scream. She wanted to yell out against the madness of the night's revelation. But instead, she just stood up and covered her eyes with both hands. Tears rolled down her cheeks as she slowly stepped back.

"Where are you going?" Heru bared his teeth in a grim smile and slowly prowled towards her. His head hung low, but his eyes stayed focused on Zenobia's paralyzed form. "If you run, I will be quick to chase."

She could see saliva drool from the corners of his mouth, and a far greater urge ran up her spine.

A voice whispered in her ear, "Run, my love. This is my land."

Without a second thought, Zenobia quickly turned and dashed for the bushes, forcing her way through the brush and bramble. She did not notice that the branches and thorns that would have torn her shawl and dress or scare her skin move to the side. She ran with such ease that when she broke into the open plains, she just kept moving.

And as he threatened, Heru instantly gave chase. But to his surprise, he lost her as soon as she entered the surrounding bush. He could hear her fearful breathing and frantic footfalls, but could not see her. To him, even the moon seemed to dim overhead to darken his vision. It was as if the gods had intervened with the moon and earth to conspire against him. But as soon as he broke through the thorns and wild brush, he sprinted straight for the solitary figure in the distance.

Zenobia heard him coming, as his heavy breathing filled her ears in the chill night air. She could feel him draw closer and closer as the weight of her impending death became too much for her to bear, she gasped in despair and fell to the cold ground. Heru growled as he prowled over to her feet. He licked her toes. She shivered, unable to scream. Puffs of steam blew from his fanged maw as he moved in and ran his tongue up past her knees towards her quivering thighs.

Until arrows snapped against Heru's brow and the rumble of chariot wheels broke the silence of the frosty night air. Heru backed away as Zenobia turned her head to the commotion. Through the light of the moon and staff-held torches, she saw Memnon with bow in hand and Juba lashing the reins.

Leading them was Ahy, whose white coat glowed like the god of vengeance himself. Zenobia ran to Ahy, but didn't realize he had something gripped between his teeth. She grabbed and hugged Ahy as Memnon sprang from his carriage, releasing more arrows at Heru, while Juba pulled on the reins and halted before her.

"Zenobia! Get in!" Juba called before jumping out of the chariot with his sword and shield. But Zenobia was too concerned with Ahy's comforting heartbeats to hear him.

Heru, unfazed, attacked. Juba, quick as lightning, pushed Memnon out of the way and met Heru's savagery with his shield braced to take the weight. They collided under the shining moon, Heru's claws puncturing the hide shield like a lion of the Nubian highlands.

Arrows broke and splintered against Heru's hide as Memnon circled them, releasing arrows at blinding speed. Arrows spent, he ran back to the chariot and snatched his own weapons before dashing back to the fray, past a sobbing Zenobia. And with spear and shield, he battered Heru off Juba, driving him back.

"What sort of beast is this that my arrows were too weak to pierce it? Juba! Let us see how it holds up against bronze and muscle."

Both sword and spear lashed out against Heru's hide. A swirl of dirt clouded the battle as they pounced and charged each other in the chaotic dance of violence, with the sting of bronze doing little to dull Heru's barbarity. Finally, Zenobia noticed Ahy had something in his mouth. Breaking free of Zenobia's embrace, he placed it on the floor and rushed into the fight to join the warriors' dance while doing all he could to keep a safe distance from Heru's deadly jaws.

Zenobia quickly picked up the bundle and discovered it was Awasi's iron sickle.

"You have the means to save them. Fear not in using it." A voice in her head whispered. She recognized the smell of rot and sulfur and the sounds from her dream of the black box. "Rise!"

A command as loud and hot as the sun drove her to her feet, and she moved quickly with the iron sickle's handle turning warm in her hand. Before anyone realized what had happened, Zenobia ducked in between the four combatants and ripped open Heru's gut. The great hyena yowled in pain and jumped back, distancing itself from the fray. Memnon and Juba paused as Ahy gnashed its teeth at Heru's bloody trail. They watched in awe as Zenobia chased after the hyena and delivered two more wounding rips into its back and arm.

"Impossible!" Heru howled.

They stopped as they heard the hyena speak.

"What god protects you so? Name your protector, so I may curse you before I breathe my last."

Zenobia paid him no heed as she took her iron sickle and ripped into his neck and shoulder. Blood rained from Heru's neck like a geyser before turning into a steady flow of black in the moon's pale light.

They all watched as the hyena momentarily transformed into Heru, holding the gash in his belly and trying to keep his guts from spilling into the dirt. He tried to speak but coughed up more blood before falling, and turning back into a great hyena in its final exhale.

"By the gods," Juba blurted out.

Memnon gingerly poked the beast with the butt of his spear. "If this is what to expect from your future suitors, you may need to reconsider marriage."

Juba approached Zenobia and nudged her. She looked up at him and sighed in exhaustion.

A cacophony of yelps and cackles broke the shared silence as hyena laughs encircled them before turning into growls and barks. Ahy, Memnon, and Juba formed a circle around Zenobia as the moon glowed brighter overhead.

Shafts of pale moonlight illuminated the savanna plains to reveal amber eyes and moving shadows surrounding them.

And as the moon-glow widened, hyenas, as big as Heru, filled their vision. Teeth gnashed and chopped as high-pitched cackles fill their ears. Until a monstrous roar silenced the feral horde, and a tall woman walked into the moonlit arena towards Zenobia. Her skin shined with the brown-black luster of polished ebony as her hair was coiffured in a halo of kinky hair. She carried the body of the disemboweled Heru as if he were but an empty pelt.

"Which one of you has murdered my child?" The woman asked.

Juba pointed his blade at her. "It was my sword—

"Lies!" the woman interrupted. "No mortal weapon can do such a thing to my kin."

Zenobia stepped forward. "Not true. This did." And she brandished the iron sickle, moving closer to the woman.

"Someone has given her the secret to our death," a voice half-growled from the shadowy ring.

The woman hissed it silent, before turning back to Zenobia and tossing Heru's lifeless corpse at Zenobia's feet. "Only one of you has the weapon. While we are many." She said as she spread out her arms and the shadows moved into the light.

Memnon counted almost thirty large hyenas, the largest he had ever seen. Juba also counted and squeezed the handle of his sword tighter with every new accounting of their number. Ahy's growls grew louder as his fur bristled with hate.

The woman moved back a step. "What hope do so few have against so many?"

Then, there was a flash from above, as if the moon itself had exploded into the sun and white light blinded the land. All but Zenobia had lost all sight. Only Zenobia could see a figure glowing as white as Ahy's coat stand between the hyena woman and herself. She couldn't see its face, but recognized the symbol of a crescent moon under a full lunar disk.

The hyena-woman growled, "Khonsu. This is not your affair."

"It is not," Khonsu admitted. "But one who has affection for this one has requested my intervention."

Zenobia noticed a bright finger point in her direction. "Me?"

"Yes, you. You have a secret admirer for your attention," Khonsu said before addressing the hyena-woman again. "And he has reminded me of your depredations. Your devouring of travelers and infringements on my roads. You were given the power to become human in a time of desperation. You have been greedy with that gift. I've been neglectful."

She screamed at the god as her body contorted and ripped with fur sprouting from her flesh. Her ears and teeth grew out of its human proportions with cracking bones and growing claws.

"You will remember the end of my silence." Khonsu said, his hand raised high. "I curse you and your kin to know the moon's kiss. When I fill the night sky, you will submit to your human disguise. Unable to turn, you will be both mortal and mad in my presence."

And with a flash, the night was restored, but for the pale sight of the moon.

Screams and howls filled their ears. With their vision restored, Zenobia, Juba, and Memnon watched in horror as the surrounding clan of monstrous hyenas and the hyena-woman fell to the ground, curling and shrinking as they painfully turned into their human forms. Many of them cried out to the moon.

"Damn you!"

"Nooo!"

"Fuq you, Khonsu!"

While the hyena-woman got up, shaking with rage, glared in hate towards Zenobia and her friends. "Kill. Them. All!"

Ahy, with a sprint and pounce, tore out the throat of the nearest were-hyena, and dashed back to Memnon and Zenobia, with his tail wagging joyfully.

"Juba! We have the advantage!" Memnon wasted no time. He speared the man closest to him, driving its bronze tip through him and out the back. They all stared at him in horror, realizing that they were no longer immune to the killing blows of mortal warriors. And Memnon pounced on them with bloody glee. Juba charged into the nearest group, swinging his sword left and right, painting his sword with hot blood.

Suddenly, Zenobia felt her body tingle with excitement at the night's carnage with an energy unknown to her, filling her heart as blood ran down her thighs, and the need for battle burning from within. She and Ahy ran to the hyena-woman, her sickle ripping a road of crimson through all who came near with her iron claw, matching the mad ferocity of her seasoned companions.

To see her children slaughtered with such reckless abandon brought such terror to the hyena-woman that she bawled with an agony no human could ever duplicate. Zenobia stopped dead in her tracks.

"Run! The gods protect them!" the hyena-woman screamed to her human clansmen. "We are unarmed and unprotected! Again, they have power over us. Back into the desert or they will slaughter us all."

Quickly, the chaotic violence ended in a route as the survivors disappeared into the night with their dead, leaving behind the blessed.

The hyena-woman pointed at Zenobia. "You would have gone blood-mad if we continued this."

"And you would be extinct," countered Zenobia.

"I am Bahiti of the Fangs. The First Bone-Cracker. And we will meet again, Consort of Chaos. Bride of the Destroyer."

"My name is Zenobia—

"Zenobia, Consort of Chaos. Bride of the Destroyer. We will meet again," she said before fading into the night.

Ahy was licking his chops by Zenobia's feet as she turned to see Memnon and Juba staring out in the distance. She couldn't help but feel a heavy sadness about their fates. She slumped to her knees as Memnon and Juba approached her.

"Sister. Are you injured?" Memnon said, noticing her bloodstained thighs.

"No. Just tired."

"You will have to explain to us what she meant by Consort of Chaos."

Zenobia ignored Memnon and stared up at Juba. The title felt too ominous to repeat. She was unsure of everything she had felt and experienced. There was a warm feeling that things could be good with Juba, but it was as a fleeting fantasy. She knew to have such a powerful enemy at such a young age was an ill omen that would foretell a strange, fearful future for her.

3

MOCHA AND MARID

BY DENISE TAPSCOTT

Morocco, 1548

MARID SCRUNCHED HIS BROAD, freckled nose at the sun as it rose in a pink and red Moroccan sky. The temps were already rising at the largest open–air market in Marrakech, and it was nowhere close to noon. Off in the distance, a few men argued with one another about the borders of their stalls while others hammered away at creating shade for their spaces. With not even a hint of a breeze, it would be another scorching day, which meant fewer visitors and fewer sales. Marid had very specific, essential tasks to achieve before nightfall, and with not many visitors, he had no idea what to do to fulfill them.

Marid arranged and rearranged statues in his stall. Locals grunted as they passed by. Some neighboring vendors mumbled under their breath and shook their heads disapprovingly. Women with small children fearfully clutched personal good luck charms and looked at the sky when he nodded in their direction. Most people gave him the side-eye and minded their own business.

It didn't bother him one bit. In fact, he savored the negative energy. As a Djinn from the Red Coast territory, he fed off people's energy. If anything, their attitudes toward him were entertaining. None of the Moroccan humans dared challenge him. They didn't know about his true form, but just like a scorpion hiding in a shady spot, they instinctively knew not to cross him.

His mindless organizing was disrupted when a heavy-set, pale-skinned couple entered his shop. They shuffled in, wearing heavy robes with poufy sleeves. Their faces were already bright red from walking around in the morning sunlight.

"Welcome to Marid's Magnificent Merchandise!" he said and bowed. "I am Marid."

"Grazie," the wife said while fanning herself. The husband frowned while his wife began picking through a pile of dusty Persian rugs.

"I detect an interesting accent. What brings you to Marrakech?" Marid asked.

"Signor Riccoboni and I are from Italy. We have been traveling for a while because he promised me an adventure. So far, I'm not very impressed with the Middle East. Everything is dirty."

"Sandy," corrected her husband. "They prefer that you say sandy, even if it is filthy."

Marid found himself staring at the foreigners in his shop. The tasks he needed to carry out might be easier to achieve than expected. The day was turning out better than he hoped for.

"Please forgive me, but you said 'travel'? So, you just move about, place to place, for leisure?"

The couple snickered.

"The Riccoboni family creates and sells art. It affords us many luxuries," Signora Riccoboni said and shrugged. "I'm not impressed with any of these things either. We should go. I'm thirsty."

The couple turned to leave. Marid jumped between them and the exit.

"What if I could promise you a special moment in your lives befitting the Shah of Arabia?"

Signora paused, resting her hands on her hips. Marid held up one finger. The agitated couple watched him run to a corner and return within the blink of an eye with a pitcher of ice-cold lemonade and two glasses.

"Go on," Signor Riccoboni said.

A crocodile smile spread across Marid's face as he poured drinks.

"I could arrange for you to relax in a lavish palace, wear the finest silk linens in the land and eat to your heart's content at an incredible feast. That is, if you truly want a great Moroccan adventure."

The wife excitedly turned to her husband.

"How much would this cost?" The husband said before his wife could respond to Marid.

"The price for me to grant your wishes is simple. All I need is something small, yet personal to you both."

The couple was puzzled.

"How about your wedding rings? Clearly, you lovers have been married for a while. Give me your outdated bands. I know a very talented jeweler not too far from here. You could buy newer, upscale rings. At the palace, we could have a small ceremony where you could renew your vows. It would be very romantic."

"I want to do this!" Signora Riccoboni exclaimed as she tugged at her wedding band.

"I promise that you will have the time of your lives," he said.

"Fine, anything for my wife," Signor Riccoboni said as he reluctantly removed his ring from his chubby fingers and plopped it in Marid's boney hand.

"No, no. Keep them for now. I will collect them at the right time," Marid said and handed the rings back.

"Rest assured, your wish is my command," Marid said.

IT WAS MID-AFTERNOON WHEN the couple stood at the entrance of a small, opulent palace. They were taken in by the view overlooking the outdoor market and acres upon acres of palm trees in the distance.

"I invite you to enjoy yourselves as much as your souls can bear. To the left, you will find sleeping quarters with closets filled with robes for you to try. The pool is heated, should you want to swim. Light refreshments await you in the shaded patio. The feast will begin at sunset."

"Grazie Marid, for bringing us this adventure. You people are more reliable than we expected," Signora said.

"Or maybe he's just different from the other Arabs."

"You have no idea, Signor and Signora Riccoboni."

Once they settled in, the boorish Italian couple comfortably sat at each end of a long table covered with bowls of fruit and plates of steamed meat.

"We changed our minds. We will pay you with coins, rather than surrendering our jewelry," Signora said bluntly.

"I don't want your coins. We agreed upon the rings. Look at all I have provided for you," Marid said.

"My wife has spoken," Signor said. Signora raised a glass of wine to her husband.

In the blink of an eye, Marid stood behind her, grabbed a handful of her thin blonde hair, and tilted her chin back. He slit her throat, ear to ear, with an engraved steel dagger. The knife was so sharp that cutting through her fair skin was like slicing butter.

Blood quickly poured from her neck. Marid casually slid a clay pot over and tipped the woman forward to collect her blood while Signor yelled and cried until his face turned purple. After several attempts, Marid chopped off Signora's ring finger and took her wedding ring. Once he slipped her ring on one of his fingers, he turned his attention to her dumbstruck husband.

The look of horror in his eyes tickled Marid! He chased the stocky man across a slippery marble floor, right into the pool. The man was the size of a baby hippo. Marid pounced onto his back and hooked his arm around Signor's neck, making sure his prey couldn't tuck his chin down to protect himself. Drowning him took a lot of energy.

Eventually, his victim passed out and Marid shoved the body in the water. He yelled as he stomped on the man's chest in the pool until he felt the ribcage give way. He dragged his body out of the pool, chopped at the fat hand until the ring was free.

To Marid's surprise, the harder part was dragging each of their chunky bodies into a sitting room at the back of the palace. Once he was sure the couple was dead, (*and why wouldn't they be?*) he admired the rings on his fingers. Energy surged through his body. He would need as much energy as possible for what was ahead.

NIGHT HAD FALLEN AND Marid stood on the balcony overlooking the Marrakech Night Market. Unlike the morning, it buzzed with energy. Moroccan humans were out in droves, buying and selling everything from fresh spices and fruit to thick woven rugs and stubborn camels. People danced in the warm air to the sounds of stringed instruments and rhythmic tambourines. Snake charmers and fire breathers mesmerized nervous audiences.

He massaged his hands and admired his newly acquired shiny gold wedding bands on his slender fingers. The residual energy from his victims was strong. It's true that he kept his word; he delivered them the most exciting time of their lives! He bet that it was just shorter than they could imagine. The energy from their deaths still vibrated in the air.

He visualized over and over in his mind the next step, a crucial part of his master plan. Turning his attention upward, his almond-shaped eyes searched the starry night sky. When he saw a thin sliver of the moon, he hoped his timing was perfect. It had to be. The love of his life, Mocha, despised the light of a full moon. It would be best that she was in a good mood when he summoned her.

MARID'S HANDS TREMBLED AS he lit a thin black beeswax taper candle. It was the last of nine candles, melting on glass plates in a circle drawn with powdered eggshells on a black and blue Persian rug. Wringing his hands, he double and triple checked his items. The nine sigils that the candles illuminated were sloppy but drawn with intensity to empower his summoning spell. Outside the circle, the food from the feast was carefully arranged. Hand carved wooden bowls were filled with her favorites.

Handpicked plump grapes, slices of sweet persimmons and dates drizzled in honey sat to his left. Platters of sweet treats and savory grilled meats, along with cases of red wine, sat to his right. In the center of the circle, a well-worn beaded necklace with nine small gold coins attached by red thread rested upon a golden square cushion. Many of the beads were cracked and at least a third of the chipped coins barely clung to the necklace.

Marid dropped to his knees to start the ritual. He reminded himself that this was what he chose. It's where he wanted to be and who he wanted to be with. He worked hard, searching far and wide across the Sahara to make this moment happen.

He'd delt with many demons. Some were shifty and weak; some were loud and gargantuan. There were even some that were small, silent killers. Mocha was on another level. The thought of being with her both frightened and excited him. During their last tryst in Madagascar, she howled and threw his offerings back at him before they had insane, animalistic sex. What mood would she be in when she answered his summons? Would he be enough for her this time?

Marid never found the right words to describe her. She was challenging and playful, murderous, and sensual. Mocha was different than any entity he had ever come across in his lifetime. Her uniqueness drew him in like a moth to a flame.

Once the butterflies in his stomach subsided, he poured Signora Riccoboni's blood from the clay pot to a brass bowl filled with dusty herbs and broken cat bones. Extending his arms, held his hands palms up and chanted his spell as loudly as he could. Flames flickered with each word that passed through his thick lips. His black and brown dreadlocks blew across his face as wind howled around the room. Nearing the end of his incantation, the air around him vibrated.

A slender, olive-skinned woman scantily draped in soft linens materialized before him. Her head was adorned with black braids interwoven with gold strands. Marid marveled as she posed and gracefully placed her hand on her hip. She wore the beaded necklace he presented with his offerings.

"Who requests my presence?" she said in a silky voice. Before Marid could respond, she faded. He grabbed matches, and re-lit one of the candles that the wind had extinguished.

"Who requests my presence?" she asked again as she reappeared. Her arms were folded, and she tapped her bare foot. "I cannot see or hear who you are. If you don't have the courage to summon me from the darkness, stop bothering me."

"It is I, Marid," he said. His shaky voice betrayed his feelings. Her image flickered a few times, and she vanished before he could say another word.

"WHO SUMMONS ME!" she boomed. The marble floor vibrated. Her image was translucent. Only the necklace with its shiny coins was solid. Marid stood his ground. He waited years to be near her. To strengthen the connection, he sprinkled blood on the pillow.

"Estremochis, magnificent ruler, ninth gate keeper in hell, I, Marid, direct descendant of the seventy-two demons commanded by King Saul himself, summon you," he announced.

"Marid, my nefarious, roguish djinn?" she asked. A sly smirk spread across her faint pink lips.

"The one and only," he said and bowed.

Mocha's form appeared solid. She flashed him a mischievous smile and played with a long, thick braid. He approached her with a chalice brimming with red wine and a platter of Baklava.

"Sweets for my sweet Mocha," he beamed.

"You remembered!" she said. Reaching out for the flaky cinnamon treat, the coins around her neck shifted. Her arm flickered and disappeared. She bellowed in anger.

"Why can't I materialize?"

Marid checked and re-checked everything. The candles were lit, fresh blood was properly spilled, the food offerings were flawless. Even the day of the week was right. He had the energy of twenty men! Everything was perfect. But when she moved...

"Stand still," he said.

"You think that you, a pesky genie, can order me around?"

Whatever nervousness Marid felt was long gone.

"Mocha." He stepped right up to her, mere inches away, and placed his hands on her soft shoulders. Pitch black eyes stared back at him as she grumbled. He caressed her soft skin. He lifted the necklace with one finger and her body flickered.

"The problem is your necklace," he said. "It's too old, and the current host is too weak to channel your energy."

Mocha frowned.

"It's my favorite artifact. I've been bound to it for centuries," she pouted.

"It's my favorite too, but you don't take care of it. When you leave me, you drop it some random place and challenge me to find it. Over the years, it has worn out. You must let the antique go. I will find you a new artifact and a new host. I swear."

There was an uncomfortable silence between them.

"In the meantime, might I make a suggestion?" he said.

"What!" she spat.

"Spend time with me in your true form. Draw energy from me if you need to. I can always replenish later."

"My true form? Never!" Mocha poked a slender finger at Marid, shifting her weight, and the necklace moved. The flickering infuriated her.

"Sweetheart. I love you, all of you. Not just the current form you take. Your tempestuous anger, your sexy laugh, your vast knowledge, and playful spirit draw me to you. I yearn year after year to wrap my arms around you and hear your stories about hell. Trust me."

"This is ridiculous. Why am I wasting my time with a lowly djinn? By the way, most demons, djinn, succubi etc. are all descendants of the seventy-two demons commanded by King Saul. There is an exceptionally long list, and your line is towards the bottom. Everybody knows that."

Marid stood perfectly still and pondered what his next words would be. He blinked three times and spoke.

"Estremochis, if you do not love me as I love you, I will break the spell and end this now. If you do not believe in our connection, I will never summon you again."

His heart pounded in his chest. He breathed through his nose, hoping not to be overwhelmed by whatever the demon would spout next. Sure, he could continue to walk the earth in search of objects to sell to humans and draw energy from them as he "granted" wishes. But would he want to? If she rejected him, he would go into hibernation and would probably stay buried in scalding hot desert sands or concealed in a damp, dark rainforest until he was over his heartbreak. It would take centuries to recover from that sort of pain.

"You really do love me, don't you, Marid?" she asked.

"I do," he said.

Mocha raised her hands in surrender.

"I need fresh blood to transform. That other blood won't work."

"I can provide it myself, while I'm in a human form." Marid found a knife and slashed the palm of his hand. She knelt before him. He dripped his blood on the top of Mocha's head and gently removed the necklace.

Her linen dress fell the floor. Smoke blew around, disturbing all but one candle. When the air cleared, a beast with dark grey leathery skin stood before Marid. Dark red tattoos swirled in its flesh, head to toe. It had four horns with smoldering tips. A tail, six feet long, with a menacing scorpion stinger at the end swished like a cat's tail when it waited to pounce. Estremochis lunged forward with black claws and bared razor-sharp teeth.

"My Mocha."

Her features softened, and claws retracted. Marid leaned forward, placed his hands on her face, and kissed the demon's forehead. There was a blinding burst of light. Marid struggled to regain his vision. Blinking through tears, he saw Mocha in her truest form, as a fallen angel. She was dark grey from head to toe, with wide-reaching, jet-black wings sprouting from her back.

"My Marid," she said.

"You trust me, and I trust you," he said with a huge smile on his face.

Bare-chested, Marid took a step back and slid his silk pajama pants off, revealing his erect manhood and naked, light brown skin. Leaning over, he took off his many beaded necklaces and gold chains. While still looking intently at Mocha, he removed his leather bracelets. Mocha eagerly watched when he removed rings from each of his long fingers. As each piece of jewelry was removed, his body changed. His taut soft skin wrinkled and faded into a leathery, ashy brown. Both feet transformed into cloven hooves. His dreadlocks stiffened into spikes. When the last ring was gone, Marid stood eye to eye before Mocha, with a green-eyed, scruffy brown desert jackal head. He smiled at her with yellow cracked teeth.

"I love you, Marid." Mocha kissed him passionately, wrapping her wings around him.

OVER THE NEXT TWENTY-FOUR hours, Mocha had her way with Marid, and he delighted in every moment. They drew from each other's energy as they explored various sacred, sensual positions one would find in the Kamasutra. As time passed, the couple's energy waned and eventually the lovers settled in and cuddled until sunrise.

The next day, Marid was up, ready to start the quest for a new host and new jewelry for his love. Mocha lay on her side and watched Marid push open heavy curtains. Sunshine lit up the room. She yawned and shielded her eyes from the bright sunlight.

"Time to get up, Beautiful."

Mocha playfully draped blankets over her head.

"I need to get myself back together or I won't have any energy to find you a new vessel," he said.

Mocha sat up and watched him intently.

"Go slow baby, let me enjoy your transformation again," she purred.

Marid winked at Mocha. He slid rings on his long fingertips with dramatic gestures. As each piece of jewelry touched his skin, his body quivered, and something changed. Freckles appeared around his broad, wide nose. His eyes regained their almond shape. Once the leather bracelets were tied, snapped, and secured, pale dusty looking skin turned back to its taught original olive shade.

With some effort, Mocha also transformed. In the sunlight, her dark grey skin grew lighter and lighter until it was a soft tan color. Her wings folded upon themselves into her spine. She shimmed her shoulders until the last of the feathers disappeared deep in her skin. Her thick curly hair twisted and stretched until it wriggled back into a thick braid that laid loosely on her back.

Marid marveled as she changed back to her favorite body, the young woman from the night before. She shook her hands, making sure her demon claws wouldn't pop out, and placed the last of Marid's necklaces around his neck. He felt the spikes on top of his head relax back into dreadlocks. Marid took Mocha by the hand and led her outside to the balcony.

"Let's watch the humans and you tell me which type you like," he said. They both intently watched people below them. "How about that young man with the blue robes?" he suggested.

"Not this time. I really enjoy the female form. Every day is an adventure within their bodies and minds. As far as strength, they are slightly weaker than men, but their inner strength is unmatched."

A slender, tall black woman caught Mocha's attention. "What about that young one? The darker female with her dog wearing the purple headscarf?"

Marid narrowed his eyes and focused until he saw the young lady carrying a basket of candies and spices making her way around the market. An energetic white basenji was at her side. She stopped and chatted with a camel herder.

"That's odd. It looks like she's talking to the camels," Marid said.

"Look at those high cheekbones," said Mocha. "Watch how she interacts with that man. She hasn't cracked a smile and yet she commands his attention."

"She doesn't look like she's from around here," Marid said. "She is too young to be out, not unaccompanied by a male. I bet no one would look for her if she went missing. I'll find out what she's shopping for and sell her the perfect item with you attached to it. Possessing her should be easy enough."

"And then we can be together. I will stay by your side. My position at the ninth gate in Hell could be assigned to another demon."

"You mean it, Baby?" Marid said.

"I do. After spending these last few days with you, I need to be with you, Marid. No entity makes me feel the way you do."

Marid kissed Mocha and dashed off to the market below.

THE YOUNG WOMAN WITH the purple headscarf was easy to spot. She stood a few inches taller than most women and a few men in the outdoor market. She picked over flowers when Marid approached her.

"Forgive me being so bold, but my dear? Your beauty is unmatched in all of Morocco."

She barely cracked a smile. Her little white dog lunged at him. Marid took a step back and bowed. "I am Marid. I guarantee that I have exactly whatever you are looking to buy today. It will change your life! Beautiful creature, what's your name?"

"I'm Zenobia. How can you know what I want when I haven't decided what I want to purchase yet?"

"I know many things about people, young lady. Allow me to escort you and your companion to my space to show you my wares. It's a few rows down."

The little dog paced between him and his master. Zenobia stood her ground.

"How about I give you a discount on your first purchase?" he said. "Buy any item, and simply chose something else at no cost to you."

Getting a good deal while shopping was the perfect motivator for Zenobia. She adjusted her basket and nodded her head. "Lead the way, Mr. Marid."

Wanting to appear friendly to everyone around him, Marid made sure to wave and speak to vendors as they passed through the flea market.

"Basheer, you are looking well today," Marid said as he passed by a man selling spices. Basheer turned his back and shook his head.

"Goodness! Your children are growing up so fast, Kito," he waved to a woman as she arranged ladies' robes in her stall. Her husband popped up and waved his finger as a warning. Marid changed his tactic.

"Once you have finished your shopping, there is a lovely spot near the exit that serves the best baklava in the whole market." He hoped she would not notice that he was winded. His energy faded a bit quicker than he expected. After a few twists and turns, they ended up in a space crammed with everything from rugs to jewelry and artwork.

"Welcome to Marid's Magnificent Merchandise," he said and plopped down on a wicker chair. His legs were tired and shaky.

Zenobia made her way around the space with her dog in tow. Handmade plates and hand-carved bowls were stacked waist high. Persian rugs of different shapes and sizes were piled next to squares of fabric. She paused at various dusty Egyptian statues on display shelves. She examined a polished black statue of Anubis with gold trim for a few moments, frowned and put it down.

Marid considered what he wanted to sell Zenobia.

Which item would Mocha want to possess and transfer herself to the young woman?

Sparkles over Zenobia's head caught his attention. There was a cluster of Moroccan lanterns hanging in the center of his space under a canvas ceiling. A lantern would be perfect! He bet Mocha would find it hilarious that she'd have to stay temporarily in a lamp like a genie.

"Zenobia don't move a muscle. I know exactly what you want," he said and glided into her personal space. Her dog howled and nipped at his ankles. He spun away from the dog, grabbed a stick with a hook attached to it. Zenobia eyed Marid.

"Ahy, sit," Zenobia said.

The dog obeyed. When safe from the dog, Marid reached up for a lantern directly over Zenobia's head.

"You must have this. Moroccan lamps are unique to this land. They are handcrafted with passion and have intricate detail. You cannot rush to make these, even if you tried. They are special, just like you Zenobia."

Zenobia flashed a small smile. Her dog growled. Marid lowered the lantern, the size of a gourd, and handed it to the young woman. It had a thin metal crisscross frame and was covered with stained glass and mirror pieces. Its rounded base was the perfect size to hold a small candle.

Zenobia examined it slowly. Marid watched her facial expressions, trying to guess what she was thinking. He needed her to want this lantern. If she didn't take it, he'd have to find something else she wanted to possess. Her silence ate at him.

"I should have just knocked her out cold and placed the first necklace I could find on her." He considered to himself. Mocha could upgrade the jewelry once she possessed the body. However, he already made the mistake of attempting to socialize with many humans with Zenobia at his side.

Zenobia's melodic voice surprised him.

"Mr. Marid, you're right. I must have it," she said. "How much is it?"

"I tell you what. Allow me to do a deep clean and polish it up. Come back at three o'clock and we can negotiate a good price and you could choose your free gift."

"See you then, Mr. Marid."

"A LAMP?" MOCHA SAID. "You want to attach me to a lamp?"

Marid rubbed Mocha's shoulders.

"It's funny."

"If you say so," she said and rolled her black eyes. "Are you alright? You look pale."

Marid was exhausted but did not dare tell Mocha. Instead, he poked out his chest and flexed his arms.

"I'm fine. The sooner we make the possession complete, the sooner we can slumber in each other's arms."

"How long do I have to stay in the lamp?" she asked.

"Not for long. The girl, Zenobia, really likes it. When she touches it, I just have to say my incantations, and she and her lovely bone structure will be yours. Later, we can find you some jewelry that you really like. Maybe earrings that glow against that beautiful dark skin. Or maybe a hair ornament? If the dog is too much, I can drain its energy and we can have a nice snack before we rest."

"Okay Marid, let's do this," she said, and blew him a kiss.

Marid scooped up the antique necklace, gingerly placed it at the base of the lantern, and laid a small candle on top of it. Mocha's form flickered and disappeared. He then wrapped the lantern in a satin bag and headed off to find Zenobia.

The marketplace was always in constant motion. Different vendors, but the same trinkets and wares. Marid looked forward to a change of scenery with Mocha. His back ached and his head throbbed, but he pressed forward through the crowd. Once Mocha took her new form, he swore he would kiss her every chance he got for all eternity. A ringing in his ears started to distract him.

"I just need to get to my space, and all will be well," he said to himself. He mumbled, "all will be well, all will be well," over and over to motivate himself. He had to make his way around one more corner and he would be in his space. When he made the left turn, his heart sank. He was on time, but Zenobia was not.

She was nowhere near Marid's Magnificent Merchandise. He knew he didn't pass her along the way, so where could she be? He held the lantern close to his chest. His knees shook, reminding him that he needed to rest and replenish his energy soon.

"No, no, no. I do not accept this!" he shouted. He closed his eyes and took deep breaths. The lantern vibrated in his arms. He held it tighter and tried to fight off tears. His ears picked up an unusual sound among the buzz of the market. A dog howled just around the corner. Not just any dog. It was the howl of the pesky white dog that accompanied Zenobia. Grateful that it hated him, he followed the howling. Frantic for energy, he touched humans he passed. The little sparks of energy fed him enough to keep moving.

Salim, the snake charmer, taunted the little white dog with a hooded Black Cobra. A small audience of onlookers gasped and cheered. Zenobia stood with arms crossed, unamused.

"Miss Zenobia, I missed you at my shop," Marid said. "I cleaned and polished the lantern just for you."

"I don't want it anymore. I have grown tired of Morocco. It's time for Ahy and I to pack up and leave."

"Ahy," she called, but he didn't obey. He was over-stimulated. His little pink tongue poked out as he ran frantically around the snake charmer and his baskets of hissing snakes in front of a captive crowd.

"Beautiful Zenobia," Marid said.

"Ahy, come. Ahmad isn't trying to hurt you." Zenobia shouted.

"My name is Salim, not Ahmad," the snake charmer corrected.

"I am not speaking to you, Salim."

Both he and Marid looked confused.

"I will deal with you, snake charmer, in a moment."

"Please, Zenobia." Marid said, trying to hide his panic. "Take one more look. Hold it up in the sun and tell me what you think. I know you won't be disappointed."

Marid took the lantern out of its satin sleeve and pressed it into Zenobia's hands. Annoyed, she raised it in the sun. The lantern buzzed. Marid said his chant as fast as he could. The crowd turned its attention to the lantern. Black smoke spewed out of it and engulfed Zenobia. She screamed and clawed at her chest.

Ahy tore away from Ahmad the snake and ran toward Marid. He sunk his teeth into Marid's left ankle, drawing blood. Zenobia stumbled backward, away from the snake charmer into a flower vendor. There were various cut flowers in buckets and vases with water.

"Stop this! It's wrong!" she shouted.

"A few more minutes Zenobia and everything will be fine," Marid yelled back, fighting the dog and resume his chant.

"I'm in danger!" she shouted, now clawing at her head.

"A little longer, Zenobia!" he said.

"No Marid, listen to me! Zenobia's voice was gravelly and low. "It's me, Mocha! I cannot inhabit this woman. She is not your average lowly human. She will annihilate me!"

Zenobia's face was distorted. Skin twisted and stretched. Marid could see Mocha's image pressing hard, trying to fight through. Marid's ears pricked up when he heard another low growl, this one behind him. It rumbled into a loud, guttural cry. He turned to see Zenobia's little white dog transform into the largest wolf–like creature he'd ever seen.

Marid and the crowd gasped as the dog's head grew over two feet in diameter. His shoulders busted wide and thick. His back was strong and bristled. His claws looked just as dangerous, if not more so than Mocha's. Ahy howled, revealing four sets of bladelike teeth. His fangs dripped with saliva.

Marid scrambled over to Zenobia. He snatched the lantern away from her and smashed it. His fingers bled as he searched through shards of broken glass and metal splinters for the antique necklace. Ahy charged Marid like a bull. Marid screamed for help, but all anyone could do was watch in horror. Ahy gripped his left leg in his jaws and slammed him around like a doll.

Meanwhile, Zenobia tripped into a shelf of flowers. A large vase with an ornate encrusted cross tipped over, spilling water all over her. Zenobia's skin sizzled. She regained clarity; she looked at the vase, then back to Marid.

Ahy attacked with a vengeance. Marid struggled free from the beast's grip. He turned his back to the beast, feeling his skin shred with each swipe of Ahy's bearlike paws. Marid managed to collect the necklace from the shards of glass the best as he could while protecting himself from the beast's blows.

Zenobia tossed water at Ahy, causing him to pause his attack. Then she slapped the necklace from Marid's hands. She stashed it in her dress pocket. She reached for another vase with a cross engraved on it, poured more water over herself. She shouted the Lord's prayer and doused Ahy with the makeshift holy water. Ahy shrank back to his small size. His white fur coat was stained with Marid's blood. Marid was in shock.

"You can't take Mocha! She belongs with me!" Marid yelled.

"You will never see this demon again, Marid."

"I will get her back and make you pay for all of this."

"Make me pay? I was minding my own business when the two of you cooked up your little plan. I didn't wish for anything from you, foolish djinn. I should have seen you coming a mile away. No matter how long you search for her, far and wide across the earth, you will never find her."

She dunked the engraved vase in a tub of water again and, once it was full, she doused Ahy one more time for good measure. As his body bled profusely, Marid curled up into a ball and watched Zenobia pick up her dog.

"Shame on you, Salim." She pushed Salim, the snake charmer, and took his basket. "If you harm one more snake, Ahy will tear your tongue out and I will seal your mouth shut."

Salim looked at Marid, who had no response.

"Come Ahmad," she said to the cobra. "Ali, Khalil, you're coming with me too," she said while opening other baskets and collecting more snakes. She walked over to Salim and took a baby snake from his vest. "And little Amina, can't forget her. Ahy and I will take you all back to your nests, where you'll be safe and sound."

Watching the strange woman talk to snakes, Marid knew he underestimated his target. As his body shut down on him, he vowed to hunt down Zenobia and retrieve his love at any cost. Within moments, he fell into a deep coma, right where he lay in the middle of the market.

4

Isla D'Ajuda

By Denise Tapscott

Caribbean Sea, 1768

A BRIGHT YELLOW SUN made its way across a deep blue sky speckled with puffy white clouds. Sweet-scented Caribbean breezes tickled young Zenobia's nose as she sat cross-legged on a soft sandy beach. Her eyes burned as she blinked from the lack of sleep over the past few nights.

She looked across a calm, turquoise ocean while her dog Ahy played in the sand with tiny brown and white spotted sandpipers. The delicate birds flew in, landing just a few feet from the small white Basenji. When he pounced, they skittered away along the edge of the waves, enticing him to follow, or they'd take flight, depending upon the distance between the flock and the dog.

The tranquil beach was a treasure hidden away from a sketchy port on Isla D'Ajuda. During low tide over the past two days, Zenobia and Ahy waded in the warm waters, searching for elusive sea slugs. She loved her time in the ocean, but dreaded the grimy town. She'd prepaid a week's rent for a small, stuffy room over a village shop, but couldn't figure out why the proprietor jumped as if scared of his own shadow every time she walked in or out of the store. Come to think of it, every single person she encountered refused to look her in the eye, even if forced to speak to her. *How could an entire town with glorious beaches be so distracted, so aloof?*

Closing her eyes, she turned her face toward the sunlight, appreciating the warmth on her face. She enjoyed running her fingers through the soft, light brown sand that surrounded her. The memory of playing with Ahy on the sands of the Nile, back when she was just a little girl, flashed through her mind. Life was so much easier and carefree before her tribe was stolen from her.

Zenobia wiggled in the sand, trying to ground herself more. A disturbing memory overshadowed her enjoyable thoughts about handsome men or delicious dinners. An altercation she had a few weeks ago chewed at her. Shopping for spices in a bustling outdoor Brazilian market, with her dog by her side, Zenobia noticed a gangly young man clutching rickety crutches making his way around different food vendors.

Every so often he'd stop to catch his breath, look over his shoulder and pick up his pace. She didn't see what the trouble was at first until he stared at her and then glanced at a rowdy small group of young men a few yards behind him. She didn't understand what they shouted in Portuguese, but they pointed and laughed at him. Assuming he might be in trouble, she followed as the young man made his way into a quiet alley.

"Do you need help? she asked.

"Young lady, you are the one who needs help," he said. He rolled his shoulders back and tossed his crutches away. He placed two fingers to his lips and whistled. The small group of men unceremoniously showed up in the alley.

"Give me your money!"

Zenobia was stunned. She thought the poor soul needed help. *How could she have been so wrong?* The men shouted at her in Portuguese and moved in, surrounding her. The thin man lunged at Ahy.

Zenobia's anger lit like a match. Most of the fight was a blur. She and her dog Ahy were unharmed, but she heard the young men scream and bones crack. She snapped the fingers on both hands of a man who managed to briefly put his hands on her. After stomping someone's skull, she charged the young man who lured her in the first place. She saw to it that he would never walk again. He would need much more than the rickety crutches he discarded.

The pain she rained down upon the robbers was justified, she reminded herself. It was self-defense. They'd never be able to harm anyone else. It wasn't her first fight, nor the first time she killed anyone. So why did the memory bother her so much?

Before her memories turned even darker and her thoughts ignited her anger, causing it to bubble and spew over like an active volcano, her eyes snapped open. Ahy stopped playing at the water's edge. He crouched and yodeled aggressively at the sea. His feathered friends were long gone.

"What is it, boy?" Zenobia asked as she rose and dusted sand off her cotton dress the best she could. Ahy ran in and out of the ocean, challenging something.

Miles of light blue waves crashed on the beach. Clusters of kelp and seagrass floated on the surf, but it wasn't anything they hadn't seen before. She was about to scoop up the ten-pound dog in her arms when her eyes tracked what excited him. A large dark figure zig-zagged in the water towards them. It was too small to be an adult shark, and too aggressive to be a dolphin.

The dark mass paused, floating a few yards from them. Ahy stopped yodeling and ran to Zenobia's side. A large round head raised above the waves.

Is that a manatee? she wondered.

Zenobia squinted; the creature was too far away for her to make out what it was. It submerged, flicked a large tail and swam closer to the shore. It resurfaced a few feet from the beach and wiggled until its fins turned into arms. It pushed itself up until it sat on what Zenobia could only assume was its large fish tail. The thing tilted its sea grass covered head slowly from side to side was creepy. Zenobia stood her ground but was grateful that her dress hid her shaky knees.

"You don't fear my presence?" The being shouted in a husky voice as it flicked its head up, tossing wet green strands behind it. It stared with jet-black eyes at Zenobia.

"I didn't say that," Zenobia said. She returned a hard stare to the figure in the water. *Was her mind playing tricks on her?*

It had the face and torso of a human woman with hair, a greenish mix of kelp, sea grass and sea snakes. The upper body had sparkly indigo blue skin. Zenobia spotted a thick, dark red band of skin around its neck. She was mesmerized by its large fish tail covered in iridescent scales.

"First time seeing a mermaid?" the woman asked.

"Yes. Honestly, I can't believe my eyes."

The mermaid tossed her head unnaturally farther back than a human could and cackled. Zenobia flinched at the sight of her sharp, pearly white teeth.

"What's your name, young lady?"

"Zenobia."

"And your little friend?" she asked, licking her thick, dark purple lips.

"This is my dog Ahy."

"Zenobia and Ahy," the mermaid repeated, emphasizing the Z and the A. "What interesting names." The mermaid dipped back into the water and floated right up to the water's edge. "Tell me, Zenobia, what year is it?" the mermaid asked after she rose again. She pushed herself up and came to a wobbly, standing position. It looked painful to see the fins of her tail folded forward and flattened in the sand.

"Uh...it's the year of our Lord 1768," Zenobia answered.

The mermaid growled and narrowed her eyes. Ahy retreated a few steps. The mermaid shook herself, the same way Ahy shook when he got out of the water. Starting with her head, she thrashed about. As water flung away, her body transformed. Black and brown dreadlocks replaced the dark green colored sea snakes, seagrass and kelp.

The indigo skin fell away, revealing dark brown human flesh, a tone only slightly darker than Zenobia's. The mesmerizing scales of her tail bubbled away, revealing muscular, curvy legs. A few scales fell into the sand. The transformed mermaid bowed slightly.

"You may call me Scarlette," she said. The mermaid's new voice sounded soft and smooth as velvet, much more enjoyable than the husky response moments before. "I was once known as Scarlette, the Bloodlust Pirate, daughter of Black Caesar." She laughed again, standing naked, a mere arm's length from Zenobia.

Her pearly white teeth weren't as sharp as before but still menacing. Small waves lapped at her ankles, revealing her iridescent feet. The sun illuminated deep scars, burn marks and ugly bruises from head to toe in the mermaid's dark brown skin. Scarlette's nails were sharp and black. The only original items left of the mermaid were her dark eyes and the red band that circled her neck.

"Allow me to get my blanket for you, to cover up with," Zenobia offered.

"That's kind of you, but not necessary."

Scarlette stepped fully onto the beach and winked at Zenobia. As Zenobia and Ahy retreated, she shook again. A black blouse, black leather vest, black pants, and black leather boots materialized to cover her flesh. A silver and onyx flintlock pistol with matching cutlass appeared on both sides of a wide leather belt that rested around her waist. She waved her hand around her head, clockwise, and snapped, summoning a black leather tricorn pirate hat adorned with clusters of shiny black cormorant feathers mixed with fluffy black ostrich feathers.

"Neat trick, isn't it?" the pirate joked. "I am granted the opportunity to appear as my former self during my legendary visits to treacherous Isla D'Ajuda. This is how I wish to be remembered when I was mortal."

Zenobia was in awe of this woman's supernatural power. She herself could move things if she focused her energy enough, but to transform clothing or physical appearance? That was something else.

"May I pet your dog? I promise not to eat him," Scarlette said. The pirate's comment was unsettling. *Who or what makes that kind of promise?* Zenobia fought the urge to attack. Her left hand twitched, ready to grab a spiritual hold on Scarlette.

After some thought, she decided the pirate wasn't a threat. Zenobia took a deep breath and flicked her fingers to break up the energy stored in her fingertips and dismissed the pirate's tone. An idea popped in her mind. Scarlette's spirit animal was probably a sleek, muscular black jaguar lurking the Amazon rainforest. Zenobia chuckled. Scarlette's fixed stare upon potential prey was unnerving.

"Ahy, come," Zenobia said. She decided she would snap the pirate's neck if she attempted anything sinister. Ahy paused, sniffed toward the pirate, then obeyed his owner.

The pirate kneeled and gently patted him on the head. "Little one, tell me what you think of your master. Is she just, or is she cruel?"

Zenobia frowned. Ahy's eyes flashed bright blue. To Zenobia's surprise, he wagged his tail and licked Scarlette's hand. The pirate's eyes also flashed a bright blue. She toppled backward as if thrown by an invisible force. She looked up at Zenobia and scrambled to a prostrate position before the young woman.

"Your Majesty, it is an honor to be in your presence. Forgive me for not paying my respects sooner. I did not know." The pirate lifted her chin but stayed on her knees. "You are Zenobia, Queen of Palmyra. I saw flashes of Ahy's memories. I saw you stand before your people in your palace, wearing a purple and white bejeweled tunic.

Your crown sparkled in the desert sun. You were honored and respected well before the Romans came. Ahy was by your side, as always. Animals do not lie. He is eternally devoted to you. You both have had many adventures. You both look very young, to be so old."

Goosebumps ran up and down Zenobia's flesh. No one in the 18th century knew her true identity. "He's a good dog," was the best she could say.

"I heard stories about you many years ago. I am in awe that you are alive and speak to me." She avoided looking directly at Zenobia.

"Please, get up." Zenobia motioned for the pirate to stand. "You don't need to kneel before me. That was a long time ago."

"The way you fought the Romans for so long was impressive! History books tell many stories of your death. From my vision, I know you were a fierce woman and respected queen. Again, I am honored to be in your presence." Scarlette rose to her feet, hat removed, keeping her head bowed. "It would be an unspeakable privilege if you joined me for dinner. I could use your guidance when I judge the townsfolk."

"Judge the townsfolk?" Zenobia asked.

"I'll explain along the way, if you choose to come with me."

"Of course I choose to come with you. This sounds interesting," Zenobia said.

ZENOBIA TURNED TO COLLECT her basket of belongings. Pirate Scarlett scrambled to her side and scooped it up, insisting upon carrying the load. After a brief bout of tug of war, Zenobia released her possessions. Scarlette was so eager to be of service, Zenobia surrendered.

The first mile, Zenobia, Ahy, and Scarlette walked in an uncomfortable silence. Once they reached the edge of town, however, Zenobia frowned. Both Ahy and Scarlette growled. The town emitted a heavy, downtrodden vibe.

"Your Highness, what brings you to such a wretched place? The last time I was here, not a single soul on this island was worthy of meeting a queen."

"The people here are different, but I couldn't say that they weren't worthy of..."

"They don't deserve the air they live and breathe in," the pirate snapped. Scarlette took in her surroundings, eyes wild with contempt as they trudged into the port.

Men shuffled past them quickly. Women held their children close. Wooden shutters slammed shut and doors locked the farther they walked into town. An emaciated, rum drenched sailor inadvertently stepped directly into Zenobia's path. Scarlette leaped between them, pushing the man to the ground. Her black leather boot dug into his dirty ribcage.

"Mr. Digby, mind where you stumble!" she threatened.

Zenobia was about to defend the drunkard when she noticed foamy wet spots appear on the Pirate's cheek and jawline, which then slid down her skin and disappeared. Zenobia flinched at the mysterious spittle.

"Your Majesty, are you alright?' Shall I kill him for his insolence?"

"No, no, I'm fine. Don't kill him."

"What's wrong? Something is bothering you."

"Nothing," she lied. Zenobia watched Scarlette rub her cheek with the back of her sleeve. "I need to rest. I thought for a moment someone, or something, spit on you. I didn't sense anyone but…"

"You can see it?" Scarlette asked, as she kicked Digby hard in his side. Zenobia watched as she snatched a shiny pendant from his neck and tucked it away in her vest.

"See what?" Zenobia asked.

"His grandfather and others spat on me, in this very street, years ago."

Zenobia shook her head. The day continued to get stranger and stranger by the moment.

"I don't understand. I don't sense any kind of presence," she said as she watched Ahy meander up the cobblestone street. Digby rolled away from the women into a ditch.

"They are echoes from the past. You are enlightened! You sense things!" Scarlette clasped her hands with joy.

"I guess you could say that. I receive random flashes of people or emotions come over me. Lately, I've been too tired to concentrate on anything. Ahy and I are here to collect sea slugs for dye and then we're…"

The pirate lunged at her. "I can help you with this."

Before Zenobia could respond, Scarlette thrust her hands on Zenobia's head. The black gloves morphed into damp, cold hands. She clasped her fingers around Zenobia's face and dug her thumbs deep into the skin between her eyes, just above the bridge of her nose.

Zenobia was done trying to be reasonable with the impossible being who hijacked her day. How dare Scarlette touch her! She crouched low and grabbed the pirate by her sides. She intended to throw her across the road. Bystanders would probably notice the display of unusual strength, but Zenobia didn't care. She and Ahy could pack up whatever belongings they had, leave the awful town, and look for sea slugs somewhere else.

Before she exercised her plan, Zenobia's ears popped. She felt an immediate sensation of someone shoving a hot poker into her skull. She held her grip on Scarlette. Ahy ran to her side as Zenobia dropped to her knees in pain. Fearing that she might vomit, she closed her eyes and drew in a deep breath. A bright burst of purple light filled her mind, and the pain disappeared as quickly as it came.

The image of a tall, dark-skinned, muscular man came to her. He had high cheekbones and a well-chiseled jawline. Small scars marked his forehead, giving him a fierce frown, but his kind brown eyes revealed his bark was worse than his bite. Standing on a sunny, white sandy beach, he held his young daughter by her waist.

When Zenobia focused, she realized it was a very vibrant, very adorably human Scarlette. Her father tossed her in the air and gently caught her, returning her carefully to the sand. The more the girl squealed in delight, the more he laughed. Her giggles were infectious.

Higher, daddy! Higher!
Alright, my magical lady.
The vision changed to the same man, a bit older with more scars, standing in a moonlit marsh, down in the Florida Keys. He aggressively pushed his daughter away.

Again! He yelled at her. *Don't let them get close enough to put their hands on you.*

Yes, Papa, a teenaged Scarlette answered, armed with a sharp blade and a torch. She had a serious but determined frown as she honed her fighting skills with her father.

The vision changed again, to the man, even older, holding an also older Scarlette, again by the waist, on a galleon ship tossed about in a stormy sea. His face was bruised and bloodied. Be strong, never let anyone see you cry, he said, as cannon balls whizzed in the air. Shrieks of sailors and the smell of gun smoke filled the air. *Safe travels, my magical lady.*

Be safe, Papa, Scarlette answered. *I love you,* they said to one another. Zenobia released her grip from the pirate and stood. She looked at Ahy and noticed he had a soft yellow glow around him. His aura was light and playful, with streaks of muddy yellow.

"I'm okay, boy, I promise," she said and patted his head. Once he was convinced she was all right, his muddy yellow faded and his aura went back to lighter shades of yellow. Looking at her hands, Zenobia noticed a purple hue hovered close to her skin. "What did you do to me?" Zenobia asked.

"I cleared your third eye. It was blocked." Scarlette said, pointing at her own forehead. Again, she kneeled before Zenobia, eyes turned downward. "I should have asked your permission before I touched you. Please find it in your heart to forgive me." Her aura was a vibrant blue.

"In time, you will be able to connect with other enlightened people through your mind and communicate with spirits. You are special, having lived for a very long time. I'm guessing that maybe you've done this unknowingly."

"It has been a gift and a curse," Zenobia said. She was comforted by being around someone else who was also different and relieved she wasn't the only one sensitive to spirits and energies. "Scarlette, please get up. You don't have to kneel before me."

She rose but kept her gaze low.

"I saw you and your father. You loved each other very much," Zenobia said. "You were his little magical lady,"

"You saw my memories of him!" Scarlette said.

Zenobia liked how the pirate lit up.

"When I was little, he always said that I was magic because I promised him there was always something possible, in impossible situations." Tears streamed down her face.

Zenobia hugged her, patting her back. Her vulnerability was endearing. No matter how abnormal the day had been, no matter how peculiar this being was, this moment was special to Zenobia.

"Are you ready to walk?" the pirate asked. "We're almost at Mister Morley's tavern."

Zenobia nodded. "Scarlette, I look forward to what happens next."

"Welcome to Mr. Morley's tavern. It's the largest bar and brothel on the island," Scarlette said as she ushered Zenobia and Ahy in.

The tavern was poorly lit, smelling like tobacco, alcohol, and ass. Various rickety wooden tables and chairs were crammed together in the dimly lit establishment. A single open path led to the rear of the bar, where a solitary table and high-back wooden chair waited for the pirate. Zenobia carried Ahy and cringed as she walked through sticky patches of unknown substances on the wooden floor.

"Mr. Morley, bring another chair for my guest and a pillow for her dog," Scarlette ordered.

The rotund, greasy looking bartender grunted, avoided eye contact and obeyed her command. A second large, high-backed wooden chair scuffed deep grooves on the wooden floor as he dragged it from the front of the establishment all the way to the back. Zenobia noted Scarlette's lower ribcage glowed red. She saw tiny white cracks in her ribcage for a few moments, then the image faded. The tips of Morley's boots also glowed the same red hue. She rubbed her eyes in disbelief.

"What do we do now?" Zenobia asked after she and Ahy settled in next to Scarlette.

"We wait for the townspeople."

"The townspeople?"

"Yes. Young and old, strong and weak."

Mr. Morley slammed two large mugs of rum on the table and shuffled away. Once he was out of earshot, Zenobia said. "I guess that explains all the chairs crammed in here."

"Those who are absent will still be dealt with."

"Dealt with?"

"No one can escape The Reckoning."

"The Reckoning?" Zenobia repeated. "I apologize if I sound like a parrot."

"With your heightened vision from your active third eye, you'll understand."

Zenobia wanted to ask more questions, but before she could, the doors squeaked open and townsfolk filtered in. The early arrivals sat at tables and chairs as far away as possible from Scarlette and Zenobia. They avoided contact with each other. Zenobia noticed different sections of Scarlette glowed a multitude of colors on various parts of her body. She saw nasty bruises, deep cuts and broken bones. The skin around her neck was perpetually bloodied and chafed.

Mr. Morley returned with a platter of braised beef, biscuits and deviled eggs. He half tossed the food on the table and made his way back to behind the bar.

Zenobia turned her nose up at the food. Judging by the sour smell from the meat and the bluish tinted eggs, the meal wasn't edible.

"Your Majesty, don't trouble yourself with this slop. In the years I've been coming here, the food is no better than poison. I don't know why he even bothers to prepare anything anymore."

Zenobia's stomach rumbled, but she knew better than to sample the food.

"Do you like fish? If we survive tonight, I will make you a meal truly fit for a queen." Scarlette eyed Mr. Morley as he poured glasses of water for weary attendees. "Bartender, stop where you are and bring us that pitcher with clean glasses."

"I can bring you another one that's fresh from..."

"No. We want that one, now, not one fresh with your saliva. And while you're at it, bring a bowl for the dog."

Zenobia watched Morley's face turn several shades of red. He obeyed and brought the pitcher of water. She watched as he fetched clean glasses along with a small wooden bowl. He carelessly tossed the bowl on the table, which bounced a few times and fell to the floor. Zenobia stared at Scarlet's rib cage as it glowed a dark red hue with broken bones poking out.

"Your behavior is unacceptable," Scarlette said. "Pick up the bowl for the dog and pour some water in it."

His boots glowed red again as he stooped over and served Ahy. Scarlette touched her rib cage and winced for a fleeting moment. Then she grabbed a silver spoon and tucked it away in her vest. Zenobia looked at the townspeople crammed together at tables and chairs in the establishment. Brown and burnt orange auras filled the room. Scarlette's body blurred sporadically.

"Are you okay?" Zenobia asked Scarlette. Scarlette offered a sympathetic smile.

"I will be, once the reckoning is over."

Church bells rang in the distance, quieting the crowd inside the tavern. Scarlette stood, adjusting her hat, and addressed the crowd.

"Ladies and gentlemen, as you all recall, I am the formidable, bloodlust Pirate Scarlette, daughter of Black Caesar, who was an African tribal war chieftain, overlord of the western Florida Keys and great lieutenant to Captain Blackbeard. This is your day of reckoning. What soul is brave enough to approach me and my company with their offering?"

Not a soul stirred.

"Who has their offering?" Scarlette repeated and took her seat. The group's auras grew darker. The overcrowded tavern was stifling.

"Foolish thief! This is ridiculous," someone shouted in the crowd. "You're just a typical water rat who shows up every year with the same stupid petition."

"This is a waste of time!" someone else chimed in.

Zenobia looked over at Scarlette, who seemed unaffected by the anger in the tavern.

"Go back to wherever you came from!"

"Get out before we drag you out!"

Men stood, pushing their chairs away. Women started yelling, inciting others in the crowd. A solemn-looking woman escorted children and the elderly to a safe corner by the bar.

"I have back up today. Should you want to repeat the brawl we had last time." Scarlette threatened, never leaving her wooden throne.

Zenobia grabbed Scarlette's hand, ready to fight alongside her. The bridge of Zenobia's nose twitched. Then a vision of the townspeople attacking the pirate filled her mind. Broken bottles, shattered chairs were all around the pirate. She was sprawled unnaturally on her table. Zenobia heard gunshots and smelled sulfur. Black holes the size of gold coins appeared in Scarlette's forehead. The flesh exploded and shards of bone poked through her eye sockets. Zenobia released her hand and fought the urge to vomit.

"Did you see what I think you saw?" Scarlette asked.

Heat rose from Zenobia's head and shoulders. Her heart pounded in her chest.

"When did these people do that to you?" Zenobia asked.

"Last year." Scarlette said.

Zenobia shook her hands to stave off her anger. She wanted to avoid another bloodbath like Brazil. She changed her focus. Watching a mirage of blood ooze from Scarlette's neck piqued her curiosity. If Zenobia could see what happened to the poor creature on her last visit, what horrible atrocity did the pirate go through to cause the blood ring around her neck?

"Do I have permission to see more?" Zenobia asked.

"Of course, if you dare."

She reached out and touched Scarlette's neck to get another glimpse of her past.

Zenobia found herself in a small, overcrowded courtroom filled with angry people. She stood a shoulder's length away from a very human Scarlette who wore torn, soiled rags. She waved a hand in front of Scarlette, but the woman never blinked, never moved. The hostile crowd, dressed in clothing from an earlier time period, didn't react to Zenobia's appearance either, so she pieced together that no one could see her.

Noticing her thin frame, Zenobia could tell the pirate suffered greatly. Her boney back was exposed, revealing deep whip marks. Dreadlocks barely hid a black eye, and a busted lower lip. Rusted shackles weighed down her ankles and wrists. An iron collar forced her to slouch. Zenobia saw where it dug into her neck, irritating the already exposed, infected skin. There were dark red patches of skin, pockets of black blood and swollen, oozing wounds.

"This trial has dragged on for a week," said a sweaty, gray-haired judge sitting high on his wooden bench. "You are charged with piracy as well as aiding and abetting; a lighter sentence would be considered if you cooperate." He pointed at Scarlette.

"For the last time, the court demands that you tell us where we can find the pirate Black Caesar. He is charged with piracy, looting, and countless charges of kidnapping, rape and murder." His cheeks were flushed with anger.

"Where's my wife?" someone from the crowd shouted.

"He stole my brother's ship and imprisoned him. Tell us where he is!" someone else yelled.

"We want our families back!"

"I don't know where he kept his prisoners or his harem. His island is somewhere in the Florida Keys. Good luck finding it." Scarlette said.

The group threw spoiled food, rocks and anything else they could get their hands on at Scarlette. She almost laughed herself to tears when a leather boot hit her in the head.

"Order in the court!" the judge commanded, pounding his gavel.

"I don't know where he is. If I did know, I still wouldn't tell any of you sons of bitches!" Scarlette said and spat at the judge.

"You are in contempt of court!" the judge yelled. The bailiff snatched Scarlette's chains, causing her to fall face forward. Zenobia reached to catch her, but she was only there in spirit. Scarlette struggled to get to her feet when a messenger interrupted the courtroom.

"May I approach, your honor?" the smartly dressed messenger asked, waving a sealed note.

"Of course."

The judge broke the seal and read the letter to himself. He tore off his glasses and shook his head in disgust.

"It has come to the court's attention that Black Caesar is dead."

Gasps and shrieks filled the courtroom.

"He was found guilty and hung for piracy in Williamsburg, Virginia, on April 15, 1718."

Scarlette held her head high and clenched her jaw, despite the heartbreaking news.

"That was six months ago!" the prosecutor shouted. The courtroom exploded in disarray. The frenzied crowd scared Zenobia, even if they couldn't touch her.

"Order! I demand order in this courtroom! In light of this new evidence, we cannot charge this woman with aiding and abetting a known criminal. However, the charges of piracy still stand. Young lady, the court finds you guilty of nine counts of piracy, assault, and treason. You will be hung at first light at Execution Dock. May God have mercy on your soul, because no one here will mourn you as your body floats with the tide."

It wasn't long before Zenobia found herself, side by side with Scarlette, standing on the gallows at the other side of town. Waves crashed against jagged rocks below them. As a warning, every few yards poles on the wooden dock had decrepit bodies of pirates, hanging from moldy ropes, dipping in the ocean. Zenobia cringed when Scarlette struggled to breathe as a man wearing a black hood and leather chaps tightened a thick rope around her neck.

Zenobia had had more than enough of this vision. Drawing in a deep breath and closing her eyes, she hoped that with enough focus, she could find her way back to the present. While her forehead ached, she listened to her own heartbeat until it was steady and strong. Opening her eyes, she was back, flesh and bone, sitting next to Scarlette at Morley's tavern in 1768. The crowd was almost as unruly as it had been in the past.

"ZENOBIA, YOU AND I are like forces of nature. People can try to break us or control us, but in the end, we will always have a fighting spirit. Focus your energy and use it as you want. You are unstoppable."

"Thank you. I really needed that reminder." Sickened at how the pirate was treated and killed, Zenobia stood and pointed at the crowd. "Lay one finger on my friend and you will regret the moment you walked in here," she threatened. "Mind your attitudes when you approach us."

"And who do you do you think…"

"Come forward, coward!" Zenobia balled up her fist and punched the air in a downward motion. People gasped as they heard the voice cry out. There was a thump on the wooden floor and a scratching sound as an unseen force dragged a burly man from the crowd. Zenobia moved her hand at a snail's pace, ensuring the man's face scraped along the filthy floor until he was front and center. She took her time returning to her seat.

"Buckley! You were warned," Scarlette scoffed.

"I am Zenobia, the Fierce, associate of Pirate Scarlette. What do you offer today?"

Buckley emptied his pockets, still prostrate on the floor. A few grubby coins rolled around at his sides.

"That is not acceptable," Scarlette said. "Clearly, you never intended to make a reasonable offering."

Zenobia shook her head at the audacity of the people. She lifted her index finger. As it rose, Buckley's head rose. As her finger fell and touched the table, his head crashed into the wood. The crowd fell silent. His fleshy head smacked the floor as Zenobia methodically tapped her finger. Several people crouched in fear as others pulled back. Scarlette cackled.

"Stop! I can send my boy to fetch a better offering," he wailed. The crowd pushed Buckley's teenaged son forward.

Zenobia snapped her fingers, releasing Buckley senior. As blood ran down the side of his face, he managed to get up by his own will. He and his son collected the coins from the floor. With one hand nursing the side of his face, Buckley stretched out his free hand and offered the money. His fingers grazed Zenobia's hand.

She examined a coin for a moment and, to her surprise, a vision of the Buckley property filled her mind. He had inherited a small plantation with livestock and slaves from his father. His father pummeled Scarlette's face back in 1718. Zenobia saw Scarlette's face transform, revealing a black eye, broken nose and busted lip as Buckley stood before them. Zenobia pointed at Buckley's son.

"Boy, bring us two bags of coins and your best cow. Free the slaves immediately. All of them. If you don't do what I say, your father will suffer greatly, and your family's property will burn to the ground," Zenobia said.

Scarlette snatched up one of the coins and leaned over to Zenobia as if they were childhood friends.

"How do you know he has that kind of offering?" she asked.

"Thanks to you, I have new insight into many things," Zenobia said. "I see past transgressions done to you and other sins that reveal themselves. You can't see that?"

"My body reflects the beatings and harassment I took from their ancestors. I feel their emotions, but I can't see much of anything else clearly."

"Don't you worry. This will be a memorable reckoning," Zenobia said.

"Who's next?" Scarlette called out. One by one, people came forward with meager offerings of tapestries, spices and tobacco.

Zenobia touched each person's hand and made her recommendations if the offerings were worthy of the Pirate. She noted which torturous acts of the past were carried out on Scarlette. Scarlette's words about no one being worthy of much in this town proved to be true.

A well-proportioned, round-faced woman dressed in a gorgeous silk dress casually strolled up and tossed a bag of coins on the table. She paid more attention to Ahy than either Scarlette or Zenobia.

"Marta Carreta, your husband has been shopping for you in Paris, I see," Scarlette said and rolled her eyes.

"This should be enough from the Carreta household," Marta said. "How much for the dog?"

Zenobia narrowed her eyes. Ahy was more than livestock. He was family. Ahy instinctively jumped into her lap.

"Hold out your hand, like everyone else," Scarlette said.

When Zenobia touched her skin, images filled her mind. Grandfather Carreta did unspeakable things to the pirate in the jail, when the sun went down, and the constable was conveniently absent. It wasn't more than a year after her hanging when his wrong doings against several women caught up with him. He never suspected his pregnant wife would slice his throat from ear to ear while he slept. Zenobia counted over thirty stab wounds to his chest.

More images of Marta filled her mind. She lied often to her hardworking husband about just about everything imaginable. He provided her with luxurious clothing and a beautiful villa. Yet she wagged her fat index finger at him and berated him constantly. She was having an affair with both a lieutenant in the French army and the Governor of the town. Worse, tonight she stole money from Morley's register when he was serving patrons on the other side of the bar.

Ahy jumped to the floor and hid under the table. Zenobia snatched Scarlette's cutlass and gripped Marta's chubby wrist. She held the sharp blade high in the air, ready to chop off the ring clad hand. Scarlette patted Zenobia on her shoulder.

"Your majesty, you are welcome to do as you please, and I am not one to give you orders. However, this woman has made her offering for the sins of her people. The grandfather was killed for his behavior."

"She's a thief and an adulteress in fancy clothes! You may as well dress up a pig."

"My friend, I thought you understood. I am here because of the past, not current sins."

Zenobia held the woman's wrist tighter, believing that she should pay for her behavior. A bunch of coins wasn't nearly enough payment. Zenobia looked at the pirate, confused. Scarlette simply shook her head. Zenobia handed over the cutlass.

"Let me go, witch!" Marta yelled.

Zenobia couldn't contain her anger. She snapped Marta's wrist.

"First of all, my dog is not for sale." Yanking her victim forward, she grabbed the back of the woman's head and pounded her face on the table rhythmically. "I. Am. Zenobia."

Crunches followed each word. Blood poured down Marta's face. Scarlette snatched a jade bracelet off the woman's meaty wrist.

"Scarlette accepts your offering. I see your sins and I've decided the rest of the town should see them, too. Try kissing a man with that face," Zenobia said and pushed Marta away.

"Tell your husband a witch shattered your face because you are an adulteress. Everyone now knows that you were sleeping with the Governor behind your husband's back, as well as a lieutenant in the French army who gave you a nasty venereal disease. I broke your wrist, so you won't steal any more from Mr. Morley's register tonight, nor another man's hard-earned money. Test me and see what else I am tempted to do to you." Zenobia blew out a cleansing breath and took her seat as people hauled Marta away.

"Your majesty, you truly are fierce," Scarlette said.

"I am tired of being nice," Zenobia said.

A boney old man, blind in one eye, ambled his way through the melee and approached Scarlette.

"Grandpa, come back here!" a young woman shouted.

"Let me handle my business!" he waved away the concerns of the woman behind him. Zenobia crossed her arms and watched the man place his hands on their table to steady himself.

"Miss Scarlette, I don't know if you remember me, but I was there the day you were hung."

"Mister Carl Freeman, I certainly do remember you. You were ten years old, and you gave me fresh water to drink a few hours before my last breath." Carl's aura lit up. Royal blue surrounded him, head to toe. Zenobia looked over at Scarlette to see if he spoke the truth. Her skin was healthy and smooth, without a single scar.

"I apologize. I haven't been to see you. I've been away for quite some time in England and when I returned to the island, I was sick. My neighbors mentioned that you were coming and against my family's wishes, I just had to see you. I have no money to offer you, but I was hoping to pay my respects."

Scarlette jumped to her feet and gave the elderly man a gentle, heartfelt embrace.

"It brings me joy to see you, Carl," she said and placed her hands on his cheeks.

"My granddaughter is looming behind me, isn't she?" he said. "She's always hovering," he said. A haggard-looking, thin woman stood a few feet from Grandpa Freeman. She rubbed her hands together nervously.

"Miss, what is your name?" Zenobia asked.

"Agatha, ma'am. I'm sorry to bother you and Miss Scarlette. He was just so insistent on coming,"

"Miss Agatha, come close," Zenobia said. She pointed at the offering table. "Take two bags of coins for you and your family and be on your way."

"Yes! This is an order, not a request." Scarlette chimed in. "Carl, it meant a lot to me that you paid your respects. You and your family are released from the reckoning. Henceforth, you and your heirs shall not appear before me with offerings."

The crowd fell silent.

"Who's next?" Zenobia asked, as a few of Agatha's children helped her collect the money and escort Grandpa Freeman home.

Once the remaining townsfolk saw the reckoning was more interesting than it had been in previous years, more people came forward. Word must have spread around town to those too scared to show, because more people appeared with decent offerings.

A timid seamstress came forward with an offering of one of her finest dresses. Her great grandmother was a bystander at the hanging who prayed for Scarlette before the pirate's neck snapped and fell waist deep into the sea. Zenobia rewarded the seamstress with a small bag of coins and told her not to return. A muscular, dark haired woman advanced to the table with children of different ages around her and a sleeping baby in her arms. Her hair was disheveled, and her eyes were dull.

"I am a single mother of five children," she announced with pride. "The best I can offer are services from my family such as cooking and cleaning and these flowers from my garden."

A thin little girl approached the table with a fresh bouquet of yellow lilies. The stoic woman held out her hand for Zenobia. Zenobia held the woman's hand for a few seconds and released it, having a good idea how this was going to play out. There was little surprise that Scarlette looked radiant.

"Mrs. Del Ray, I sense that you recently lost your husband," Zenobia said. "We are sorry for your loss." The woman gasped. Her hardened face softened as she fought to keep tears from rolling down her cheeks.

"How do you know my name? How do you know about my family?" she asked.

"Don't ask," Scarlette said.

Zenobia continued. "Elizabeth, you and your beautiful family are welcome to take two bags of coins, a few chickens and the cow outside; the animals are healthy and will provide food for you and your family for many years. I also recommend you hire a few of the newly freed people to help you with your land."

"I also request that you continue to grow those beautiful flowers," Scarlette added. "They brighten up this island. You and your family are cleared of the reckoning." She tucked a single yellow flower in her vest.

"Thank you, Zenobia. Thank you, Pirate Scarlette." The Del Ray children, who were old enough to understand what happened, tried to fight back their tears, like their mother.

"We are grateful for what you've done for us," Mrs. Del Rey said and smiled at the women as the family left. A soft orange glow from the morning sun crept through the windows of the tavern. The last few stragglers presented their offerings and left peacefully, with their heads held high.

Mr. Morley cracked open a window and propped open the doors to air out the building. The tavern stench and muddied energies swirled away with soft ocean breezes.

The tavern felt lighter and welcoming. Ahy yawned, which made Zenobia yawn, too. The women laughed.

"I think we're done here," Scarlette said. "You need to rest, your majesty."

"Yeah, this has been quite a day. I already know that this will be the first time in a while that I'm gonna have a good night's sleep. Just one more thing. I almost understand your day of reckoning," Zenobia said to Scarlette. "It's not about their wrongdoings?"

"Your Majesty, you saw my past. I was a good person, but I did many bad things to many people. I paid for my sins and made my peace long ago. I don't choose to come here. My heaven is freedom in the deep blue waters of a vast, beautiful ocean.

Zenobia shook her head.

"It's the townspeople's guilt and shame that beckons me back, year after year. The sooner they let go of the past and forgive themselves, the sooner they will be healed, and I won't reflect any marks. Leaving an offering usually helps humans release their guilt and pain and opens themselves up to accept gifts and blessings. Until your visit, this town wouldn't even allow themselves to leave a worthy offering. It was easier for them to hold on to the past than it was for them to forgive themselves and heal. It's bittersweet that Isla D'Ajuda means island of healing, in a few languages."

"I'm not perfect either, Scarlette. I guess none of us are."

Scarlette leaned in close to Zenobia. "I see what disturbs your sleep. You did the right thing, defending yourself in Brazil." Zenobia teared up as Scarlette continued.

"Those young men took advantage and hurt many people before you came along. You probably saved lives. Your majesty, I know you have fought many battles. Forgive yourself. Have a nice treat and let that heavy memory go."

Zenobia remembered there were times when many people suffered and died because of her outbursts of rage. There were other things she did in the past not as costly to human life, but still bad. Some were justified, some were not. Most of them she repented for or paid a price for. Her time here on the island with Scarlette taught her she needed to let the thoughts and memories of her sins go. It was time for her to release the past and heal, too.

Scarlette cackled and clapped her hands. "Thank you, Zenobia. This reckoning was the best ever!"

Zenobia noticed there were still some offerings left on the table.

"Mr. Morley, thank you for the use of your tavern. You are welcome to whatever is left."

"Thank you, Miss Scarlette, and thank you, Miss Zenobia," he said, rushing to the table to collect the bounty.

"Miss Zenobia will be back later with freshly caught fish. Is there a way to make sure they are prepared and served properly for her and her dog?"

"Of course. It would be my pleasure," Mr. Morley said with a huge grin while stuffing fistfuls of coins in the pockets of his apron. His aura changed from dark brown to vibrant green. His healing had begun, and the money would ensure a successful future if he were smart with it.

"All the years I've come here, I have never seen that man smile until today," Scarlette said.

ZENOBIA, AHY, AND SCARLETTE stepped out into the morning sunlight. People's windows, once locked, were open to let in fresh air. Birds sang as they flew overhead.

"What now?" Zenobia asked. She desperately needed sleep, but she wanted to enjoy her time with Scarlette.

"Time for me to go back to swimming around my beautiful home in the deep blue sea," Scarlette said. She looked vibrant and young, just like in Zenobia's memory of her and her father Black Caesar.

"Ahy and I would be honored to escort you back," Zenobia said.

They turned and headed through the town, back to the ocean. They passed by the village shop, where Zenobia rented a room. The owner and his wife were outside sweeping up and getting ready for the day. When the trio passed them, the couple smiled and waved. There was no longer a dark brown aura emanating from the city.

It was a lighter tan color, with streaks of green. There was hope for the town, Zenobia thought. It wasn't long before they found themselves back on the soft, sandy beach where they first met. Ahy dashed off to chase sandpipers.

"Queen Zenobia, the fierce. This place is different because of you," Scarlette said.

"Scarlette, the Bloodlust pirate, my dear friend. It's different because of us. I will always remember the adventure Ahy and I had with you."

Scarlette tiptoed into the water. As the waves crashed over her boots, they became scaly, iridescent feet and legs. She turned back to Zenobia.

"You must be exhausted and starving for a good meal. There will be a basket of fresh fish for you in a few moments, over by the rocks."

"Thank you, I appreciate it," Zenobia said.

"Oh! I almost forgot! I have an offering for you for spending time with me." The pirate jogged back onto the beach, shedding scales with each step.

She lifted her tricorn, took out a yellowed folded piece of paper tucked in her dreadlocks and handed it along with a few shiny feathers to Zenobia.

"Open this in three months," she said. "It will be a map of sunken treasure for you. I have to collect a few things first before you find it."

The pirate reached into her vest and pulled out an oval-shaped pendant. It had a man, a bull, and a lion engraved on it. "It's shiny, and I liked the faces on it," Scarlette said. For some reason I feel that I should give it to you."

"It's the pendant of Chronos. I saw it once, in Greece." Zenobia reached out and gingerly touched the shiny ring shape in Scarlette's hand. "I was told that supposedly, to make it work, you must first hold it close to your heart, then think back to a specific time and place you want to be. Use as many senses as you can. Remember how you felt, what you smelled, what you heard and what you saw. The more you can recollect, will make the time more vivid. Once you arrive where you want to be, you have exactly eleven minutes and eleven seconds before you are brought back to your natural time. 11:11."

Scarlette stared at the pendant.

"You should use it yourself! Say a proper goodbye to your father. If it really works, give it to me in the future as a keepsake of our adventure today." Zenobia said.

"But it's a gift for you."

"It would make me happier if I could do something special for you. Could I give your old body some kind of proper burial?"

"That's thoughtful of you, but my bones were washed away years ago. The sweet Lord above forgave me my past and blessed me with who I am today."

"I will find a way to honor you, I promise," Zenobia said. Ahy returned to her side.

Scarlette smiled widely.

"Zenobia, may the sun shine upon your face and the wind blow in your favor. I hope you are blessed every day you walk the earth." Scarlette removed her hat and bowed as low as possible one last time to honor her friend the queen.

Zenobia watched as Scarlette dropped to one knee, patted Ahy, and kissed the top of his head gently. Where she stood, more iridescent scales fell into the sand. She stepped back into the warm ocean, shimmied a few times, then extended her arms and leaned backward into the ocean. As the waves engulfed her body, she transformed back into a mermaid. A small voice behind Zenobia gasped. She turned to see a little boy a few yards behind her.

"What's your name?" Zenobia asked. The little boy took a few steps back. "It's okay, although I'm fairly certain someone so young shouldn't be wandering around this town alone. Did I see you earlier at the town meeting?"

"Yes, Ma'am."

Zenobia's little white dog wagged his tail and ran circles around the boy. The boy laughed and clapped his hands.

"Then you know I am Zenobia, and he is Ahy." Ahy sat and allowed the little boy to pat him.

"My name is Ambrose Freeman, Ma'am. My grandpapa Carl hugged that... that pirate lady? My mother sent me to say thank you for blessing my family." Ambrose slowly approached Zenobia, watching her scoop up some of the mermaid's scales. She put some in her pocket and tossed some into the ocean, where they dissolved into foam.

"Can't believe you saw a mermaid, can you?" Zenobia asked. "I couldn't believe it either. Want some scales?"

Ambrose nodded. Zenobia sat in the sand and motioned for the little boy to sit next to her. Together they shifted through soft brown sand, picking and choosing perfectly shaped scales. Her hand brushed against his hand, and she had a flash of Ambrose as a middle-aged man wearing white gloves, dusting small marble statues on pedestals and polishing jewelry in glass cases. Her stomach flipped a few times, and her forehead throbbed. She looked up at the sun and drew a deep breath to take in the scent of the ocean breeze.

"I see you like to collect shells and things. I like to collect things too," she said once she felt somewhat normal.

"I wish I could take them all home," he said.

"Take what you need, to make space for more collectible things you might find. Trust me on this."

Ahy ran to the ocean and yodeled. Zenobia noticed a wooden trap filled with fish by the rocks, just as Scarlette said there would be.

"Ambrose, it's time for Ahy and I to collect our fish and return to town. Would you like to walk back with us?"

Zenobia stood and extended her hand. Ambrose smiled, took her hand.

"When we get back, ask your family if they'd like to join us later for dinner. I'd like to get to know them better."

5

LE CHANT DE LA MORT (THE SONG OF DEATH)

BY JOHN PALISANO

WE BEGIN IN THE dark of night, as so many of the best and most frightening stories do.

A baby born in dirt. Offerings gathered and raised to the high priestess. A new vessel from which sundry things will grow and blossom. The air smells of tattered ragweed and lavender. In the long grass, just beyond the thatched walls, a shaker sounds, freezing me in my spot. Is it an Eastern rattlesnake?

Or someone who has made a rattle from the invasive bamboo, using pebbles from the shallow, green river? Is this all just what is expected of a story set in the deep south? Minds turn to curses, and rituals, and that beautifully glistening mixture of the supernatural, the French, the darkness, and a form of Christianity called voodoo. This is the image that haunts me. Each time it arrives, more details come with it, while others fade. Maybe, I thought, it'd be a good idea to write some of this down so I won't forget.

I take the water bottle from my makeshift nightstand and look at the yellow moonlight coming through my window. I really should remember to close the shade before I pass out. The copy of Toni Morrison reminds me each night I plan on losing myself in a few pages—a salve for the rote frustrations and humiliations I go through daily.

La Gourmandise has kept me sheltered and fed, I remind myself. So what if I'm a line cook and prep cook and whatever else is needed to keep the place running? I got all the food I needed at the restaurant, anyway. It's not the medical or doctor position I'd always dreamt of. Those were dashed during my first year at Tulane. I just didn't have it in me. I don't know what I have in me.

Except for the venom. That's something I know is still in me, even though the counter measures were supposed to have neutralized it. But I still feel it in me, hiding like a sand crab on the shores of the Gulf, ready to pounce when a biting fly lands too close.

THE MILLIPEDE'S FACE LOOKED like it was grinning—like an old smiley face cartoon. Only it wasn't benign. That was a trick. It crawled up on me, as heavy as a serpent, and nearly as long. Who knew they got so big? I felt its pointed feet moving ever so slightly, keeping it balanced, checking me for any sudden movements. And it was the same deep red color as day-old blood left to dry.

My leg shifted. I couldn't help it. Instinct. I wanted to shake it off. It knew, and so it bit me, right in the middle of my belly by my navel and was gone in a blink. Under my bed. Under a cabinet. Inside a closet. I don't know. My efficiency didn't have too many hiding places, and I didn't even have a stove or fridge. Not back then. It was bare bones.

IT STUNG LIKE FIRE where it'd bitten me. I got up and went to my bathroom sink. I had some Castile soap and rubbed some on, but the mint made it worse. At least it was clean. Or so I thought.

An hour later, I had the worst fever of my life. I waited through it all night, tossing and turning, trying to find any kind of almost-comfortable position. No dice. It was one of the few days I was glad to go to work. Mister Jeffries would know what to do. They'd probably have a tincture there to set me right.

While I was blacked out, I remembered my uncle Lucas. "You're something special, Antoine. Don't let anyone make you think different."

"How so?"

"Your momma's white and your daddy's black. So, you've got a lot of mixed blood in you."

"That's good?"

"It is to me. But it's not for everyone. That's why we got you hidden down here. Where no one will question you or give you a second look."

"Am I Creole?"

Uncle Lucas didn't give himself away. "I'll tell you everything when you're seventeen."

He was gone long before. I still don't know my history.

EDGAR JONES STOOD OVER me. I thought I was hallucinating. Maybe I was just a little. What was my boss doing in my room? He rented it to me, sure, but he never came near it.

He put the back of his hand on my forehead. "You've been hitting the sauce?"

I couldn't speak. Couldn't move.

"Nah. Not you. You've got some kind of fever."

There was someone next to him. A very well put together woman. "His hand's on his stomach," she said. "Like he's covering something."

"Hope he ain't been stabbed or shot."

He moved my hand away from my stomach. His eyes went wide. "What in hell?"

The woman looked down. Nodded. "He's been bit."

"By what?"

"By fate, it seems," she said. "We better act right away, or he won't make it, but for a few days."

My heart raced. I was paralyzed and couldn't do a damn thing to help myself.

"It's gonna cost him, though," she said. "You think it's worth it?"

He nodded. "Yes, I do, Zenobia. I do, indeed."

THERE ARE BRANCH-LIKE THINGS crawling, seeing, searching. For me. They stick into me in places, and I feel them. My veins hurt near where they go inside me. They say you can't feel when blood is taken except where the needle pokes you, but I felt this. I was sure my veins were being pinched like paper straws. It hurt and made them sore, and I wanted them to stop.

Other branch things slid into me in other places. The most tender was under my belt, where my privates were. They went inside somehow.

This is when I first heard the song.

I can't play an instrument. Wish I could. Maybe I'd write it down. But I can remember every movement. Every instrument. Some I've never heard before. Cosmic stuff.

I'm so high up in the air. How can this be possible? When I look down at the crisscrossed streets, many lit with streetlamps, it seems remarkable I can walk and step and look down as easily as if I were on Decatur peering down at the sidewalk.

The clouds break and there are large, gray spheres that appear. They are at once smooth and perfect but texturized and imperfect up close. Like a face that looks young from far away but that you can make out the age as you get closer. The skin, mottled. The lines, apparent. The illusion, broken.

And the millipede returns.

The kids wear flared jeans and listen to long songs with shuffling beats. It's like they're accessing that same place the venom brought me. Almost. Just not as deep.

And the millipede comes back.

This time it wants to take me on the forever journey. I'm ready for it. We end as we began, in the dark of night, as so many of the best and most frightening stories end.

I'm a young man dying in dirt, my suffering and soul the offerings gifted to the high priestess. From my beaten vessel, new sundry things will grow and blossom. I glimpse them as I fade. I recognize the scents of tattered ragweed and lavender, familiar, but I'm not sure why.

And then, sounds. I hear music. A song for one.

The song of death. Le chant de la mort.

I rest in darkness.
How long, I'm not sure.
Days. Months. Years.
I cannot move.
I cannot breathe.
Somehow, my blood feels energized.
Rising, I push away the cloth laid upon me.
Sit up on the small, wooden bed.

I am alive.
Once more.
Once again.
My hands twitch.
I must find a way to play the song
looping in my head.
A piano. A guitar.
And I will play it for her...
Zenobia.
An offering...
A song for two...
who've cheated death...
escaped by the light of...
the purple crescent moon.

FIN.

6

THE DEVOTED DEFENDER

BY DENISE TAPSCOTT

The South, 1863

UNION SOLDIER NEIL PORTER flinched at imaginary gun-fire erupting around him as he drove his horse-drawn wagon down a dusty road. The deep booms of cannons and high-pitched screams of dying men filled his mind, followed by a shrill ringing in his ears.

"You alright?" his best friend Alvin Simmons asked, sitting beside him.

With shaky hands, Neil pulled the horse to the side of the road. He removed his dark blue Union cap and rubbed his face. After a few moments, he shook his head in hopes of clearing the sounds that haunted him.

"Honestly no. But when I have some of your wife's precious home cooking you bragged about, I think I will be just fine," Neil joked.

"Yeah," Alvin admitted.

They exchanged weary looks. The sun was too bright; the air was too humid, and they had too many miles to travel, starting from Maryland going all the way down to Virginia. Both men stank of blood, mud, and gunpowder. As Alvin adjusted in his seat on the wagon, Neil noticed he winced.

"You alright?" Neil asked.

"No, but like you said, when I have some of my wife's home cooking, I will be just fine." Both men laughed. Alvin shifted again.

"Lemme take a look," Neil said and leaned over. Alvin cautiously removed his hat. Neil gingerly checked the bloody bandages wrapped around Alvin's head. Small buckshot wounds speckled the right side of Alvin's face and ear. A few bright red droplets of blood gleamed in the sun through his thick, nappy hair. "They almost got you in Antietam." Neil said. "Almost."

"Nah. With you by my side, Lieutenant, they couldn't get me." Alvin laughed.

"First Officer Simmons, with the Negro infantry men fighting side by side like brothers, them damn southerners couldn't get hardly any of us," Neil said with satisfaction.

"We were proud to have you with our regiment. You are a strong leader. Some of them white Union boys were reluctant to fight side by side with us until they saw how fierce we were. We got those Confederates good."

Neil shook his head in disgust.

"I don't understand it. It burns my soul that white people treat y'all differently. You are a man; I am a man. You fear God, I fear God. So, we look a little different. It don't matter none. I'm proud to call you my brother any day. Hell, I don't claim the kin that I do have."

"Don't get too soft on me now," Alvin joked.

"I'm serious! Trust and believe that I consider you and yours as my family. When you showed up on the field without a decent weapon, I knew had to give you my daddy's cutlass pistol. Seemed like the right thing to do, especially because you saved my life a few times out there."

Both men sat in silence, thinking about the hideous battle they endured. The nightmarish battle of Antietam would haunt them for years. Eventually Alvin spoke up.

"I appreciate you, brother Neil," Alvin said. "You have a heart of gold underneath all that dirty blonde hair."

Neil laughed heartily.

"I appreciate you too, brother Alvin."

"Let's get a move on. My wife has some cooking to do!"

"I hope she makes peach cobbler. I sure could use some right about now," Neil said.

Chicago, Illinois, 1926

SIX-YEAR-OLD DAISY PAXTON PEEKED around her father's waist to look at a pale stranger who knocked on their door. It was right after lunchtime on a Saturday afternoon when her father shooed her away and invited the man into their cramped, stuffy apartment. Between boxes of Madam C. J. Walker's black hair products and piles of half-read books, there wasn't much space for the man to have a seat.

Except for the police, it was rare that white people came to their Chicago neighborhood. Daisy certainly never saw one visit the Paxton home. When the guest removed his hat, Daisy stared at his thin salt and pepper hair that barely covered the pulsing blue blood vessels on the sides of his head. He was very boney and had many wrinkles in the corners of his blue eyes. She thought he could use a good meal.

She was supposed to be helping her mother wash and dry dishes, but instead she strained to see what was going on. Her mother, Valerie, nervously smoothed out her apron over her handmade house dress.

"Daisy May, stay out of grown folks' business," she warned. Valerie eventually pointed at Daisy and then their bedroom.

"Yes, Ma'am," Daisy said as she slowly crossed from the kitchen. Her mother's stern look burned in the back of her head.

Daisy didn't sleep in her parent's room, but whenever the adults had things to discuss, it was where she was banished until they were done. She closed the door as slow as humanly possible until her father Amos slammed it shut. Pressing her ear against the door, she could barely make out the muffled tones of her father's and the stranger's voices. The downstairs neighbors were yelling very angry, nasty things at each other, as usual, and the neighbors on both sides were blasting unappreciated jazz music. The constant rumbling of traffic that bled through the windows didn't help much either.

The low tones of the men's voices were interrupted by Valerie shouting, "Oh my Lord, are you serious?"

Daisy dared to open the door, where she found her father energetically shaking hands with the thin man. Her mom danced as if she were in church, stomping her feet, rolling her shoulders, and clapping her hands.

"What's going on Mommy?" she asked.

"Mister Ryder here is a lawyer, and he's come to tell us that we've inherited a house all the way out in Virginia. It's on a few acres of land, with lots of rooms and plenty of fresh air." Valerie explained, as tears streamed down her cheeks.

"A house? A real house?" Daisy asked. She had always dreamed of living in a home with a front yard and a backyard where she could play for hours on end.

"Yes, little lady," Mr. Ryder said with a broad smile. "By all accounts it looks like you'll get your own room," he said as he saw his way out of the Paxton's home. The rest of the details were a blur when Amos swooped up Daisy and danced with both of his ladies in their tiny living room until his knees ached.

"We should take a moment and say a prayer of thanks," Valerie said. "We have been truly blessed."

As Daisy was gently returned to the linoleum floor, she watched her father kiss her mother passionately. And then, with grateful tears, the family held hands and bowed their heads.

"Heavenly Father, we take the time to thank you for our new house in Richmond, Virginia. We also give thanks that we can leave Chicago for new beginnings down South. We are grateful to the man who honors our family lineage, and we pray that he found peace up there in heaven above with you. We give you all the glory, in Jesus' name."

The family said amen and laughed themselves silly with joy.

IT WAS WELL PAST bedtime and there was absolutely no way little Daisy was going to sleep. Wearing her favorite soft pink nightgown, she trembled under a pile of blankets on her new bed. Things were very different tonight than they had been in the last two weeks.

It felt like a lifetime ago when the family held hands and said a prayer of thanks for their newly inherited house. The first day they arrived at the new house, they stood together on luscious green grass under a fresh blue sky. The abandoned two-story house looked lonely, as if it was waiting for just the right family to fix it up here and there, showing it some love.

Richmond was such a wonderful change from the hustle and bustle of their overcrowded, smelly, old apartment building in Chicago. Daisy was excited about having her very own room that she could decorate any way she wanted! At her insistence, wallpaper with pink and white daisies, just like her name, covered the walls. Auntie Brenda made her a quilt with white hand stitched daisies.

No matter how much she loved her room, not even the butterfly lamp her dad found for her at a local store could keep away the disturbing growling from her closet or the creepy, constant scratching inside the walls. She trembled when invisible footsteps stomped around her bed.

Unlike the rest of the house, her room was always cold, day or night. She heard the muffled voices of her parents and she wanted to run to them, but she didn't dare leave the safety of her bed.

"Tell me again that this is real, not a dream," Valerie said to Amos as she laid her head on his chest. The two were downstairs, cuddled up on a large couch with a heavy wooden frame. Although they now had a small library across from Daisy's room, small stacks of books still made their way into the salon.

"This house was owned by the first-born son of the Porter family. In his will, he insisted that after his death, whoever lived here had to be a descendant of slaves the family once owned. He felt that it was his responsibility to make things right for what happened back in the day. Once an occupant moved out or died, someone from the family law firm would find other families, descendants of the slaves, and invite them to live here as long as they wanted. Thanks to our roots, the house…"

"…and the car," Valerie interjected.

"Yes baby, the house, and the car, that horrendous weapon over the fireplace and all the land they sit upon is ours." Amos said. The couple glanced up at a menacing-looking cutlass pistol with a thick, sharp blade attached to the barrel. It was on display in a glass case high over the fireplace mantel.

"This house is a dream come true," Valerie said. Footsteps and pounding above broke the quiet moment between them. "Speaking of dreams, let me check up on that little girl and see why she's still awake," Valerie said. She kissed her husband and headed upstairs.

Valerie's soft knock upon Daisy's bedroom door stopped the hissing under the bed, the flickering light as well as the other random paranormal activity in the little girl's room.

"Honey, can I come in?" Valerie asked.

"Mommy!" Daisy burst into tears. Valerie rushed in to her daughter's side.

"Sweetie, why are you still up, and why is it so cold in here?" Valerie asked. She frowned at the dark circles under her daughter's eyes. "We talked about you going to sleep at a decent time. You shouldn't be up running around and playing with your dolls. Your father and I heard you making a ruckus. You should be asleep."

"It's not me! There's something wrong with my room," Daisy said in between sobs.

"Now Daisy...." Valerie started.

The invisible heavy footsteps pounded across the floor, from the door to the closet. Valerie looked at Daisy and back to the closet. Her bedroom window slowly slid open and then banged shut. An underlying stench of decay and gunpowder filled the room.

"Get out!" an angry voice shouted. An unseen force crashed into the foot of Daisy's bed, followed by heavy footsteps scuffling around until the bedroom door squeaked open.

"Daddy!"

"Amos!" Valerie shouted, while holding Daisy close.

Amos, belly full of his wife's delicious cooking and weary from a long day of teaching at the local elementary school, trudged up the stairs towards his daughter's room.

"I'm coming," he said. "Hold your horses." As he reached the top of the staircase, a vase full of flowers flew out of Daisy's room and crashed into the hallway.

"What the devil is going on here?" he asked as he rushed in. Although the room was eerily quiet, Daisy's clothing, books, and dolls were haphazardly strewn all around. Valerie and Daisy clung to each other on her small bed.

"There's something wrong," Valerie said.

"I told you, mommy," Daisy said.

"Sweetheart, I know the move has been a big deal for all of us, with your mom selling Madam C.J. Walker's hair products and me teaching at your new school. However, there's no reason for you to act out like this."

"Amos, you are not listening. She's right," Valerie said. "There is something wrong with the house."

"All I know is that it's late and…" Amos started but was interrupted by the bedroom door slamming shut, followed by more heavy footsteps running around the room.

The scent of burnt flesh and rotten eggs filled the air. A miniature white and blue ceramic pitcher from Daisy's tea set rose in the air and flew across the room at Amo's head. It stopped in midair, inches away from his nose. Slowly, it lowered to the floor. Daisy burst into tears again when they all heard growling and hissing from the walls.

"Come on girls, we're leaving," he said, sweeping Daisy up in his arms. Valerie followed closely behind him.

AFTER SPENDING AN EXHAUSTING week with Valerie's sisters, Brenda and Myrna, and their incredibly large families two hours away in Danville, and after many exasperating calls to the local church in Richmond, Daisy and her parents eventually returned to their country home. They sat in their inherited Ford Model T and stared at their inherited two-story home.

Although Amos had repainted it and Valerie hung fresh drapes in all windows, the house wasn't as charming as the first time they gazed upon it. The flowers Daisy tended to on the front lawn (with her father's help, of course) drooped and wilted. Daisy wondered if maybe the house needed love from a different family.

"Daddy, do we have to go back inside?" Daisy asked while clinging to a doll one of her uncles made for her. It had a pink dress and matching bows in its curly black hair made of yarn.

"No, baby. We're all going to sit out here and wait for Pastor Stewart from the church to show up. He's going to bring his best bible and strongest prayers to clear out our house," he said.

"This has to work," Valerie said. "We can't afford to go back to Chicago, and there's no way we can continue to stay with my sisters. Last week was stressful enough for all of us and they already have more folks expected to come through their place next weekend," she said.

"I know," Amos admitted. "Plus, I had a few choice words with Brenda's husband, so we aren't welcomed back."

"Why? What happened?"

"Frankly, I didn't like the way his son Cornell spoke to you, or Daisy, and I told him so. Then yesterday he accused Daisy of beating up the boy and..."

"My little Daisy? He must have been mistaken," Valerie said.

"Sorry Mommy," Daisy admitted. "He was mean to me, so my friend slapped him a few times."

Valerie looked at Amos, who shared a quizzical look. They turned around and looked at Daisy in the back, seated behind her mother.

"Your friend?" Valerie asked.

"His name is very long, so I just call him Ten-Ten. He doesn't scare me anymore."

"Baby, who is this 'Ten-Ten'? " Amos asked.

"What does he look like? Have we met him?" Valerie asked.

"He said he owned our house. I don't know what he looks like, but I can hear him. He said he's here to protect me from the bad man and anyone else he doesn't like."

Valerie and Amos stared at each other for a moment.

"You know that Daddy and I will always protect you," Valerie said.

"He said he knows you're doing your best, but there are some things that mommies and daddies can't fight as good as him. That's why he followed us to Miss Brenda and Miss Myrna's house. He says that summa na itch Cornell is good for nothing, and he had got what was coming to him. He also says that his daddy is a yellow bellied…"

"Daisy! We don't use that kind of language!" her mom said.

"But that's what he said just now," Daisy said.

"Just now? Where is Ten-Ten?" Amos asked.

"Right here, next to me in the car."

"Nope!" Valerie exclaimed. "Everyone out of the car, right this minute." The back door on the driver's side squeaked open by itself.

Valerie burst out of the car from the passenger's side and opened the back door for Daisy. She scooped up her daughter in her arms and backed away from the vehicle. As Amos joined his family, the car shuddered and rocked from side to side. The doors opened and slammed shut, and the horn honked sporadically. Daisy cried and Valerie screamed. Although at his wits' end, Amos consoled his family the best he could. As he wiped Daisy's tears, she looked over his shoulder.

"Look daddy, the churchman is here!"

The family turned to see a well-dressed African American man approach the family on a donkey pulled wagon.

"Isn't he a sight for sore eyes?" Valerie said.

"Looks kinda young to be a pastor of a church," Amos noted. The visitor was dressed in an all-black suit, including his wide-brimmed hat.

"Pastor Stewart, I presume?" Amos asked when the man was close.

"The pastor sends his regards," he said and flashed a bright smile. "Our pastor had other obligations, so he sent me instead. I'm Deacon Ezra. Nice to meet you," he said and tipped his hat.

UP IN DAISY'S ROOM, Valerie and Amos nervously watched Deacon Ezra set up for a protection ritual. After he prayed Psalm 91 and polished a golden amulet of Saint Benedict around his neck, he strategically set out his large, worn-out bible, a handful of white candles and a bottle of holy water on their daughter's small desk. Daisy was instructed that regardless of what she might hear, it was important that she waited downstairs in the salon until the grownups were done banishing the demon in their house.

Lurking at the bottom of the staircase, Daisy strained to listen. She heard the deacon announce that he was going to begin with the Lord's prayer. She toyed with the idea of sneaking upstairs to watch the ritual of banishing a demon when there was a startling, distinctive knock at the front door. Her parents were obviously busy, and she knew better than to let strangers in. On the other hand, they hadn't had a single visitor since they moved into the new house, so she dared to tiptoe over and peek out of the front window.

A tall, dark-skinned woman in a tailored dark purple dress and matching wide-brimmed hat waited on the front porch. A little white dog sat at her feet.

"Doggie!" Daisy exclaimed and opened the front door.

"Hello young lady. I'm guessing that you are Miss Daisy Paxton," the woman said.

"Yes Ma'am." Daisy said.

"It's nice to meet you. My name is Grandmother Zenobia, and this is my dog Ahy. Your auntie Myrna said you might need my help. May we come in?"

Daisy hesitated.

"From what I was told about your parents, I know that you are a smart young lady and that normally you wouldn't dare let a stranger into your home. I think they will understand that it's okay to let us in. This is a special case."

Daisy heard the Deacon chanting his prayers upstairs. Every now and then, her parents would answer yes, Lord. She carefully considered the options of a dreaded spanking or random help from a stranger with a cute puppy dog. She decided to let the woman in.

"Ahy, come," Grandmother Zenobia said to the dog. He sniffed Daisy as he made his way into the house.

Grandmother Zenobia paused and smelled the air when she entered the home. Daisy decided to sniff the air too, out of curiosity. To her, it smelled dusty and stale, with a slight aroma of the last dinner they had before they ran out. Grandmother Zenobia sat on a loveseat in the salon. Daisy sat next to her, copying the way her guest sat tall, with her hands folded in her lap. They both listened to the Deacon chanting a bible verse.

"May I pet your dog?" Daisy asked.

"Thank you for asking! Ahy would like that very much," Grandmother Zenobia said.

However, when Daisy reached to touch Ahy, he backed up, growled, and yodeled. Daisy snatched her hand back. Ahy ran circles all around the salon and then charged full speed at the staircase. He stopped at the first stair and continued to growl. Grandmother sniffed again, so Daisy did too. This time, she smelled a faint musty and sweaty odor. Daisy was upset at the dog's behavior.

"Well, that's not what I expected," Grandmother Zenobia said and wrapped her arm around Daisy's shoulders. "Sweetheart, I need to you to be a very brave girl. Can you do that for me?"

Daisy grew more anxious.

"I promise that you are safe with us."

"Safer than with Ten-Ten?" Daisy asked.

"Most definitely," Grandmother assured her. "Speaking of which, here he comes now," Grandmother said and nodded at the staircase.

Daisy watched as Ahy backed up, baring his teeth. He then stopped, sniffed the air, and wagged his tail. His head slightly bounced up and down, which looked peculiar to Daisy. But then she saw a large, muscular white hand appear, petting the dog's head. Then there was an arm, a torso and then an entire white man knelt, scratching the dog's ears. A blond, blue-eyed man with a scruffy beard wearing a tattered Union soldier uniform materialized. He turned and looked at Daisy.

"My sweet girl," he said. The apparition smiled and put his hand on his chest. He then looked over at Grandmother Zenobia suspiciously. He flickered sporadically.

"So, soldiers don't have manners here in Virginia?" Grandmother asked in a disapproving tone. He disappeared for a moment and reappeared in front of Grand-mother Zenobia. He waved at her. She didn't budge, but Daisy smiled nervously and waved back at him. His face twitched a few times, and he patted the back of his head.

"Hmm," Grandmother said.

"Wait, Miss Daisy can see me?" he asked. His image continued to flicker.

"Yes sir, we both can," Grandmother Zenobia said.

"Oh, my lord! Please forgive me, Madam!" He bowed deeply and removed his hat. "I am Second Lieutenant Neil Simmons. I am more than honored to make your ac-quaintance." He then stood proudly, puffing out his chest.

"It's my friend! Ten–Ten!" Daisy exclaimed. "Ten–Ten, this nice lady is Nana…"

"You may call me Grandmother Zenobia."

"It would be my pleasure. It's been a long time since anyone has seen me," Neil said.

"Miss Daisy, you know this spirit?"

"Yes Ma'am. He protects me from the bad man."

Before Grandmother could ask, Ahy growled and yo-deled again at the staircase. A raggedy, dark–haired man wearing a shoddy gray Confederate uniform stormed down the stairs. He lunged at Neil.

"Get back here, you son of a…"

"Language!" Grandmother Zenobia warned. Daisy put her hand over her mouth. The Confederate soldier stopped in his tracks. He also flickered at a quicker pace than Neil. Grandmother Zenobia raised one eyebrow at the spirit.

"They can see us?" he asked Lt. Neil.

"Yes sir, they sure can."

"Of course, the first one to see me in this state is a Negro," he said. "Of all the people on this here planet and I have to converse with a bunch of…"

Lt. Neil tackled the Confederate soldier and punched him in the face a few times.

"Do not speak about my guests in that manner!" The Confederate soldier vanished. Neil stood and straightened his uniform. "I'm so sorry Grandmother Zenobia, Miss Daisy. That is my brother Earl. He truly has no manners."

"Daisy, would you be a dear and fetch me a glass of water? I need to have a word with your friend," Grandmother said. She watched as Lt. Neil shook his head slightly and cringed as if he heard something from far away. He faded in and out.

"Ahy will make sure his brother doesn't bother you."

"Yes Ma'am," Daisy said. She was still shocked and slightly relieved that she could see her friend. As she entered the kitchen, she wondered how her parents were doing with the Deacon.

WHEN SHE AND AHY returned with a glass of water, she found her mother in the salon speaking to Grandmother Zenobia. Valerie's hair was a bit disheveled. There was no sign of Lt. Neil.

"Mommy!" Daisy beamed.

"Hi sweetheart," Valerie said.

"Miss Daisy, I think your mother could use that glass of water more than I." Grandmother said. Daisy handed the glass to her mom.

"Thank you," Valerie said. Daisy watched as she guzzled down half the glass of water.

"You have a lovely daughter, and a lovely home," Grandmother Zenobia said. "Just so you know, Daisy was not going to let a stranger in, but I explained this was a very special circumstance. Your sister Myrna contacted me and told me about your situation. Your other sister, Brenda, had some wild accusations about Daisy beating up some boy twice her size. It seemed very odd to her, and she asked me to do a supernatural check up on you and your family. I don't leave my home in New Orleans much, but when I heard a child was involved, I had to come and see for myself."

"A supernatural checkup?" Valerie asked.

"Yes. It might be hard to understand, but..."

"No, I think understand." Valerie paused quite a bit before she continued. "I've heard rumors about you. The incredible root worker, voodoo woman, Grandmother Zenobia. I didn't think you were real."

"I see. Well, here I am, in your home. If that's okay?"

"Mommy, can she stay? Please?" Daisy asked.

"Yes, of course, just as long as you behave yourself."

"I promise," she said. Daisy beamed and then thoughtfully pet Ahy. Valerie was surprised at how much Daisy took a liking to the stranger in her house.

"Grandmother Zenobia, what's your opinion about what's going on?" Valerie asked.

"Your house is not possessed by demons. Are demons real? Unfortunately, yes, but you don't have to worry about that today."

Valerie clutched her pearls. "Today?" Valerie asked.

Grandmother Zenobia continued without missing a beat.

"There are two ghosts haunting your home. It's two brothers fighting like cats and dogs, making a huge mess of things. One of them, the one with some manners, has taken a liking to your daughter. I'm guessing that he's the one who beat up that boy at your sister's home. The lieutenant is very protective of her."

As if on cue, Lt. Neil appeared like a mist in the salon.

"Ma'am can Miss Valerie see me?" he asked Grandmother Zenobia.

She looked over at Valerie and shook her head no.

"Sorry Ten-Ten," Daisy said.

"Please tell her that those pearls are lovely on her. They used to belong to Miss Ruthie, Alvin's wife. Once she passed, no one dared wear them. People have come and gone in this house and that necklace has been sitting all alone, collecting dust for years, until now."

Valerie had a strange look on her face.

"More importantly, please tell Miss Valerie that she's an outstanding mother and that she and Mister Amos are raising a delightful young lady. Miss Daisy reminds me so very much of Miss Sabrina, Alvin and Ruthie's youngest daughter back in the day. When Alvin was on his deathbed, I swore to him that I'd protect her and his entire family. I will do everything in my power to protect Daisy as well."

Valerie looked at Grandmother Zenobia, then Daisy, then around the salon.

"Uh, did I just hear Ten-Ten?" she managed to ask.

"Lieutenant Neil Simmons at your service, Miss Valerie."

Daisy thought her mother was going to faint.

"I should get my husband and the deacon. Do you mind keeping an eye on my daughter?" she asked.

"Daisy is in good hands," Grandmother Zenobia said. Daisy sat close to Grandmother Zenobia and Ahy sat at their feet.

Moments later Valerie led a worn-out looking Amos, and an energized looking Deacon Ezra, armed with the word of God, into the salon. Before any introductions could be made, the temperature in the room dropped quickly. Earl appeared and body slammed Neil, causing books to fall off a bookshelf. Ahy yodeled and lunged at Earl, who picked up a book to throw at his brother.

Amos and Valerie watched in horror as books flew off bookshelves. Some crashed into walls while some levitated around the room. The sounds of growls and grunts bounced around the room. The air smelled like sulfur and sweat. Deacon Ezra opened his bible and started shouting verses from the Old Testament. Daisy clung to Grandmother Zenobia when Earl grabbed a candlestick.

"Daisy, don't be frightened. You see those two silly fools fighting in your beautiful new house?"

She tightened her grip on Grandmother but watched the two men fight.

"All they are doing is making a lot of noise, and a big mess for your family to clean up later. I don't know about you, but I have had enough of this. Silly white boys wasting our time. Shame on them. Lord knows they both need a bath and a good spanking."

Daisy loosened her grip. Neil snatched the candlestick from Earl and pushed him hard, causing him to tumble and fall hard on his backside. Daisy giggled.

"Am I right, or am I right, young lady?" Grandmother joked and then continued to fuss. Ahy backed off and sat next to Daisy. Valerie, Amos, and Deacon Ezra were puzzled.

"Can you hear them?" Valerie asked. Amos and Deacon Ezra nodded.

"Let's get to the bottom of this ruckus," Grandmother said. She reached into a pocket and took out an embroidered cotton handkerchief. Daisy beamed when she saw it had little daisies along its borders. Grandmother Zenobia opened her hand, revealing a shiny pile of small buttons.

"Neil and Earl Simmons, I demand your full attention. Stop with all that catty-wompass nonsense."

Neil disappeared into a mist and reappeared in front of her. He stood at attention. Grandmother noticed his right eye twitched sporadically. Earl faded in and out near the mantle, growling.

"What did that bitch say to me?" Earl said and charged Grandmother Zenobia from the back of the salon. Daisy and the rest of the group gasped. Grandmother Zenobia calmly threw three buttons at the spirit. He howled and sizzled away into a puff of smoke.

"Is he gone?" Valerie asked.

"Temporarily. He'll return after he collects himself." Grandmother said nonchalantly.

"She's right, he'll be back in a moment," Neil said. "I usually count down from ten. He appears around four or three, depending on how feisty he is." As he counted backwards from ten, Valerie, Amos and Deacon Ezra watched the Union soldier faintly materialize before them. Valerie gasped. Amos stepped in front of her and took a protective stance. The deacon rifled through his bible for another appropriate verse.

"So, you are Daisy's friend Ten-Ten?" Valerie asked, interrupting his countdown.

"You all can see me? I am so pleased to make all of your acquaintances. I apologize for my brother's disrespectful behavior." Neil said. Daisy thought his eyes were as blue as the sky was on the day they moved into their new home.

Like clockwork, Earl reappeared, and everyone could see him.

"You are back, I see. I suggest you behave yourself," Grandmother Zenobia warned.

"How dare you call me out of my name!" he shouted, flickering violently.

Daisy noticed that Grandmother Zenobia was irritated with the unruly spirit.

"I am merely a guest in this house, but I bet that this family will not tolerate that kind of behavior here. Especially that kind of language."

"I don't care who you are."

Grandmother picked out three more buttons and handed them to Daisy. Neil appeared at the young girl's side, ready to attack his brother.

"My darling, throw these iron buttons at the bad spirit. If you miss, don't worry, I have plenty more."

Earl growled and charged Grandmother Zenobia. Daisy tossed the small pieces of iron at the spirit. Once again, he howled and sizzled away. Neil bellowed with laughter. Daisy giggled and her parents relaxed. The deacon kept reading bible verses.

"That's what he deserves! He should know better. My goodness, I haven't laughed like that in God knows how long." Neil wiped his ghostly tears on his cheeks and sighed. Everyone watched as his demeanor changed.

"You know, we weren't raised to be that disrespectful. I regret that our family used to own slaves. It hurts my heart. Earl didn't seem to care one way or another, for quite some time. He eventually changed into someone awful before the war." Neil said to Grandmother Zenobia.

Earl popped back up.

"Are you ready to speak with us now?" Grandmother Zenobia asked.

Earl growled and then mumbled.

"Speak up when spoken to," Grandmother Zenobia said and offered Daisy more buttons.

Earl flinched.

"Yes ma'am. I was trying to say my name is Earl Porter. P–O–R–T–E–R. He's got everything all wrong. We ain't even from around these parts. We hail from South Carolina. This damn fool always has to be different from the rest of the family. Stupid blond hair, perfect blue eyes. He is the only one in our family that fought for the Union. Me and my six brothers fought for the confederacy. I heard Daddy tell Momma that Neil was a disgrace to our family."

"Don't you bring up Momma," Neil warned.

"This Judas bought property here and changed his name to Simmons because of some..."

"Watch what you say," Neil threatened. "I will continue to fight you in front of these nice people if I have to."

"It's the damn truth!" Earl whined.

"Yea, you right."

Everyone turned their attention to the Union soldier.

"I changed my last name to Simmons, not that my family acknowledged it, in order to protect and defend my best friend, Alvin. We fought side by side in the war at Antietam. Things were very hard for him and his family; come to think of it, it was difficult for all the freed people after the Civil war ended. I swore back then and continue to swear to this very day that I will assist, protect and defend any and all Black people to the best of my abilities. Especially any descendants of those we enslaved. I cannot abide by anyone who treats Black folk less than equal, including my own flesh and blood."

"Is that why the two of you have been quarreling after all these years, instead of going into the light?" Grandmother Zenobia asked.

"No ma'am," Earl said. "This son of a…"

Daisy cocked her arm, ready to throw the iron at him.

"I mean, my so-called brother gave my cutlass pistol to…Alvin." Earl gritted his teeth and clenched his fists as he spoke, dragging out each word with his southern drawl. Daisy thought he looked like he was trying to choke down something awful like cod liver oil.

"You had already passed away at the Battle of Belmont. Your clumsy ass got struck by a cannon ball! My best friend needed it," Neil said.

"Daddy gave ME that gun, not some gator bait darkie." Earl yelled.

Before Daisy could throw silver at Earl, Neil unleashed his rage. He jumped on Earl and stomped on his head repeatedly.

"Do not speak about Black people that way! Ever!" Neil screamed. Grandmother Zenobia covered Daisy's eyes and tossed iron buttons on both spirits. Amos looked at Grandmother Zenobia as an idea popped into his head.

"You see that ugly thing over the fireplace?" he said as he pointed at a menacing-looking weapon in a glass box over the mantle. It was displayed high on a small ledge.

"We hate that pistol with the knife attached to it. I feel awful every time I notice it," Valerie mentioned. "We haven't unpacked the rest of our belongings, let alone had the chance to do some serious redecorating."

"I wonder if that's what Earl is talking about?" Amos said.

"It could very well be. Sometimes spirits attach them-selves to objects. Maybe that's why Earl is still here on earth." Grandmother Zenobia said.

"If we take it down, I could sprinkle some holy water over it, to help the transition," Deacon Ezra chimed in.

"I don't care what you do with it. I know I don't want it in my house," Valerie said.

Daisy nodded in agreement. She thought the sharp knife in the glass box was scary.

"I love that idea," Grandmother Zenobia said, and patted Daisy on the back to comfort her. "The bigger problem is that those two spirits have been here on the Earth too long. Spirits start to decay and get all twisted up if they take too long to go into the light. We have some convinc-ing to do and we don't have much time. I think both of them have deteriorated considerably. They are losing their human spirit, and turning more demonic, especially Earl, with all that growling he does."

Deacon Ezra loosened his collar.

"Let's start with taking down that weapon."

IT WAS NEIL WHO appeared first in the dining room, where everyone nervously waited. Grandmother Zenobia noticed the specter's hands shook when he spoke.

"Miss Daisy, everyone, please excuse my behavior. I know it was unacceptable, and I beg of you to find it in your hearts to forgive me. Earl gets me so fired up."

Earl showed up right after Neil and simply stared hard at everyone. Daisy noticed ghostly drool leaking from the corner of his mouth. Had it been real drool, she would have hated to be the one to clean it up. Earl didn't say a word until Ezra removed a piece of linen in front of him, unveiling the infamous firearm with an eleven-inch curved blade attached to the barrel. It gleamed under the light of a dusty chandelier as it sat in the middle of the dark wood dining room table.

"There's your gun. The one Daddy gave you," Neil said.

"That's not just any 'gun'. I will have you know that it is a Cyrus B. Allen cutlass pistol." Earl's demeanor softened. "Do you see that beautiful walnut wood grip? Daddy said not many were made, and he got this one special, just for me. That's how I knew I was special, too." He smiled brightly when he spoke. His uniform looked a little cleaner, and he stood taller.

Earl barely noticed that the Paxton family and Deacon Ezra quietly prayed over the pistol.

"Earl Porter, I have a proposition for you. We can bury your gun with your bones down in South Carolina, on the condition that you pass into the light." Grandmother Zenobia said.

"How do I know this ain't some trick?" he asked.

"No trick. You've been here long enough. Aren't you tired of fighting your brother? You finally get what you've wanted, and you get to heal. You will have peace of mind."

Earl looked at the gun again.

"And if I don't go?" he asked.

"I will dump a ton of iron in your grave and a mound of salt on your bones. You want that kind of agony?" Grandmother warned.

"We done quarreling here, Earl. You know you want to hold that pistol again," Neil said. "These nice people will gladly make things right."

"I will put the pistol in your hands myself," Deacon Ezra assured him. He picked up the weapon and held it out.

"Take a close look at it," Grandmother Zenobia said.

Earl leaned in close and examined the gun.

"Would you look at that! Right there. Daddy had it engraved with my name on it. I never noticed that before," Earl said.

"I don't know how many times I had to tell you he loved you," Neil said. Daisy and the rest watched as Earl fought back spectral tears. Ahy wagged his tail in approval. A shimmering light appeared, swirling behind Earl, roughly the size of a doorway. Everyone gasped. Grandmother sniffed the air, Daisy copied her, smelling a sweet scent of roses.

"Hmm," Grandmother Zenobia said and furrowed her brow.

"Neil, I'll see you on the other side, you goddam son of a bitch," Earl laughed while wiping his face. Grandmother Zenobia and Daisy shook their heads simultaneously. Daisy raised her hand to throw the iron buttons, but Grandmother stopped her.

"Earl Porter," Neil said. He gave his brother a big bear hug before Earl turned and vanished into the light. Daisy heard a popping sound when the light disappeared.

"Hmm," Grandmother said again.

"What is it?" Daisy asked.

"I'll explain it to you later." Grandmother said. She then turned her attention to the Union soldier.

"And as for you, Neil Simmons, what can we do for you?" Grandmother Zenobia asked.

"Nothing, Ma'am. I'm here to stay, to protect Miss Daisy and her family. It's what I do."

"Sweetheart, I know the family appreciates you, but your services here are done. Daisy has her parents. They don't need a white savior to watch over them."

"But I can serve her better than they can!" Neil said. "Aren't I right, Daisy?"

Everyone watched as Daisy waved for Neil to come to her side. He knelt in front of her.

"Ten-Ten, I promise I'll be safe. Nana said you need to go into the light to get better. She said your nightmares would go away."

"I don't understand," he said.

"We see how the war has affected you." Grandmother Zenobia said. "I know you still hear the gunshots and the screams. Your hands shake and your face twitches. You need to rest and get right."

"But it's in my soul to stand guard and defend my people," he protested. "I have to fight for those who can't fight for themselves. Plus, I don't want to say goodbye to another loved one."

"Son, let me be very real with you for a moment," Grandmother Zenobia said. She motioned for him to come close to her, similar to what Daisy did. "I know what drives you." Grandmother Zenobia whispered in his spectral ear.

Neil snorted and folded his arms. "With all due respect, I don't know what you mean," he said loudly and stood tall. "You don't know what you're talking about." His image flickered like a candle.

"Actually, I know a lot more than most people. Your father regularly took advantage of the light-skinned slaves. It's why Earl and a few of your brothers have darker hair and tan skin, while you and your brothers closer to your age have blonde hair and fair skin. When you were just a young boy, a slave girl bore your father a daughter. Your half-sister Matilda was dark-skinned, and your father hated it. You two were as thick as thieves. However, when she was old enough, Matilda was sent to work in the fields. You couldn't do a thing about it, no matter how hard you tried. Eventually, your father traded her off, even after you fought him tooth and nail. It has always been more than just a mission for you. It's a deeper calling for you to protect those who could not protect themselves."

"How could you possibly know all of that?" Neil asked.

"You kept a few of your mother's close possessions here, not just a dusty set of pearls or a menacing weapon. It took a little work, but I had a nice chat with her."

Neil's spirit flickered.

"Ten-Ten, I really wish I could hug you, to make you feel better," Daisy said.

Ahy yodeled at Grandmother Zenobia and pawed at her feet. She blinked a few times, considering what she heard.

"You're right. That's it!"

Everyone looked at the dog and back to Grandmother Zenobia in confusion.

"Neil, if you'll allow it, I can bury some of your bones on my property and leave the rest here. Ahy and I would appreciate all the protection we could get. Once you're healed up, you can come and go as you please on my land as well as here on the Paxton's land. Stand guard and defend us as needed. Daisy and her family can set up a small altar for you, to guide you home, and I'll do the same. You would be free to visit both places. How does that sound?"

"How do I know you're telling the truth? How do I know you won't pour iron and salt on my bones?" Neil asked.

"I won't let her!" Daisy shouted.

"Daisy May! Mind your manners with grown folk!" Valerie warned.

A wry smile crept up on Grandmother's face.

"You continue to impress me, young lady." Grandmother said. "Neil, spirits come back and forth from the other side all the time. Back in New Orleans, we honor our ancestors with candles on our altars. They are like beacons in the darkness, to show them the way back to us."

"Daisy could learn how to make your favorite dessert and leave an offering for you if she wanted," Valerie said.

"You need to go into the light. Otherwise, you'll end up angrier and meaner than your brother, Earl. Eventually, the Deacon here will in fact have to exorcise you because you will lose all of your humanity and become an awful demon. You don't want that, and you certainly don't want Daisy to see you like that," Grandmother warned.

"Daisy, do you want me to go into the light?" Neil asked. Daisy reached out. To everyone's surprise, he appeared vibrant and bright, almost as if he were a flesh and blood man. Daisy smiled approvingly.

"Ten-Ten Neil, Mamma will teach me how to make the best peach cobbler just for you and Daddy. I promise. That way, you have to come back to me." Valerie nodded in agreement. However, Amos and Ezra stood ready in case things went differently.

"I do love a good peach cobbler," Neil said.

"Son, where are your bones?" Grandmother Zenobia asked. Neil sighed deeply. He looked at the Paxton family and Deacon Ezra. Ahy trotted over to him and pawed at his boots. Finally, he conceded.

"My remains are under the Black Oak tree, over yonder," He pointed out west, to a large tree in the distance.

"Very well," Grandmother Zenobia said.

Deacon Ezra felt a warm energy behind him. When he turned, another shimmering light appeared. Everyone gasped. Grandmother sniffed the air, Daisy copied her, smelling a sweet scent of roses.

"Hmm," Grandmother Zenobia said, and Daisy copied her.

"Mister Amos, Miss Valerie, it has been my honor watching over Miss Daisy." Neil said and tipped his hat.

"The Paxton family appreciates you, Lieutenant Neil Simmons," Amos said.

"We look forward to seeing you back, real soon." Valerie said.

"God bless you, Mister Neil," Deacon Ezra said.

"Son, you will be in good company soon enough, and you will feel more like yourself again. "Grandmother Zenobia said. "You might even see Alvin and his family for a quick spell. Please hug your mother for me if you see her."

Neil knelt down before Daisy. His uniform appeared brand new, and he was well groomed.

"Thank you for watching out for me, Ten-Ten." Daisy said.

"I hope to see you soon, Miss Daisy." Neil stood and turned towards the light. Daisy watched as a young Black girl roughly her same age poked her head outside of the shimmy portal. She had a huge smile and waved excitedly at Neil and at Daisy.

"Oh, my Lord, it's my sister Matilda!" Neil said in shock. Neil took a few steps back and drew a deep breath. The group watched as he transformed into his younger, twelve-year-old self, then jumped into the light. Amos, Valerie and Deacon Ezra cheered.

"Hmm," Grandmother said, again, and took a seat on one of the dining room chairs.

"What is it, Nana?" Daisy asked.

"Well, my darling, you might be too young to understand this, but both of those men did very bad things when they were alive. They killed a lot of people in the war."

Deacon Ezra, Amos and Valerie heard Grandmother Zenobia and stopped celebrating. The weight of her words filled the room.

"If I were a gambler, I'd bet that brother Earl did a lot of terrible, unspeakable things to good, innocent people too. And yet when the light appeared, there was no screaming or gnashing of teeth like the good book says."

"What do you think will happen to Ten-Ten?"

"I have no idea. Time will tell. Maybe there's hope for all of us, in the end." Grandmother Zenobia said.

7

DIANE'S FLOWER

BY DENISE TAPSCOTT

New Orleans, Louisiana: Present Day

IT WAS A TYPICAL hot and muggy Saturday, mid-August in New Orleans, Louisiana. The sun played peek-a-boo behind dark storm clouds looming across a blue sky. Armed with an umbrella, Diane Sparks hoped summer showers held off for a few hours.

Diane and her husband Cassius, along with their four children and what felt like half the city of New Orleans, attended the inaugural Moon Pie Festival in Jackson Square. Music blared in two areas of the park while smells of festival food filled the air. Everything from steamed crawfish and southern deep-fried gator bites to sloppy burgers and spicy sausage cornbread tempted the Sparks family.

Diane marveled at how food vendors managed to offer culinary delicacies of gooey marshmallow, crunchy graham crackers and sweet chocolate. There were "Deep Fried over the Moon" slices of pie, Moon Pie Pancakes on a stick, and even frozen Moon Pie non-dairy gluten-free smoothies. Who knew Moon Pies could be so versatile? Her stomach growled as she considered the options.

As she surveyed her surroundings, it dawned on her that she was surrounded by children of all ages. A huge smile bloomed across her lips. She always had a soft spot for kids, delighting in their infectious laughter and curiosity for life.

"Mama could a cat talk if it eats a talking bird?" asked Tommy, the four-year-old, as a man wearing a bright Hawaiian shirt with a parrot on his shoulder passed them by.

"No, sweetie," Diane said.

"Mama, where do the sun and moon come from?" asked Lucas, the seven-year-old.

"Where do you think they come from, sweetheart?"

"I want to be a bear when I grow up," continued Tommy.

"I'm not sure you can do that. Maybe you can help bears when you grow up."

Luna, the two-year-old, clapped her hands furiously, causing everyone to laugh. Diane believed that until children grew older, there was something special about how light and free their spirits were. Their joy was her joy, too. Chubby faced Tommy stared at representatives from the Moon Pie Company, dressed as coal miners in baggy overalls, in homage to the treat's origin.

"Minions Mama!"

"Tommy, stay close, please."

Seven-year-old Lucas, who was tall for his age, repeatedly tapped his mother's shoulder.

"Can we get closer to the stage? Please?" He pointed at ladies wearing tan WWII dresses who sang about a bugle and Company B, as the treat was also famous for being sent to troops during the war. Diane was tickled pink watching him shuffling his feet, mimicking Lindy Hop dancers near the stage. He would need dance classes, regardless if Cassius approved or not.

Baby Luna wiggled in Diane's arms, reaching out towards a stationary Mardi Gras float where shiny plastic beads, stuffed animals and mini Moon Pies were tossed out to an eager crowd. Diane's back screamed in pain and her knees ached. Sweat ran down her backside as she shifted Luna to her right hip, pretending to ignore the never-ending discomfort. Her oldest child, Candace, dashed off to meet up with her teenage friends near the main stage, waiting for the headliner to appear.

Excluding children, of course, Diane hated gargantuan crowds of local folk. She could barely move without someone bumping into her kids or yelling behind her. People were inconsiderate, smoking in a non-smoking area and loudly blabbing on cell phones. She preferred to be in nature, listening to bird songs and looking to spot deer in the distance.

Presently in the distance, she watched her high-school sweetheart Cassius queued up in a long line of adults at a makeshift bar. He stood, sexy as ever, hands on his hips and laughing. His bright smile made her smile, too. He didn't break a sweat in the 90-degree weather while chatting with ladies nearby. They waited for the adult beverage of the day, a Moon Pie Surprise, a shot of Irish Cream, Banana, and Coffee liqueur, with an RC cola on the side. Cassius lifted his designer sunglasses, blew a kiss in Diane's direction, and waved.

"Wave at Daddy," Diane said to the kids. They half-heartedly waved back, distracted by a woman painting blue butterflies on a little girl's face.

Diane noticed the chatty ladies. Her smile melted when they gestured at her feet and then their own. Diane loved her earthy Birkenstock sandals, even if they weren't trendy. Running a busy household required her to be comfortable, not fashionable. It was probably her imagination, but when the women waved their hands in the air and shook their heads in disapproval, it looked like they scolded Cassius. The thinnest and most stylish of the women laughed and pointed at Diane. Cassius replaced his sunglasses, crossed his arms, and stared at his expensive shoes.

Diane hadn't seen him appear defeated since he was repeatedly passed over for a promotion at the furniture store. She wasn't sure why he always needed to impress people. As a teenager, she was quiet, studious, and solitary. He was athletic, boisterous, and popular. Back when he was failing algebra, he asked her, the smarted one in class, to tutor him. He was more concerned with approval from his basketball coach than his grades.

When algebra started to make sense, though, he took more notice of her. Diane sighed deeply as she remembered the first time he professed his love for her. They both were so nervous! The idea he was more than a dumb athlete gave him a new view of himself, all thanks to Diane, he told her. Now he stood as a middle-aged adult, seeking the approval of others again. She caught herself growling and gritting her teeth.

"What I wouldn't give for a chance to sit in a forest, surrounded in wildflowers. No aches, no pains, just fresh air," she thought.

She knew her husband flirted a lot; he was a sucker for attention. He was always dressed to the nines. Everything he wore and how he moved in it was sexy. Earlier, he stood shirtless, wearing black boxer briefs, ironing for an hour to ensure his cream linen suit was perfect. If the kids hadn't been home, and if she had more energy, she would have peeled those boxers right off.▢

When she got the kids ready to leave the house, he mentioned something about her raggedy sundress and nappy hair. She dismissed him. Making sure the kids looked presentable was a higher priority. She had too much to do rather than pamper herself.

Diane knew Cassius loved her. They had four beautiful children to show for it. Still, she wished that he'd ask, "How was your day, Diane" or say, "I love you" more often. She also understood that men and women communicated differently. Although he flirted with anyone, male or female, he provided for the family and brought home nice treats for her and the kids.

It stung when people judged them. Everyone knew opposites attract, didn't they? He was energetic and athletic.▢She was quiet and curvy. As a storm cloud blotted out the sun, Diane wondered why people cared what other people thought about them. She was told by her parents repeatedly that she could have been an amazing nurse. Nevertheless, she was happiest being a great mother.

Diane turned away from Cassius and moved the kids closer to the Mardi Gras float. Maybe shiny plastic beads or stuffed animals for the kids would lift her spirits before the rain started.

A FEW DAYS LATER, Cassius stared through a dimly lit jewelry case in Tyrell's Treasures, a shop owned by his longtime friend Justice Tyrell. Dusty shelves were crammed with old books, glassware, and figurines. Glass counters were stuffed with previously worn gold and silver rings, necklaces, and earrings. Racks of shabby clothes pressed against the back wall.

"Can I help you, handsome?" Justice asked.

"I need something nice for Diane. Her birthday is coming up, and I don't know what to get."

"You're still with her?" He asked and rolled his eyes. "How about a makeover?" Justice said while leaning across the display case towards his only customer. The shop was never busy during low travel season in the French Quarter. Cassius watched his friend run his small, manicured fingers through thick blonde hair, batting his blue eyes.

"Aren't you naughty," Cassius said. He liked that Justice adored him, even if nothing would ever happen between them. Attention was attention, as far as he was concerned.

"If you only knew," Justice giggled. "How about some jewelry?"

"No, the baby tries to eat anything shiny."

"I can't stand rug rats. I don't know how you deal with them," Justice bemoaned with his southern drawl.

"Time for me to go before you say something horrible about my beautiful children and ruin our friendship. Candace, Tommy, Lucas, and Luna are my gifts from Diane. If anyone insulted my family, including you, they would regret it."

No longer entertained by the little man's flirtations, Cassius turned to exit when bells on the front door jingled and jangled. A man with olive skin entered, clutching a black bejeweled walking stick. Despite it being August, he wore a thick burgundy coat with a wide black velvet collar, a salmon-colored blouse and a gold silk vest with silver stars embroidered on it. His navy pin-striped slacks swished as he limped toward the two men.

"Good afternoon, Mr. Marid. Happy Tuesday," Justice said.

"Happy Tuesday to you too, Mr. Tyrell."

Mr. Marid stood eye to eye with Cassius. He couldn't have been taller than 5'9" but his presence was dynamic. His thick dreadlocks moved from side to side, although there was no fan blowing inside the store.

"Cassius, this is one of my dealers, Mr. Marid. He wanders in from time to time with things to sell on consignment."

"Nice to meet you, Mr. Marid," Cassius said, as he stared at the man's perfect, freckled cheekbones. He unconsciously touched his own face in comparison.

"What treasures have you brought me today? My friend here needs a gift for his wife. She needs something, anything, to make her look almost as good as him," Justice said.

Mr. Marid placed his hands on his hips and gave a deep, hearty laugh.

"Cassius Sparks, today is your lucky day."

Before Cassius questioned the stranger about knowing his last name, Mr. Marid opened his coat and removed a red velvet roll. He placed it on the counter and unrolled it, revealing various hair accessories. The room temperature dropped.

"Sounds to me like your wife needs something different." He cocked his head as if he heard something. "I suggest one of these. The history of hair ornaments is quite fascinating, especially in Chinese culture." Mr. Marid smiled; his full lips revealed large white teeth. Cassius wondered if his own smile was as dazzling as the man's smile. It had to be! Cassius was the handsomest man in town. At least he was until today.

Cassius couldn't place where Mr. Marid was from. His almond eyes suggested he was Asian, maybe Pacific Islander, but his accent suggested he was French, African, or Australian. Was he British? The more he tried to figure him out, the more his head swam. Mr. Marid was so exotic. Cassius was just all American. He felt inferior and jealous of this mysterious man.

Mr. Marid waved his hand adorned with silver and gold rings, over hairpins, barrettes, and bows.

"Let me take a closer look," Cassius said.

"I'll show you anything you want to see," Justice mumbled.

There was a variety of hair accessories. Some hair pins were made with Swarovski crystals, some were gold plated, and some made of pearls. There were red silk bows, sterling silver hair claws, and barrettes with shiny black feathers.

"She won't like any of these," Cassius said.

"She is…well, kind of earthy," Justice said.

"What's her name?" Mr. Marid asked.

"Diane,"

"Ah yes, I should have known that. Diane, as in the Greek Goddess Diana…huntress, ruler of the moon, forests, and fertility. I have just the thing for her."

Mr. Marid snapped, and the velvet roll unfurled a bit more by itself, revealing a simple white and pink porcelain rose barrette with metallic leaves. Cassius and Justice flinched at the sudden movement.

"She likes flowers, doesn't she? All women like flowers," Mr. Marid said.

Cassius felt dizzy when looking at the barrette.

"How much is it?" he asked.

"We can negotiate a fair price. I aim to please."

"Justice, what do you think? I could take it to that nutty Voodoo woman and maybe she could work some magic on it for Diane." Cassius said as he studied the flower.

"Your wife will need more than a hairpin to make her pretty. I'm just saying," Justice chimed in.

"Enough. She's my wife and I love her," Cassius said.

"Stand down Justice Tyrell," Mr. Marid warned. "You've had more than enough fun for one day." He stared at him with coal–black eyes.

"Yes Mr. Marid, Sir. Sorry Cassius," Justice apologized. Cassius noticed his friend's face turned bright red. "Let me get you a gift box," Justice continued, turning his back to the men, fiercely wiping away tears. Cassius turned away from Mr. Marid to watch Justice rush off to the back of the store. He was tired of the flirting, but never meant to upset Justice. Who was this Mr. Marid?

"Voodoo woman?" Mr. Marid asked.

"Yea, there's a local woman, Grandmother Zenobia. I've seen her at church every once in a while. People say she has a way about her. I don't really believe in all that mumbo jumbo stuff, but what the heck?. I can see if anything comes of it."

Mr. Marid shuddered and almost lost his balance. He adjusted his bejeweled cane to steady himself.

"You alright, Mr. Marid?" Cassius asked.

"I'm right as rain, dear boy. If the Voodoo woman can't perform for you, I may have a trick or two for you."

"So, how much do I owe you?" Cassius asked again as he searched for his wallet.

"Cassius Sparks, leave whatever you think is a fair price with Justice. He'll give me what's mine later. All will be well," Mr. Marid said.

Justice screeched like a little girl from the back of the store, followed by a few curse words.

"Sorry, I saw a rat," he yelled.

When Cassius turned back to Mr. Marid, he was gone.

THE ROSE BARRETTE BELIEVED it was literally nothing. It had no value, it did not exist, until they arrived in front of a shotgun style house with a purple front door. A sparkly ruby red, high-heeled shoe rested upon a wooden pole, part of a fence guarding the property. The man who held the barrette mumbled something about being happy to see the shoe. It meant the Voodoo woman was available to see clients.

When he stepped on the property, soft vibrations ran through the barrette. The rose pulsed rhythmically, echoing the vibration, releasing small waves through its petals. A sense of being a part of the world throbbed within it, right down to the metal hair pin it was glued to. The man paused and adjusted his suit. He cracked open the clear plastic box the barrette sat in, to admire it in the sun.

"Zenobia… Zenobia," a giant oak tree whispered as breezes swirled through its branches. The barrette's ceramic petals relaxed. Vibrant yellow and pink tones rushed to their edges. The delicate scent of jasmine filled the air. Its metallic, diamond encrusted green leaves unfurled and sparkled. Before the man closed the clear case, doves sang songs of Zenobia and her glory. The barrette could hardly wait to meet Zenobia.

The man jogged over to the side of the house. Above the door was a sign that read, 'Prayer Room'. He knocked several times. Bells clanged on the other side of the door with each energetic fist pound.

"Why Cassius, how nice to see you. Come in and have a seat," a melodic voice said as the door opened.

"Thank you for seeing me, Grandmother Zenobia," he answered as he stepped into the room. He tossed cash in a cigar box labeled 'Donations' by the door.

Cassius lingered when entering the domain that smelled of cinnamon cookies. The barrette thought he hesitated because of the vibrant presence that ran around the property, and everything inside the home. But no. He noticed a wall mirror. He flashed a smile at his reflection and smoothed his wavy hair. He then sat on the edge of a metal fold-up chair, placed the barrette before him, and leaned in.

There were shelves with thick religious books in different languages, statues of all shapes and sizes, a few crosses (some with and some without Jesus), a large brass pentagram and a hand-carved jade statue of a dragon perched on a shiny black rock. Each item had a story or a song to share if the barrette listened closely enough.

"You don't need to check yourself. You're always well put together."

Grandmother Zenobia sat in all her glory on a purple and gold throne. To Cassius, she was a mysterious, dark-skinned woman who didn't look old enough to be a grandmother. His mortal eyes couldn't see the real Zenobia and her history. The rose barrette saw her scars. There were battles she won and lost over centuries. It saw an ethereal crown bestowed upon her by an Egyptian God. The simple man couldn't fathom the powerful being he addressed.

Cassius noticed Grandmother didn't smile when she looked at him, but seemed to be in a good mood.

"What brings you by today?"

Cassius displayed a toothy grin.

"Diane's birthday is coming, and I got her this. I'm hoping you could bless it or put a spell on it to make her prettier." He pushed the barrette to her across a black velvet card table that separated them.

Grandmother raised an eyebrow and crossed her arms. "What now?"

His smile faltered.

"Don't get me wrong. Diane is lovely. She's an obedient wife, and a great mother. It's just that, well, folks keep saying she's plain looking, at best."

"Let me see..." she said and lifted the barrette out of the box. When Grandmother Zenobia, Queen of the land, held the rose in her cool hands, it knew why it was awakened from its slumber. It was meant to be with her.

"Beautiful," she said. The barrette begged to wrap its ceramic petals around her fingers. How could it thank her for its life? The rose glowed when her kind, dark brown eyes studied it. "Diane will love you," Grandmother said. It wanted to tell her it wanted to be with her, not some Diane person. Before it could manage to find words of adoration, Cassius interrupted.

"I figured if you could do your hoodoo voodoo thing, Diane will be more presentable. She should look good on my arm when we go out. Ladies at church whisper about why a handsome man like myself would settle down with a woman so drab. Guys at work make fun of me because she's so…"

"First of all, that's not how Voodoo, nor Hoodoo, works. Secondly, who cares about what other people think?"

Grandmother's harsh tone caught Cassius off guard. He sat back.

"All that matters is what you think of your wife and what she thinks of you. You still love her, don't you?"

"Of course I do."

"Then it shouldn't matter what other people say. Love is a sacred bond between two people."

Cassius snatched the barrette from the Voodoo woman. If it wasn't so shocked, the barrette believed it would have found its voice, and screamed at him. A metal leaf sliced his thumb, but it wasn't enough to stop him. Blood ran down its backside and stained its white ceramic belly. The barrette was stifled when he shoved it back in its plastic coffin. His grip crushed the edges of the box.

"You don't understand what it's like, Zenobia."

"You will address me as Grandmother Zenobia."

"Yes, Ma'am."

"Shall I remind you that I was at the church when you both stood before the powers that be and shared your vows?" Grandmother waved her hands around like swatting a fly as she spoke. It hurt the barrette to see her Goddess agitated.

"But she needs help in the beauty department. A good-looking guy such as myself should have a good-looking woman next to him. She admires me, but I need more."

"If you meant what you just said, then you don't love Diane. You don't deserve her, you selfish man. Get out the good book and read 1 Corinthians 13:4–8. Love is patient, love is kind. Read all of it. You trying to change her because of what others think, is ugly and hateful."

Cassius stood.

"I love my wife, and I want what's best for us. Does this mean you won't bless this flower for me?" He shook the gift. Rattling around in that box was horrible for the little rose.

"I can't believe you didn't hear a word I said." Grandmother paused before enunciating her words. "Listen to me. I will not put a spell on that barrette for you. She is a perfect gift for your wife, just as your wife is perfect for you, as is."

He didn't like that she spoke to him like a little boy.

"She? Don't you mean it?"

"Cassius, do not try to change Diane. It will be bad. Very bad."

"Grandmother Zenobia, I spent good money on this gift. I can't believe you won't help me. I'm special, and I expect people to think my wife is special too. Good day to you, ma'am."

"Suit yourself."

Cassius looked at his reflection again before storming out. The vibrations that had filled the barrette with joy, faded with each step away from Grandmother Zenobia. When Cassius passed the threshold to common ground, the delicate rose petals went rigid. The colors faded, and the sparkles dulled. There was nothing but darkness for the barrette.

LATER THAT AFTERNOON, CASSIUS found himself standing once again on Royal Street, staring at the storefront of Tyrell's Treasures. He decided to return the barrette but was baffled with what to replace it with.

"Welcome back, Cupcake," Justice announced. Cassius noticed the aging blond man giggled and blushed. He was in brighter spirits since their last meeting. "Mr. Marid said you'd come back to me."

Cassius bristled when hearing Mr. Marid's name. He was already defeated from his meeting earlier and his self-esteem was low. He couldn't hold a candle to that man's charm.

"He said that when you returned, I was supposed to prepare the barrette a special way and then hand it back to you." Cassius noticed Justice's hands shook as he spoke. "I'm sorry. He makes me so nervous sometimes." Justice admitted. His smile faltered. Cassius handed the clear box to Justice. Maybe the barrette was enough to give his wife, after all.

"Follow me to the back," Justice said. "I promise to be on my best behavior."

"Where is Mr. Marid?" Cassius asked as he scanned the empty shop. He wondered what tricks Marid could do, that Zenobia wouldn't do.

"Don't you worry about him. He's long gone, thank good-ness."

Cassius relaxed. He followed Justice as he sauntered to the back of the store to an unorganized office. Next to a desk covered with letters, bills and invoices, the small room had a smaller counter littered with jeweler tools, fabric, and boxes of sewing knickknacks. Justice took the barrette and dropped it in a coarse cloth bag filled with black powder. He mumbled a few words to himself as he shook the bag.

"What's that horrible smell?" Cassius asked.

"It's some weird concoction Mr. Marid left for when you returned."

"How did he know I was coming back?" Cassius asked.

"I have learned not to question him. His instructions were to recite a weird poem he gave me and to make sure I covered the flower with this stuff. He said it'll enhance your wife's natural charms and make the barrette look nicer, longer. When you give that hair pin to Debbie, I bet the odor will be gone before ya know it and she'll look, oh, so lovely."

"You mean Diane," Cassius corrected. Whatever Mr. Marid was up to, he didn't care. Cassius Sparks was his old playful self again.

"Whatever, Cutie pie. You know I love you," Justice joked. "I should be on your arm, not her." He handed the gift back to Cassius. "Be a good boy and good luck."

"Aren't you sweet? That crazy Grandmother Zenobia wouldn't help me. I'm glad I came back to you. I need all the luck I can get." Cassius winked.

Unbeknownst to the chatty humans, Mr. Marid's spell that Justice recited woke the rose barrette from its slumber. The concoction dusted on the rose was made with chili peppers and other irritants, including powdered snakeskin and graveyard dirt. Sulfur was the worst. The black powder grated against the flower's ceramic paint, and it burned as it stuck to Cassius' dried blood on the back of the rose. Its leaves itched and ached.

When the barrette, still in the black bag, was returned to its clear plastic coffin, it gathered they were in some establishment, with old objects on shelves. The difference between these objects and the ones at Grandmother Zenobia's was easy to see. Her items hummed and sang. These items screamed and wailed. The love-struck blond human wrapped paper over the clear box, obliterating light for the rose.

THE SMOLDERING SENSATION CONTINUED until the barrette was freed from the darkness. The clear box was handled by calloused, dry hands. The rose believed these were hands of a gardener, a cook, or a dishwasher. It turns out they were the hands of someone who ran a household.

"Happy Birthday, Baby. Do you like it?" Cassius asked.

"It's beautiful, too extravagant for me," Diane said.

"Nothing is too good for my woman!" Cassius said as he took his turn and handled the barrette. Compared to Diane, his hands were too soft. Diane was the strong one.

The barrette needed revenge. Why did the foolish man take it away from Grandmother Zenobia? It was poised to strike Cassius. If it couldn't cut him again, perhaps it could drop from his grasp? Maybe it would fall and roll under some piece of furniture, never to be seen until it could plot its escape. It tried to slip from his manicured fingers. Almost free, Diane took it from him.

When her fingers brushed the ceramic petals, a strong, constant energy surged through the barrette. When placed in her kinky hair, the burning and itching stopped. The barrette sat, perched on the left side of her head, grazing her scalp, experiencing a new view of the world.

Hello, Diane.

The barrette understood why Grandmother Zenobia allowed it to leave her presence. Diane was its goddess. It was meant to be with her. The rose barrette connected with Diane. It felt her heartbeat, overflowing with love. Her body was exhausted from everything she did throughout the day for her children, for her man, for their home.

She loved what she did because it was all for them. Through the aches and pains, she pushed onward. There was no time to care for herself, and she was okay with that; her spirit was full of joy and peace. It was the barrette's job to take care of her.

Diane was naturally charming and graceful. No smudge of make-up, no piece of clothing could add to her beauty. It radiated from within. The barrette was blessed to be with her. As Diane admired the hairpin in a mirror, it glowed. Its petals softened and its metallic leaves sparkled. If it had actual eyes, it would have winked at her; Diane instinctively winked back at her reflection.

The golden metal hair clip, caked in black powder and blood, nestled into her head. The barrette wasn't sure why it did it. It just knew was that it was there to stay.

"Look at you," Cassius said, while rubbing the left side of his head. "The flower is perfect. If I didn't know any better, I'd say you're glowing."

Diane covered her mouth with her hand as she laughed. The barrette dug deeper. Cassius patted his head again and then shook it side to side.

"Honey, are you okay?" Diane said.

"I have a small headache. I'm fine. I have a great idea! Let's drop the kids off at my cousin's place. I'm taking you out for a nice birthday dinner." He grabbed his phone.

"That's not necessary. I've already baked a nice cake for all of us to enjoy after supper."

"Nonsense! We're worth a night out." he waved her off.

AN HOUR LATER, DIANE wore a clingy, royal blue dress, one that her husband insisted she wear, so they'd have matching outfits.

"My God, look at those curves!" he said.

Diane blushed. She liked the silky soft fabric against her skin. It had been a while since she wore something that made her feel sexy. The barrette's pink and yellow petals changed to royal blue with a thin yellow stripe in the middle of each petal, complimenting her outfit.

"That's a neat trick," Diane thought.

Cassius pinched his nose and rubbed his head again.

"Baby, do you need some aspirin?"

"I'm fine. Let's go," Cassius said.

AFTER AN EVENING OF wining and dining, Diane woke up refreshed. She couldn't remember the last time slept like a baby. Cassius, on the other hand looked horrible. He woke up with several blue veins that ran across the left side of his face to his left, bloodshot eye.

"Good morning," the couple greeted each other.

"You look awful." Diane said.

"Don't look at me, look at you!" he dismissed her. "You look even more wonderful than last night!"

"All the attention last night was nice," she admitted.

"I was impressed when the chef came out to wish you *Happy Birthday*. The complimentary bottle of wine was great."

"I felt like royalty."

"I'm surprised you slept with the flower in your hair."

"I forgot it was there." Diane touched the left side of her head. The rose buzzed.

"It's naturally beautiful just like you." Cassius said and rubbed his head.

Diane's concern for Cassius grew.

"Take the day off. I don't like how you're wincing every time you blink. I should call the doctor."

"Naa. It's probably an allergic reaction to something I ate. I'm fine. Let's get up."

Reluctantly, Diane kissed him and got out of bed. She noticed her back didn't ache as usual from holding the baby. Her knees weren't sore from kneeling while picking up after the kids or scrubbing the kitchen floor. Taking away her ailments was the least the barrette could do for its Goddess.

Diane went through her daily rituals of getting the kids ready for school, ironing her husband's suit, preparing breakfast for the family, making lunches for the kids, and dropping them off at their different schools. As Diane ran more errands from grocery shopping to picking up Cassius's dry cleaning (and everywhere in between) everyone said she was breathtaking. It made her uncomfortable.

"That must have been some birthday," shouted Ethel, the nosey next-door neighbor, and head of the neighborhood watch. She stood on her porch while Diane wrestled with the baby's car seat.

"For a forty-year-old woman with a bunch of kids, you make a t-shirt and sweatpants look like a new fashion trend. What's your secret? Your skin is flawless."

Diane politely smiled and escaped with the baby and groceries in tow. She was grateful the house phone rang, so she didn't have to socialize for long. Her smile faded when she recognized the strained voice of Mr. Brown, Cassius' boss. He worked with him for decades.

"Diane, I'm glad you're home," he said.

"What's wrong?" Her heart sank. She knew her husband should have stayed home.

"It's Cassius. He shouted inappropriate things to his female co-workers. He yelled at customers on the showroom floor. Luckily, his friend Jay came by because they had lunch plans. Jay stopped him from jumping on the sample mattresses. Right now, he's howling and scratching himself."

She could hear Cassius screeching in the background.

"I'm so sorry, Mr. Brown," she patted the barrette softly in her hair. "He insisted on going to work today. He needs a doctor. Did he hurt anyone?"

"Diane, you have such a nice voice. I didn't notice it after all these years." Mr. Brown paused. "You're so sweet to worry about other people. Everyone is fine. Jay is taking him home. You'll probably see them at any moment. If you need anything, call me. I mean it. Don't hesitate if you need anything from me at all."

"Thank you for your understanding, Mr. Brown."

Mr. Brown's tone at the end of the call disturbed Diane. Was he flirting with her? She didn't need a damn thing from him, she thought. A silver sedan skidded into the Sparks' driveway. Cassius moaned when Jay dragged him out of the car.

"Thanks for bringing him home," Diane said as Jay struggled to get Cassius through the front door. "I just called my sister to take care of the older kids."

Jay took one look at Diane, holding the baby, and he lowered his eyes. Diane didn't like that he wouldn't look directly at her. She'd deal with his strange behavior later. Right now, Cassius needed her. The barrette noticed a familiar scent from Jay that it couldn't place.

"Uh…it's not a problem", Jay said, struggling with Cassius, who refused to stand on his own. Jay was shorter but more athletic than Cassius.

"But yea, he needs help. Did you call the doctor?"

The baby cried.

"Why are you talking to Diane like that? You trying to steal her away, too?" Cassius accused. The entire left side of his head pulsed with thick black and blue veins. He clawed at his bloody scalp every few minutes. His crusty left eye was swollen shut.

"Don't look at her. Don't talk to her. Get out of my house before I kill your black ass! She's mine."

Cassius swung at Jay, who stepped back, letting him fall to the floor.

What was that scent? The rose wondered.

"This is ridiculous. I'm calling 911," Diane said, fumbling with Luna in her arms.

The Maid of New Orleans! That's it! Jasmine! Diane wasn't aware, but the barrette remembered. Evidently, Jay had seen Grandmother Zenobia that day. *Grandmother Zenobia,* the barrette whispered to its Goddess, stopping her in her tracks. *Take him to Grandmother Zenobia.*

Diane nodded her head in agreement.

"Take us to Grandmother Zenobia," Diane ordered.

Jay looked her in the eye, puzzled at the command. He smiled at her, and she forced a smile back. His smile was the biggest grin she'd seen all day. It sickened her.

"Anything for you."

Diane's younger sister entered, shocked at seeing Cassius splayed on the floor, Jay looking at Diane like a love-struck teenager, and baby Luna bawling her eyes out.

"What the hell is going on?"

"Bia, I'm so glad you're here. Take the baby over to Penelope's place. She has the other kids. I'll get them all once I figure out what's wrong with Cassius."

Bia stared at Diane when the barrette changed from a perky daisy to a large yellow rose.

"Bia, the baby."

"Right. Is that a new perfume you're wearing? It smells like roses." Amidst the chaos, Bia took the baby but didn't move to leave. She reached out to touch the barrette. "So, this is your birthday present. I can hardly wait to borrow it." There was no way on earth she was gonna get a hold of the rose. Menacing thorns sprung from its leaves. Bia retracted her hand and held Luna closer.

"Come on, people. Get moving. Cassius is getting worse by the minute." Diane demanded. Both she and the rose were anxious to see Grandmother Zenobia.

IT WASN'T LONG BEFORE everyone stood in the sweltering heat outside the house with the purple door. Jasmine filled the air. Jay struggled with Cassius. The rose was delighted to be back. Other flowers, ones that sprang from the ground, waved from a distance. There was no red shoe on the fence. Grandmother Zenobia would not see unannounced visitors.

The barrette sensed soft vibrations radiating from the land. Her majesty had to be home. Its leaves flexed, and with some effort, two additional rose buds formed, covering half of Diane's head. Maybe if the rose barrette were bigger, it figured Grandmother Zenobia would see them outside of her domain. Cassius convulsed and clutched his head in agony.

From the back of the house, Diane heard someone humming. With each passing moment, the humming grew until she saw her. Grandmother Zenobia wore a large straw hat and gloves while holding a basket of ivory roses. Her little white dog trotted at her side.

"Well, look who we have here," Grandmother Zenobia said.

Grandmother, something's very wrong with Cassius," Diane said.

"I see."

Grandmother took a long look at the group. She waved her left hand, and the gate opened by itself. "Jay, bring him out back. We'll all sit a spell."

Grandmother and her dog Ahy went inside while everyone else made their way around back to her gazebo. It was covered with dark pink roses in the middle of a luscious garden. A welcoming cool breeze blew around. Jay sat close to Grandmother's empty chair, Cassius sat across from it slumped over in his seat, on Diane's right.

With Ahy at her side, Grandmother returned with towels, a tray with four glasses and a crystal pitcher filled with ice water. It had a bejeweled cross in its center, and small etchings of crosses at the base.

"Jay, sing that song you wrote, the one you shared with me earlier." Grandmother said.

"Without any music?" he asked.

"Yes. Your song comes from your heart and that is what we need right now. It won't be easy but sing until I tell you to stop."

Diane's stomach flipped. She didn't need a song; she needed her husband healed. Jay sang a sweet song that he wrote for his wife. The melody came from his heart; the lyrics came from his soul. Rather than question Grandmother Zenobia, Diane sat back as Jay started to sing. Cassius bolted upright and stared hard at Diane. He foamed at the mouth like a rabid dog. Diane clutched her chest. Ahy cocked his head and crouched low.

"Cassius, what did you do?" Grandmother Zenobia demanded.

"Nothing Grandmother." His voice sounded deeper than usual to Diane. He grunted and growled. Ahy bared his teeth.

"Boy, look at me when I speak to you."

His head twisted unnaturally toward her.

"What did you do?"

He squirmed and laughed as though he heard a joke.

"I bought the barrette from some man named Mr. Marid at Tyrell's Treasures in the French Quarter. When you wouldn't bless it to make Diane more beautiful, I went back to the store. Mr. Marid left something with Justice to help me."

"You dealt with Makhadie Marid?"

Cassius shrugged. Ahy yodeled and stood on his hind legs.

"Was he an odd-looking fellow with all kinds of jewelry?"

Cassius snickered. Diane patted her head, unintentionally causing her husband to dry heave.

"Lord have mercy, this is much worse than I thought. Ahy go inside right now. I mean it." Grandmother Zenobia said. The little dog sneezed three times. "Don't you test me. Go, now." Ahy trotted off, making his way back inside the house.

Diane raised her eyebrows in confusion and disbelief. Her husband's words cut her deeply.

"You are a foolish, hard-headed man. I warned you something bad would happen." Grandmother started to scold Cassius.

"Zenobia look..."

Grandmother held up her right hand, interrupting Cassius. "Do not speak again until you are spoken to. Listen to the song." She made a fist. Cassius slumped in his chair. Grandmother Zenobia placed a towel over his head and another on his shoulder.

"Is it true?" Diane asked, straining to contain newfound anger.

"I don't have to tell you that your husband is not the smartest man, Diane. When we're done, remind me to check up on Justice Tyrell. There's a good chance he's laid up in the hospital if he isn't already dead."

The idea made the barrette growl and shake. Grandmother smirked, looking at the barrette.

"Jay, keep singing. Diane, listen to the words, and sit still."

Diane wanted to flee. Screw Cassius. She didn't need him. She could go back to nursing school and provide for her babies. She could get huge dogs to protect her and the family. Grandmother Zenobia pulled her chair around and patted Diane's shoulder.

"Breathe, Darlin'. It's gonna be okay," she said, placing a towel on her shoulder.

"Hello Beautiful." Grandmother said to the rose barrette. The petals turned purple, matching the front door. Cassius twitched.

"It's nice to see you, too. I am so sorry you were hurt. We're gonna fix this, little one. Now, I need to get a good look at you to see what's going on." Grandmother petted the petals of the center flower as she spoke. Small currents of electricity buzzed from her fingers like a honeybee.

"I can't leave my goddess. She needs me." The rose barrette spoke out loud in a tiny, clear voice. Diane gasped, Jay choked, and Cassius vomited. Grandmother chuckled.

"Sweetheart, trust me. I will put you back where you belong. Listen to the nice man's song."

Jay sang of undying love. Like Jay's song, it would do anything for her. The rose obeyed Queen Zenobia, releasing its grip from Diane. There was a thick pop and a soft crunch before the barrette slid from Diane's head into Grandmother Zenobia's hands.

Dark blood gushed from Cassius' head. His towels turned red. He screamed at the top of his lungs as chunks of meat and bone fell to the ground. Diane rose to help him, but Grandmother motioned for her to sit. Grandmother got up and poured water on Cassius until the shrieks stopped. Unharmed, Diane sat still as instructed while tears streamed down her cheeks. Everyone knew not to cross Grandmother Zenobia.

"Keep singing Jay, you're doing fine." Grandmother lifted the barrette and twirled it around before flipping it over to look at the back. "Poor thing. Look at what he did to you." She lifted the glass pitcher that refilled itself with water.

"This is holy water. It will hurt, but I promise your pain will go away."

She poured the water on the rose. Places where the black dirt and blood were stung like a thousand wasps. The barrette howled. Two of the three flowers crumpled. The purple color washed away. The metal leaves and hair pin disintegrated. Everything faded until there was just a song, and a small pink and yellow rose in Grandmother Zenobia's hand.

"Your turn," she said to Diane. "Lucky for you, it won't hurt." Grandmother poured holy water on Diane's head. She braced herself. Grandmother, still cradling the flower, parted Diane's thick curly hair, exposing a hole the size of a quarter, bored into her skull.

"Did I do that? I didn't mean to hurt her. I love Diane," the flower whispered. "It's alright, Beautiful," Grandmother whispered back. Grandmother Zenobia leaned over, showing Diane the flower. Diane dared look briefly back into the mysterious woman's eyes before examining the flower.

"Do you still accept your husband's gift?" Grandmother Zenobia asked.

"I do, "Diane said, the words reminding her of her wedding day. With no hair clip and no metal leaves, how would the flower manage to stay in Diane's hair? Grandmother Zenobia mumbled a few words and pressed the flower to Diane's head. As it grazed her scalp, the hole closed, kinky hair grew, holding the flower in place. Diane patted the rose, glad that she was back.

"Thank you for singing your song, Jay. You can stop now. Please enjoy the ice water." Jay stopped and guzzled the water as fast as he could. Grandmother removed the bloody towels from Cassius. He sat upright, looking more like himself. Some of the angry, pulsating veins were gone, but most remained. His bloodshot eye was open.

"Cassius, you'll be okay. Your full vision will return in a few hours. There's not much I can do about the scars or hair loss. Marid tricked Justice Tyrell into using Goofer dust."

"Goofer Dust?" Diane asked. As she spoke, she knew she and the flower weren't entirely as one. Still, she sensed that it felt her heartbeat and continued to heal some of her pains.

"Honey, for safety reasons, I won't go into too much detail. Basically, it's a working used against one's enemy. Your husband flirted with the wrong person. We all know how sweet Justice is, like it or not. Sadly, he's desperate for love. He made some deal with that shady Marid, hoping to curse you, to get close to Cassius. Who knows where Marid got the barrette and clearly, he didn't know how special the barrette is. On top of that, Marid probably didn't know that the pin had Cassius' blood on it. The curse attacked your husband while the flower protected you."

Cassius fell to his knees before Diane.

"Baby, I'm sorry," he begged. "I shouldn't have tried to change you. I love you. Can you forgive me?" Diane touched her husband's cheek. She still loved him, even if he was foolish. "I'll forgive you this time." Diane said. "But I won't forget. Grandmother Zenobia, are there any other side effects?" she asked.

"Well, like his remaining scars, your beauty will never fade. You'll have to deal with the attention you both receive from others."

Diane dreaded hearing that she would draw more attention to herself.

"The curse was strong; never, ever remove the flower or Cassius will die. I'm fairly certain she isn't going anywhere, anyway."

Diane patted the flower. Its petals, now soft and silky, caressed her fingertips.

"I can make a spray for you to use daily," continued Grandmother Zenobia. "It's a blend of hummingbird tears, rose oil, cinnamon and the feather of a Nicobar pigeon. It'll moisturize your skin, your hair will grow, and your little rose will love it." Grandmother drank her own glass of water.

"For extra protection, I suggest you get Blue Tick Coonhounds. They're great hunting dogs and the kids will love them. I can recommend a breeder in Arcadia."

The rose knew its goddess wanted hunting dogs at her side.

"If that Mr. Marid ever comes back around, don't talk to him. Don't even look at him if you can help it. You call me or come find me right away, day or night," Zenobia warned. She mumbled something under her breath and took another sip of water.

"Lastly, and this goes especially for Cassius, take time to love each other. Make time to be with one another, not just sex. Tell and show each other how much you mean to one another other. The good book says, 'three things will last forever—faith, hope, and love—and the greatest of these is love'. Diane doesn't need you, but she loves you. Appreciate her. If it weren't for her love for you and Jay's beautiful love song, we'd be planning your funeral, Cassius."

"I'm glad I could help," Jay said.

"Cassius, tell people about Jay's show in a few weeks. Get a proper babysitter and take Diane out. Have dinner and buy front row seats. Artists want to entertain people and feed their families too."

Diane looked off in the distance, admiring the land. Grandmother smiled.

"You and the kids are welcome to sit in my gazebo and play on my property during visiting hours. We both know enjoying nature feeds the soul."

"Thank you, Grandmother Zenobia," Diane said. The rose knew it would be back to see Grandmother on her glorious land, once everything was "normal" for the Sparks family.

"I'll fetch that spray for you and some cookies to enjoy before everyone heads home." Grandmother Zenobia said. She stood, kissed Diane's flower, and made her way back into her home.

8

LOVE SICK SOLES

BY DENISE TAPSCOTT

Carrolton, Louisiana: Present Day

A FEW SCATTERED SUMMER storm clouds loomed overhead as Grandmother Zenobia and her faithful dog Ahy waited on the porch of a charming cottage just upriver from the French Quarter. It was a sleepy Tuesday morning in Carrollton, Louisiana. There wasn't much traffic, and not many people were out and about. It was late August, so there weren't families ushering children off to school. People were relaxing on vacations rather than dashing off to jobs. Instead of the hum of leaf blowers by landscapers, birds sang, and an occasional soft breeze offered the sweet smell of magnolias.

Grandmother Zenobia admired the well-manicured lawn in front of the small shotgun-style home. Twin light pink myrtle crepe shrubs highlighted the steps to the porch. A handful of smaller bushes with little white and blue flowers accented the front yard. Small pink and purple petunias lined the sides of a gravel walkway to the street. A large wreath with purple, yellow, and green braided ribbons hung on the front door, inviting guests into the home.

She sifted through her pockets, reconfirming her small inventory of Hoodoo tools she might need for the day, as she and her dog Ahy continued to wait on Mr. Justice Tyrell's brick porch. The alarm set on her cell phone had already buzzed twice, reminding her they'd been waiting for over ten minutes.

"Why is she here?" a muffled female voice asked from the other side of the front door. The visiting Tyrell clan was unaware that Grandmother Zenobia could hear quite clearly everything they said in their twangy Georgian accents from where she stood.

"Well…I invited her," a softer, toned female voice replied.

"Hope! Why would you do that?" a masculine voice asked.

"Why are you even here? Shouldn't you be running your candy store?" a huskier female voice said.

"Our family has a history of bad blood with that woman and her people," a deeper male voice said. "Don't you ever forget the story of how Zenobia's Great Gramma attacked our beloved Great-Gramma at a prayer meeting back in the day."

Grandmother Zenobia stifled a giggle. She didn't have a Great Gramma, and she remembered her battle with legendary, overbearing-holier-than-thou Miss Beulah Mae Tyrell as if it were yesterday.

"Great Gramma Beulah Mae must be rolling over in her grave right now. Thanks, Hope," said the first female.

After picking up on the tones of her voice, Grandmother guessed the first female might be Charity Tyrell, one of the older siblings chastising Hope.

"Honestly, she's not that bad. She helped me open Hope's Honey Pot and Sweet Treats," Hope said.

If Charity was present, Grandmother suspected sister Patience, brothers Malachi and Levi were also present. The four siblings of the large clan were as thick as thieves.

"What?" Levi asked.

"How could you accept help from that woman?" Malachi chimed in.

"Not one of y'all helped me with my store when I asked," Hope said. "Just like not one of y'all helped Justice with his thrift store."

Grandmother smirked at the pregnant pause.

"Mmm-hmm. Good for you, Hope." Grandmother barely whispered. "I'm glad you're sticking up for yourself. Miss Beulah Mae would be proud of you."

"Maybe if we wait long enough, she'll just leave," Patience said.

Grandmother cleared her throat loudly, reminding them that she was there to stay.

"Grandmother Zenobia called me last night, very concerned about Justice. She said she'd like to come spend a little time with him and pray over him, with my permission."

"Pray over him? Really?" More like case the joint."

"Malachi stop it. Like the good book says in Matthew 18:20, "when two or three are gathered in my name...""

"You trying to challenge us with Bible verses, young lady?" Levi accused. "Because you cannot hold a candle to what I know."

"Our brother is in a bad way, and you think that..." Malachi interjected.

"In a bad way?" Hope's voice rose. "Justice is dying! I can't imagine that Grandmother Zenobia could do any more damage."

Grandmother Zenobia knocked on the front door, as another reminder she was still waiting. After two clunks, a click, and a chain sliding across wood, the front door opened, revealing sour faces.

"Good afternoon, Grandmother Zenobia. Happy Tuesday," Hope said. "So glad you could come by and visit with Justice." Grandmother bent over and hugged the petite woman.

Patience, Charity, Malachi, and Levi glared at Grandmother as she and her dog entered. Although they varied in shapes and sizes, each family member had their great grandmother's corn silk blonde hair and piercing blue eyes. The home was unusually warm, heavy with the scent of gardenia incense. Grandmother fought the urge to gag.

"Tyrell Clan," Grandmother Zenobia said and nodded to everyone in the foyer. Hope greeted her with a sweet smile. As Grandmother passed through, the rest of the family members avoided her gaze. She gritted her teeth, trying to contain herself.

"I can't believe the nerve of her to show her face here," Patience grumbled, leaning her heavy frame towards her older sister Charity. Grandmother stopped and turned abruptly to the pudgy woman.

"I see you're down two dress sizes, Patience. You look good as a size 20. I'm glad the Bible verse and the holy water spell I gave you are working. You'll be at your ideal weight in no time."

"Uh yes, thank you Grandmother Zenobia." Grandmother chuckled at how quickly Patience turned bright red and bowed her head.

"Malachi and Charity, how are the fertility treatments coming along for your families?" Grandmother continued. "I haven't heard from either of you in a while."

"My wife is due in five months. Thank you for asking. I'll remind her to come by sometime next week to pay her respects." Malachi said as he nervously adjusted his horn-rimmed glasses.

"I found out last week that my husband and I expecting twins," Charity said. Although she was almost as tall as Grandmother, she slouched and also stared at her shiny black Jimmy Choo heels in embarrassment.

"Levi, how's work?" Grandmother asked.

"I got the promotion that we discussed, Grandmother Zenobia." Levi frowned and shoved his hands in the pockets of his Dickie's cargo work pants. "I started as assistant foreman two weeks ago." Grandmother rolled her eyes at his bitter response. "Congratulations to each and every one of you and your successes." Each family member scowled at one another. Their visits to the Voodoo woman were no longer clandestine.

"Grandmother Zenobia, let me show you to Justice. I don't know how much time he has left with us," Hope said.

"I'll see what I can do, if he'll let me," Grandmother said. Hope escorted Grandmother Zenobia to the master bedroom. Ahy trotted inside the room and Grandmother closed the door behind him. Charity attempted to follow when Grandmother stopped her.

"Hope, be a dear and fetch me a broom," Grandmother said while eyeballing Charity.

"Yes ma'am, of course."

When Hope scampered off to the kitchen, Grandmother pulled a paper napkin from her pocket. She opened it and blew a dark red powder in the air towards Charity and the others. The family coughed and sneezed like patients in the lobby of the free clinic down on Magazine Street.

"Justice should see only Hope and me. I'm sure you understand," she said. Charity squinted and shook her head. Her eyes were unfocused as she turned away from Grandmother and stormed toward her siblings. "Why are the two of you just standing around? Lazy sons-a-bitches," Charity said.

"As if you are any better!" Patience accused.

"Don't start with me, Fatty Patty. You're the one that's been raiding the kitchen the past few days. You should be ashamed, eating Justice out of house and home!"

Hope returned, startled by the flailing arms and hostile insults that flew around the foyer.

"Leave the broom by the door and mind where you step," Grandmother warned. "You don't want to get caught up in the confusion powder. We'll sweep it away when we're done."

Hope scurried into the master bedroom.

"Bless your hearts, Tyrell family," Grandmother joked as she entered Justice's room.

THE ROOM SMELLED OF sickly human sweat and disinfectant. Justice Tyrell was barely recognizable. His face and neck were bloated. His arms were bruised and swollen. His usually well-manicured hands were black and drawn up as if he were an arthritic old man. His face was strapped with a steamed-up mask, attached to an oxygen tank. One finger was pinched with a fingertip pulse oximeter to record his oxygen levels, and one arm was strapped with an IV.

A large flat screen TV across from his bed displayed various images of landscapes in hopes of soothing him when he was awake. Ahy whined and clawed at Grandmother's feet until she picked him up and placed him at the foot of the bed.

"Behave yourself," she warned the little dog as she cracked open a window to let fresh air in. "That's much better," she lied. She twitched her nose, detecting an underlying scent of urine, then folded her arms in disapproval when Ahy disregarded his master. He crept up the bed until he could lay his head on Justice's stomach.

"Justice, it's Grandmother Zenobia and Ahy," Hope said. He moaned and attempted to roll away from Grandmother. The white Basenji was just heavy enough to prevent him moving too far over.

"Your friend Cassius Sparks and his wife Diane came by my house yesterday. Seems they were affected by a cursed object he bought from Tyrell's treasures." Hope gasped. "Once I treated them, I had a bad feeling you wouldn't be well. I came to pray over you and give you a treatment if you allow it."

"I can't imagine that you'd have anything to do with cursed objects or anything of the dark arts. But something has got a hold of you," Hope said. "Please say yes to her. She's not making any promises, but I believe she can help you."

"Fine," Justice managed to say through the misty oxygen mask.

"Thank you, my darling'. I'm guessing doctors don't know what to make of you, and they're probably warning that you don't have much time left on this earth. I'm here to tell you I know what's going on. That handsome Cassius said there was a strange man in your store that sold him the gift. Your condition is because of your dealings with that shady Mr. Marid and the beautiful Rose barrette a few days ago. Makhadie Marid is an evil djinn who tricked you. He lied and told you to read a poem and sprinkle stuff on the present. What he really did was convince you to say a curse and handle deadly Goofer dust."

Tears streamed down Justice's puffy face.

"Trust me, sweetheart. I've dealt with him before. You're in good hands now. I'll make it my personal mission to see he doesn't come back." She removed the oxygen mask from his sweaty face and tossed aside the oxygen reader that clamped his middle finger. "We're done with these uncomfortable contraptions." Grandmother took out a floral embroidered lace handkerchief and wiped his face.

"I know you had no idea who or what you were really dealing with. Those tricky genies can be so nasty. I bet he told you that the gift would break up Diane and Cassius. You were hoping that your love for that good-looking Cassius Sparks would be returned to you and shady Marid took advantage of that. Don't you worry, I'll take care of him at the right time."

Grandmother noted that Hope put her hands over her mouth to stifle her emotions.

"I understand you are lonely. I'm not here to judge you about who you want to be with. I do know, very well, that we all want to be loved. Other than your little sister here, your family doesn't understand what's in your heart.

Frankly, it's none of their business. Don't mind those busy bodies. You two keep looking after each other and things will be okay." Grandmother Zenobia said.

Justice tried to cover his face as he sobbed, but he couldn't raise his arms.

"It's okay. Let it out. I know everything hurts." Grandmother cleared her throat a few times to shake off feelings that stirred within her. Hope patted her brother's shoulders and dabbed his tears, trying not to cry too much herself.

"I've done some ugly crying myself, back in my younger days. I'm so sorry that Cassius misled you. He thrives on attention, anywhere he can get it. Mind you, he paid a steep price for his foolishness. He tried to change his wife, and it backfired. He'll be scarred for life. I'm also sorry you have to go through this kind of pain. It's physical and emotional. The heart wants what it wants and when it's denied? Lord have mercy. That pain runs deep. I've been around a long time and to me? Heartache is the worst kind of pain anyone can endure."

"Grandmother Zenobia, what can you do for him?" Hope asked. Grandmother fished in her purse until she retrieved a small Mason jar filled with a bright orange substance.

"This here is a special concoction I came up with. It has herbs and roots from my garden for healing. You aren't allergic to Goldenseal or Papaya, are you?" Justice shook his head no, best he could.

"Good. I also petitioned a spirit at 3 o'clock in the morning who allowed me to take sacred dirt from around where she is laid to rest, over at St. Anita's. Lastly, I collected blood from a Demon and an Angel."

Hope frowned. Grandmother held up her hand.

"Don't ask, because you wouldn't believe me if I told you the truth." Grandmother opened the jar, releasing a delicate floral scent, and offered it to Hope.

"Justice, we are going to slather this cream all over you, from head to toe. It will be ice cold at first, but the ginger I mixed in should eventually give you a soft, warm sensation. Cinnamon will speed up the process. Either you will get to living, or you will get to dying. Not that I'm a gambling woman, but my money is on you living." Grandmother didn't like giving the truth sometimes, but everyone had to be prepared for whatever came next.

Hope put on a pair of latex gloves and moved closer to the smallish looking headboard thanks to the mound of sweat stained pillows that cradled her brother's swollen head. Ahy squirmed a bit but continued to lay on the patient's stomach. Grandmother also put on a pair of gloves and moved to the foot of the bed. She pulled back the blankets, revealing blackened flesh, from above Justice's knees down to his toes.

Large pasty pustules were scattered along his legs. Grandmother shook her head and pursed her lips. Hope gasped in horror. When Justice saw the blood drain from his sister's face, he strained to look at his feet to see the damage. Ahy wiggled and pawed at Justice.

"Look at me, sweetie." Hope said.

"It's bad, isn't it?" he asked. "I can't feel anything below my waist."

"Stop trying to look. It'll give you a lifetime of nightmares," Grandmother warned. "Don't you worry, I'm here to make things better. We'll recite a bible verse together, and then Hope and I will apply the salve. We'll find something to talk about, to take your mind off the pain." The trio recited *Psalm 23* in unison.

Hope gingerly applied the bright orange cream on her brother's face while Grandmother Zenobia started on his feet. Red, craterlike ulcers on the pads of his feet and heels oozed clear fluid. She paused and quietly prayed a second prayer and continued. His toes were as cold and hard as ice when she massaged them. Grandmother sympathized with Justice as he cried. Her little Ahy whimpered.

"I just thought of a lovely story to tell," Grandmother said. "If my memory serves me correctly, Justice is the only Tyrell family member who hasn't been to my house out in Carrefour Parish. You've never seen the red strappy high heel I put out when I'm seeing clients. It's there as a shingle for business and has sentimental value."

"It's a lovely shoe," Hope said as she worked the cream into her brother's skin. "Did you used to wear them?" she asked.

"Oh, goodness no. The pair belongs to Shula, the Famous Fire dancer. Way back in the day, when my grandson was about three years old, I had the pleasure of making her acquaintance. That had to be what, the fall of 1873 or so?"

"Don't you mean 1973? We're already in the 21st century," Hope said. Grandmother burst out laughing at the puzzled looks Hope and Justice had. "I'll answer any questions you may have after I share the story.

As I WAS SAYING, it must have been September because it was harvest season and I remember I was low on salt. I needed to prepare some beef and pork to stow away for winter. Back then, we didn't have freezers like we do nowadays. I actually said out loud, "I need to get me some salt," when there was a faint knocking at my front door. I can't stand unannounced visitors, so I wasn't going to answer it. The knocking continued, and I heard soft voices, so I took a peek.

On my doorstep was Alice, a vibrant young lady from church and some plain looking white girl wearing glasses. She had jet black hair tied up in a bun so tight I could see her scalp. Alice sewed dresses for me on occasion and I wasn't expecting her for a few days, but there she stood with two baskets of clothes. Naturally, I opened the door. Both ladies had sticker weeds all over their dresses. The prickly plants didn't deter them from walking up to my porch as I had hoped.

"Why Alice, what a nice surprise. I wasn't expecting you until Wednesday or Thursday of this week," I said to her.

"I know Grandmother Zenobia, but I was so happy with how your dresses turned out that I just had to bring them over to you right away."

I let the ladies in. To my surprise, Alice's friend took a moment to remove her black leather boots and leave them by the door before entering my home. It was a charming gesture I hadn't seen in a long time. I pointed them in the direction of my kitchen and offered them some tea and cookies.

Both ladies were courteous and polite. Alice introduced me to her friend Beatrice, who was in a little dance troupe. They were performing all week at the Crescent City Harvest Festival, down by the river. Beatrice was just as sweet as could be, but I saw that her aura was dark blue and cloudy, with specks of pink. She put up a nice front, but she was distracted and sighed too much.

"Miss Beatrice, don't mind me, but I'm picking up that your spirit is heavy."

"It's true, Grandmother Zenobia," she said. "Alice was saying you had a way about you, but I didn't believe it."

"Would you like a quick reading?" I offered. Alice encouraged her, so she accepted. "Shall we do this in private?" I asked.

"Alice is my new best friend. You can tell me whatever you like with her here," Beatrice said. The three of us moved to the living room and got more comfortable. I shuffled my tarot cards three times, for the Father, the Son and the Holy Ghost, and pulled three cards.

"My darling, this is a fairly easy reading. The first card representing the past, is the Three of Wands. It shows expansion and travel. The second card, representing the present, is the Lover's Card. That's an obvious one. It's about relationships. The Third card, representing the future, is the Four of Wands, which is a good omen. It represents families, weddings, celebrations and surprises. That sort of thing. If I didn't know any better, based on what I see in the cards, you've started something new, and a romantic relationship is definitely on your mind."

I wish you could have seen this girl's face light up. Alice giggled at her friend's excitement.

"Grandmother, I'm new in town and I recently got a job as a bookkeeper over in Iberia. There's someone at work that I adore, but he doesn't give me the time of day. Quite a few men work there, but he's special. I'll say hello and he's polite enough to say hello back, but that's it. He's so handsome and my heart just pounds in my chest when I see him." Beatrice said all that as fast as her mouth would let her form the words.

"I tell you what. Give me a few minutes and I can make a sweeting jar for you. It will literally sweeten this man to you. All I ask for is a ticket to one of your shows as payment." Beatrice agreed, needless to say. I collected herbs and flowers that represent love and attraction, added sugar, water and mixed them in a mason jar. After reminding her to shake the jar often, I sent the ladies on their way.

Later that afternoon, once again, there was someone, annoyingly unannounced, on my porch. Lucky for him, it was that nice man, Russell from Avery Island, knocking on my door. Had it been anyone else, I would have given them a piece of my mind and put a small hex or two on them. He also had the sticker weeds stuck to his pant legs, and bees swirled around his head. I admit I was disappointed that my bees didn't deter him from walking right up to my porch. After opening my door, I blew a kiss to the bees and waved them away.

"Russell, what brings you by?" I asked. "I just put my grandson down for a nap and I almost didn't answer the door."

"I'm so sorry to disturb you, Grandmother Zenobia," he said, removing his hat in my presence. He had the thickest head of beautiful red hair I had ever seen. "Your name was on next week's delivery list for Tabasco and salt, but I was already crossing the bridge back from a delivery in Slidell. I felt I should just stop by and give you your request now. I can come back at the scheduled time if you want. I would hate to bother you, and little Will."

Russell's cheeks burned bright red.

"That's okay, young man. You're already here. Just don't make a habit of dropping by unannounced. You can go ahead and bring the items in."

A few minutes later, he carried in over his broad shoulders a large bag of salt from the Avery Island salt mine, and several bottles of Tabasco. He placed the bag in my pantry as if it were light as a bag of feathers.

"So, how are things at that Tabasco farm and their beautiful gardens?"

"Work is fine, I guess," he said. I noticed his aura was brown. Usually, that's a good sign because the boy is down to earth. This shade, though, was too dark and muddy, indicating feelings of worthlessness and self-doubt.

"What's troubling you, Russell?"

"Grandmother, I went to a vaudeville show last night, and I saw the woman of my dreams on stage. A Spanish lady named Shula the Fire dancer has stolen my heart and I don't know what to do about it."

"She must really be something to catch your attention like that."

"She takes my breath away."

"Well, I won't give you a love spell to work on someone that doesn't know you. It wouldn't be right. But, in exchange for some flower seeds, I can give you a little spell to do at home to help draw her to you."

"I would like that, Grandmother Zenobia," Russell said with a small smile.

"To get this young lady's attention, write her name and your name on a piece of brown paper. Fold it towards you three times and place it under a candle. Say a little prayer of love and light the candle for half an hour or so every day until the candle burns down. If it's meant to be, she should at least give you the time of day."

"Thank you for the advice, Grandmother Zenobia. I will be back next week with some of our finest seeds. I promise that you will have the best garden this side of the Mississippi river!"

GRANDMOTHER STOPPED HER STORY and offered Justice some water. She was pleased that his tears finally stopped and his extremities warmed a bit. By now, most of his body was bright orange from her cream.

"Grandmother, if I get through this day, what will you want in return?" Justice asked in between deep, wet coughs.

"Let's get you through today and we'll discuss it." Grandmother said. "Hope and I are going to apply this cream until your natural color comes back."

"I'm happy to offer up anything it takes," Hope said.

"It's funny you say that. Beatrice said the very same thing to me, way back then. It was barely two days when my sweet Ahy was yodeling up a storm at the front door."

"Grandmother, do you name all your dogs Ahy? There's no way he was around in 1873, or 1973," Hope said.

"Like I mentioned, I'll be happy to answer questions at the end of my story," Grandmother said, and continued with her tale.

AHY YODELED HIS LITTLE heart out by my front door late one afternoon. The sun was just about to set. I was out back having tea with my dear friend Priestess Rina, who was visiting from up north. Before we were so rudely interrupted, she was explaining to me how she learned to specialize in clearing and sending healing energy. I was intrigued because I definitely needed more of that in my life. Lately, I questioned my spell work and wanted to know if I needed to do some personal fine tuning.

Ahy kept on, poor thing, so she and I approached the front and found a young lady at the steps leading up to my porch, arms crossed, looking sadder than ever. A chubby skunk waddled circles around her and every few minutes, she swatted bees that flew past her. Apparently, Waylon wasn't enough to deter strangers, either.

"What brings you by, Miss Beatrice?"

"I came to drop off tickets to the show, as I promised."

"Stay where you are. I'll get a treat for Waylon and send him on his way." I grabbed some catfish from the icebox and tossed it out to my skunk friend. Once he meandered off, she came right up with tickets in hand. She handed them to me, not looking me or my guest in the eye. After many years, you'd think I'd be used to people not looking at me directly.

"Thank you," I said. Miss Beatrice turned to leave, hesitated, and turned back to us. She scratched her head nervously a few times, turned to leave again, and paused. I waved my hand, dismissing the bees. "Is something wrong?" I asked, half knowing what she was gonna say.

"Yes, Ma'am. I'm so sorry to disturb you."

"Come join us up here," I told her, and after introductions, the three of us sat together on my porch.

"I appreciate you, Grandmother Zenobia, but the sweetening jar didn't work. The man at work is polite, but still doesn't really talk to me. I feel as if I am drowning in loneliness. My heart aches."

"How long have you been working the sweetening jar?" Priestess Rina asked. I always admired how she always had perfect hair, perfect makeup, and a perfect attitude.

"About two days," she replied.

"About two days? Girl, love work is like making a peach cobbler. Once you add all the right ingredients and put it in the oven, you don't keep checking it every few minutes. It'll will never come out right. The same goes for love spells. Give it some time."

"Beatrice, she's absolutely right. Focus on other things that make you happy," I told her. "What about you and your little dance troupe? That sounds like it would be fun." I watched her as she sat with us. We could almost see the words sink in her head.

"There's nothing like dancing. When I'm moving around, I kind of hear the audience, but it's really just me and the music."

"Feel how her energy changed?" Priestess Rina pointed out to me. "It's different than just seeing the colors of her aura."

"Dancing is something you should think about when you feel sad or lonely. It feeds your soul, which is wonderful. I wish you could see what we see and feel what we felt. Your happiness is heavenly."

Beatrice flashed a sweet smile.

"If you'd like, we could whip up a spiritual bath to cleanse your aura and brighten your mood even more."

"Thank you, Grandmother Zenobia. I'll be happy to offer up anything it takes to ease my heartache."

"This one is on the house, precious. We all want love and happiness. Just don't pop up here again unannounced. I can't guarantee that Waylon won't spray you next time. Do me a favor and pour us all some lemonade while we get to work. You'll find it in the icebox." The girl's aura glowed pink and yellow, which warmed my heart.

Priestess Rina grabbed a few lilies from my garden while I mixed some fresh basil and rosemary together with rose water. After adding some fresh salt for cleansing that I got from Russell, we put all the items in a larger mason jar.

"Say the Lord's Prayer, mix half a cup of milk with this mixture and pour all of it over you when you bathe. Let it run from the top of your head all the way down to your toes. Imagine your bad thoughts being washed away."

Beatrice sniffed the mixture and smiled even brighter than before. She hugged us both and scurried off. Not too long after I sent Priestess Rina back home with a few supplies for her work, there was a loud ruckus, once again, in my front yard. It was early in the morning, right before dawn, and I was hotter than fish grease that someone was trespassing on my land. Cries for help filled the air. I didn't want anything to disturb my grandson, so I ran to the front.

"Help me, please!" Russell cried. He managed to get himself caught up with a pair of fat gators. They circled around and hissed at him.

"Do you have any idea what time it is?" I scolded him.

"I'm so sorry Grandmother. I know I shouldn't be here right now."

"There is a reason Gertrude and Aloysius guard my property at night. I don't want people all willy-nilly on my property."

I'm fairly certain he was only half listening as the gators roared at one another and lunged toward him. I went back in the house and rummaged through my icebox until I found some chicken. I returned to find Russell frozen in place while the gators toyed with him.

"Boy, you owe me a nice dinner some time," I warned as I tossed my chicken toward the side of the house. "Thank you for your service, Gertie and Al." The gators tore up that chicken quicker that I could spell Tchoupitoulas.

"Come on, get up here." Russell bolted up my steps and into my kitchen. "What on God's green earth brings you by at this hour?" Russell sat with his shouldered scrunched up and bit his lip.

"I am beside myself. I tried to get an autograph from Shula, but she acted like I wasn't even there. I'm devastated."

"What did she do?"

"Well, nothing. That's the problem." He ran his fingers nervously through his hair.

"So, you never actually spoke to her?"

"No," he said and covered his face with his large hands. It broke my heart to see that sweet man weep.

BOTH JUSTICE AND HOPE covered their mouths in unison, stifling their gasps of disbelief.

"Children, I swear it's true," Grandmother said.

"That man's love for that woman was overwhelming, similar to the way Justice felt. It was more than lust. To me, it was a positive sort of obsession, if that's even possible. The desire to love the person they had their heart set on was powerful," Grandmother explained.

"What happened then?" Justice asked.

"There was only one thing I could do, just like I'm doing now. I consoled him the best I could and tried to get him to change his focus," Grandmother said.

"Justice, you would have loved this man. He was tall and strong, and honest as the day is long. He knew nothing about this woman and yet he was so distraught. He knew he had to be with her. It broke my heart. After he collected himself the best he could, I sat him down and poured him some chamomile tea. Justice, I know our families have a certain history, but if you would have come to me about love, I would have done the same for you."

Grandmother noted that his clenched, blackened fingers and toes had softened. Her patient's skin, although still swollen, was closer to its natural color. The ulcers stopped oozing and the skin on his feet was smooth.

"Oh lord, I'm scared to ask what happened next," Justice said. His eyes were brighter, and his speech was clear. Grandmother Zenobia continued with her story.

"Well, Russell kept beating himself up. He was embarrassed and ashamed of his behavior. Worse, he thought he wasn't worthy of having love in his life."

I poured him more tea, offered him one of my handmade handkerchiefs. "Russell, tell me three things you like about yourself," I asked him while he blew his nose.

"I like my hands. I work hard and they never let me down."

"You do wonders helping things grow, I might add."

"You're right. I believe I'm fairly smart. Some of the men I work with out in the gardens come to me for advice about working their own land and fixing stuff. It makes me feel good that they trust my opinion."

"Those are all admirable qualities." I noticed some movement with his aura, but I couldn't tell which way it was going.

"I dunno, Grandmother. I'm a simple farmer at heart. I'm probably too boring for the fire dancer."

"You listen to me, Russell Bixby. It's her loss if she doesn't connect with you. You are very handy, smart and handsome. You have a warm, friendly soul."

Russell blushed.

"I do try to speak to everyone, even the ladies in the front office at work. The men think they are all too high falutin' to pay us any mind. I think they are just busy in a different way than us. That's why they don't speak that often."

I looked that young man right in the eye and did something I hardly ever do. I made him a promise for something I couldn't guarantee.

"I promise that you will find love."

"Really?"

"Yes, but I need you to stop a minute and breathe. You have to get a hold of your emotions and take care of yourself first."

"Okay Grandmother Zenobia," he hesitated. Judging by his frown, he only half believed me.

"How about I make you a mojo bag? It's something small you keep in your pocket, to bring you good luck in love and prosperity."

"I'll take whatever I can get," he said.

"It'll take me a little time because I want to make a very special one for you. Come by Saturday morning, just before sunrise. I'll have it for you by then. Do not show up at my house unannounced. Do you hear me?"

"Yes Ma'am! You have my word. Thank you for being patient with me Grandmother Zenobia. I am grateful you took the time to sit me down and not let those gators get me."

EARLY SATURDAY MORNING, THERE was a knock at my front door. Assuming Russell showed up on time, I carelessly opened it. Instead of that handsome red-headed man, there was a woman in a provocative red dress. It revealed lots of skin and emphasized every one of her curves. She was slouched over so much that her long, curly, black hair covered her face.

"Ma'am, can I help you? Are you hurt?" The woman looked up at me. Low and behold, it was Miss Beatrice. "What on earth are you doing here, dressed like that?"

The girl could barely get any words out in between her sobbing. I had no choice but to let her in. The poor creature could barely stand. Before she entered my house, she removed her shoes. They were a beautiful pair of red, high heeled strappy flamenco shoes. They had shiny glass crystals glued on them, in the shape of flames on the toes. We managed to get to my kitchen when she fell to her knees before me.

"Grandmother Zenobia, I'm begging you to put a spell on me. The man at work is in love with some woman and I just can't take it. I saw him sneaking a peek at a picture. He kissed it, he folded it up like it was extra special. My heart broke into pieces like shards of glass. I performed tonight, and I could barely focus. My rhythm was all wrong. I almost fell off the stage and I'm fairly certain I burned my hair once or twice. If Saturday night wasn't closing night, I would just run away, never to be seen again. If I can't be with him, I don't want to live. It hurts too much, Grandmother. I can't bear it. Could you please make this pain go away? Make me forget I ever laid eyes on him?"

She cried so hard that she made me cry, too. I've never seen anyone this lovesick, or so I thought. Before I could ask her more questions, there was a knock at my door. "Come in," I replied.

"I wasn't sure if I should come in. I saw some red shoes on your porch that don't look like they belong to you," my favorite farmer, Russell said.

Beatrice shot up and pulled her hair back into a bun. She roughly wiped her tears away. Russell stood with his mouth wide open.

"What's going on here?" he asked.

"My friend Miss Beatrice just stopped by for a little advice. She gave me some tickets for the show Saturday night," I said and took a second look at the tickets on my table. I don't know how I missed something so obvious. "Apparently her stage name is Shula, the fire dancer."

"Russell, what brings you by?" Beatrice asked, trying to cover herself with her hands on her chest.

"I...uh, gee. I came by to see Grandmother Zenobia." His cheeks burned as red as her dress. "Miss Beatrice, if you don't mind me saying, I am shocked that you are Shula the Fire dancer."

In the next moment, if that man said anything disrespectful, I was ready to pounce with a quick spell that would make him beg for mercy.

"You were amazing tonight. Every night this week, actually."

I sighed in relief.

"You came to my show every night?" Beatrice glowed.

"Yes ma'am. I wish I would have known. I would have told you at work. You take my breath away. I am inspired by the way you sway back and forth with the music and light up with the flames. The way the flames dance around your head and run up and down your arms and legs is mesmerizing. I don't know how you don't just burn right up. The way you move around on stage and your incredible smile set my heart on fire."

The two of them stood right in my kitchen and beamed at each other. Everything clicked. I couldn't believe I missed the signs. They worked together at Avery Island, out in Iberia, so they knew each other. She was a burly dancer in her free time, in the vaudeville show that he attended at the Crescent City Harvest Festival.

"I'm gonna give you both advice and then send you on your way. First, one person should never be your only source of happiness. Love them, but do not depend on them to make you happy. That is your job. Second, never, ever show up at my door, ever again, unannounced. You both worked my last nerve."

We all laughed a lot about my second rule.

"How about I give you my shoes? They can be a sign it's okay to come by. I have several pairs." Beatrice offered.

"I LOVED HER IDEA. They were such a sweet couple and eventually had a beautiful family." Grandmother took a moment to reflect on her story.

"That day we agreed they could come by anytime her red shoe was out. Once I started that, it just stuck for any-one coming by. I put a spell on the shoes to make them last as long as Russell and Beatrice loved each other. When either of you come by my house, you'll see those shoes are still just as beautiful as ever, especially when they sparkle in the sun.

"Grandmother, why didn't the sweeting jar and other spells work?" Hope asked. She nudged Justice in hopes he was paying attention.

"The spells weren't effective because true love was already in motion. They were already 'sweet on each other'. He was in love with her, and she was in love with him. They just didn't know it. Recently, I had a nice sit down with my favorite spirit guide, Papa Veneur. He has a powerful, vibrant presence. He can be kind-hearted and insightful if you make time to listen to him. He's so wonderful. I talk to him about everything, just about any time. Anyways, I'm going off track. There was a time when I questioned my spell work and he reminded me about the red shoe story. Spell work is fueled by intention. My love work was fine. It didn't work the way I expected because the love and passion were naturally there. He said the lovers' behavior was escalated because they spent so much time on that big salt dome with all that fiery hot pepper. Pepper intensifies and heats things up, including emotions. Avery Island, with its beautiful gardens, is a magical place. That's another story for another day."

Grandmother noticed that the sun was setting. She was pleased that Justice was more alert, and the swelling had gone down. She excused herself to the restroom and washed her hands. When she returned, she took a long look at Justice.

"So, Justice, find what makes you happy and enjoy the good emotions that pop up. It's not always easy, but you'll have a much brighter path in life when you try. I'm repeating myself to make sure my message is getting through to you. There is no man that should be in charge of making and keeping you happy, and you should not be in charge of making and keeping some man happy. Understand?"

"Yes Grandmother, I understand. I cannot thank you enough for coming by to pray over me. It means a lot that you gave me a treatment and spent time with me and Hope. This is a moment that makes me happy, and I promise to keep it in my heart."

"I'm grateful to the powers that be that you chose to fight and live. For a minute, I thought you were going to give up. Ahy saw to it to keep you here with us. He's sensitive to spirits and souls too, you see. Speaking of my dog, Hope, would you be a dear and get Ahy a bowl of water?" Grandmother asked. "Be mindful of the confusion powder in the hallway."

"Of course! Forgive my manners," Hope said. Ahy jumped off the bed and followed her out of the room. Justice managed to wiggle around until he could lean forward.

"What do you want in return for my treatment?" he asked. "Nothing in life is free. Hope has done so much for me, and I know she wants to pay you back for me. She has been marvelous looking after me when I caught ill and I don't want to burden her any more than I already have." Justice said.

"Hope will be taken care of. Something tells me her candy store is gonna have a lot more business very soon. Good people like your little sister prosper."

"God bless you, Grandmother Zenobia," Justice said, tearing up again.

"I'm not done with you, mister. Strictly between you and me, once you are back to yourself, you will pay me a different kind of offering. In a few weeks, once you are nice and healthy, I want you to invite that cute brunette bag boy at Rouses market on a date. You know who I'm talking about, the one who always offers to carry your bags to your car, no matter if you have three bags of groceries or a small pint of ice cream. This is an order, not a request. I'm fairly certain he will accept your invitation. Make a reservation at Queenie's Place in Iberia and mention that you are my guests. When you get there, ask specifically for Seraphina. I expect you will be treated to a lovely dinner and a fabulous show, right down to exotic fire dancers. I refuse to force someone to love another, but I can point people in the right direction."

Grandmother winked and patted Justice's hand. Hope and Ahy returned to find Justice clear eyed and sitting taller in his bed. His color was coming back in his cheeks.

"The others are long gone, thank goodness. Did I miss anything?" Hope asked.

"No, my dear. I was getting ready to tell your brother here that we can keep this little visit to ourselves, if it helps. The family doctor is gonna be shocked at how his health suddenly turned around. Our families have feuded quite a bit over the years and probably will continue to do so in the future. Being the good Christian folks that you are, it won't look good if people knew you were visited by a Voodoo High Priestess. Mind you, I've seen many of them in private, but you know how it is. Keeping up appearances is important for us Southerners. It'll be our secret if you like. It's up to you."

Grandmother's cell phone buzzed in her pocket.

"Well children, time for Ahy and I to get home. My god daughter is checking up on me. If you need anything, please call or come by when you see that red shoe on my fence."

"Grandmother, is there anything I can do to repay you for what you've done for my brother?" Hope asked.

"Your brother and I knew you were gonna ask that. You are such a sweet woman. You looking after your brother is more than enough. He did most of the work and didn't know it."

Justice squeezed Hope's hand.

"I will see myself out. When I get home, I'm gonna light a candle and have a nice chat with Mrs. Beulah Mae Tyrell about you two. Your Great Grandmother will be pleased to hear about you. Be good, children." Grandmother kissed Justice on the forehead and hugged Hope before leaving the room. A light mist shimmered over her right shoulder.

"Papa Veneur, you're right on time," Grandmother said. The mist transformed into the image of a well-groomed bearded man wearing a tailored royal blue three-piece suit.

"Zenobia, I'm here to make sure you get home safe. You're a little farther from home than usual, and there are too many distractions along the way."

"Ahy and I appreciate you looking after us."

"I know you love your stories, but you almost told them too much about yourself. Their mortal minds can't fully understand who you really are or how long you have been around."

"As usual, you're right. I have walked the earth a long time and I try not to say too much, about too many things. That's why I get to share my many stories with you," Grandmother said and laughed. "I'm almost ready to go." She sprinkled a few pinches of fern leaves and mustard seeds by the front door as they exited. Justice and Hope wouldn't remember the specifics of her story that day, but they'd remember how they felt around Grandmother Zenobia.

9

Rusty Memories

By Steven Van Patten

"There is something different in your voice," Grandmother Zenobia said. "It would be easier to pinpoint if we were together in person, but I sense it will be a long time before that even happens. It's in your voice. It has changed."

On the other end of the cellphone call, sitting in his office in New York, Christian Brookwater sighed. "Don't miss much, do you?"

"Do you want to talk about it, or will you keep your troubles to yourself like the stoic vampire lord that you are?"

Christian smirked. Outside of his wife Melody, there weren't too many women who had him as pegged as grandmother did. "You've got enough to do deal with," Christian answered. "Plus, I don't think there's anything you could do to help for me. Or if I even need help in the traditional sense."

One of her eyebrows twitched as her intuition kicked in hard. "In other words, you want me to concentrate on this new friend of yours?"

"If you don't mind."

She nodded and sucked her teeth. "When would this friend of yours get here?"

"Now that you agreed to help, I'll put him on my jet. He should be there in a few hours."

"I'll be here waiting for him."

"Oh! And I should warn you about something. He's a zombie..."

"I beg your pardon?"

"And he smells pretty bad." For the first time in their association, the vampire lord sounded sheepish.

"Christian, that would be the least of it! How is a zombie even considered a friend?"

"Well, this particular zombie can talk. In fact, he's a pretty good singer."

"Wait! You're not talking about that zombie that was on America's Next Country Star, are you?"

"The very one!"

She laughed at herself for having seen the episode, yet being quick to dismiss it. "I thought that was a fake! The news coverage said as much!"

"As immortals of color, I think we both know not to believe everything we hear on the news."

"True indeed, my friend."

"Anyway, he seems to be having a tough time remembering how he died."

"I would think that a blessing."

They both chuckled. "Under certain circumstances, sure. But I'm afraid he doesn't think so."

"Send him. I'll see what I can do."

"Thank you, Queen."

"You're welcome, Lord Brookwater."

"You know you don't have to call me that. Plus, I... am kind of leaning towards retirement."

"You are definitely going to have to explain that when I see you next. Also, if he even looks like he's trying to bite me, I will vaporize him, friend or no, great singing voice or no."

"I understand." There was a very telling pause, as if Christian wasn't entirely sure when he'd see Zenobia next, or ever again, for that matter.

Her instincts ablaze, she decided to let the matter lay. She could always meditate on the situation and gleam whatever Christian wasn't telling her from the universe later. As terrifying a proposition as that may be, her curiosity and possible worry over her beleaguered friend outweighed. "Be well, Christian. I'll do what I can for your friend."

"Thank you, Queen!" his cheerfulness sounded forced, which is something she normally despised. But she knew he meant well. The call ended.

DUSK HAD SETTLED IN with an array of orange and purple filling the sky above her house. Zenobia absorbed the peace and quiet one content breath at a time as she rocked back and forth in her chair. Ahy, in the hold of a doggy nap, snored. He was equally tranquil as his mistress. At least, that is until they both stirred from the sound of a large vehicle crunching the gravel in the driveway in front of the house.

Zenobia sighed. She knew there would be no calming Ahy while a monster was in the house, no matter how harmless the monster may or may not be. *Hell, Ahy doesn't even like Christian. I can't even imagine how he'd treat a zombie.*

"Ahy, go upstairs!" The dog looked confused, his head held tilted like the dog in the RCA logo of old. But I'm supposed to protect you, the look seemed to say. "I'll be fine."

Ahy looked almost disappointed at losing the chance to fight a zombie. Yet, after a moment, the dog obeyed, his scampering ending just as the knock on the door sounded.

Zenobia, sensing no danger, opened the door. Rusty's stench hit her like a punch. His visage partly blocked by a KN-95 COVID mask. She could see from the look in his eyes that he was painfully aware of his offensive order.

"Ma'am, I do apologize," Rusty said. His voice reminded him of so many southern gentlemen of long ago.

"We all have short-comings, Mr. Nail," Zenobia said as she graciously recovered. As the smell seemed to subside, she opened the door. "Please come in."

She stepped aside, noting the guitar strapped to Rusty's back and the seemingly brand-new leather outfit. As he passed her, he quickly took off his cowboy hat and the guitar. She helped him stow the guitar near the front door and hung his hat on the nearby coatrack before leading him into the parlor.

"You can take off the COVID mask," she said with a smirk. "COVID doesn't seem to be a problem either of us have.

"I was wearing it more for the benefit of the driver and the vampire staff on the Brookwater jet," Rusty explained as he unhooked the COVID mask's straps from his ears and placed the mask on the coffee table that separated the parlor chairs. He did not sit.

"A gentleman to the end," she observed. "Would you like some tea, Mr. Nail?"

He smiled. At least she figured it to be a smile. "I'd love that."

"You sit with peaceful thoughts, Mr. Nail," she said. "I'll be right back."

"Thank you, Ma'am," he said with a nod as he took the seat, a wooden chair padded with pillows.

She left the parlor and entered the kitchen, performing the necessary steps for tea preparation. As the water boiled, she could hear that Rusty had retrieved his guitar, presumably getting some practice in while waiting for his tea. Then she heard a scampering that could only be Ahy bounding down the stairs to check Rusty out and probably protest the noise or, for that matter, Rusty himself. Her eyes narrowed.

"Disobedient little so-and-so," she sighed under her breath. Making her way back to the parlor to intercept the dog, she was further irritated to see he'd outpaced her. However, as she turned the corner, what she saw was something of a surprise.

Rusty stood in the pantry playing a very bluesy melody on his guitar, facing Ahy, who quietly sat on his hind legs with his tail wagging in sheer happiness. The dog's head was tilted again, but this time the tilt conveyed amusement. Zenobia observed and laughed to herself as she retreated to finish making the tea.

"CHRISTIAN EXPLAINED YOUR REQUEST, but I can't imagine this being anything but a painful experience for you," Zenobia said as she sipped her tea. It was a little colder than she normally preferred. But after she had sat the tea down, she took the time to light some incense candles to mask Rusty's scent. Then there was the matter of calming Ahy down once Rusty stopped playing.

"Sorry, Little Baby," Rusty said to Ahy with a shrug.

"Oh, don't apologize to this spoiled dog," Zenobia chuckled as she finally sat down. She watched as Ahy settled down on the carpet in front of them, keeping his usual watchful eye as he would with any guest in the house, but exhibiting no outward hostility.

A couple of blues cords and you're in love? You're not even agitated by the vampire limo driver waiting patiently in front of the house. You teach me something new every day, Ahy.

Rusty acknowledged not needing to apologize to the dog, then closed his eyes. "You see, Ma'am, I recognize how fortunate I am to become a sentient zombie, even though the origin of this gift came from sinister hands."

"Enemies of Christian Brookwater?" Zenobia asked for the sake of clarity.

Rusty nodded. "Yes, Ma'am. You may or may not have heard, but there were zombie surges in every major part of these United States, and that was, in fact, a part of a larger assault on the vampires and werewolves."

"I did," she admitted. "I also know my friend and his vampire soldiers handled it."

"They did, but there were some losses. But that's not my story to tell. It's Christian's."

"So, I gathered," she said with a nod.

"My problem is I have no story to tell. My song about getting kicked out of heaven is, as far as I know, a fabrication, something planted in my head by a vampire scientist. I want to know what really happened to me. How did I get here? Why am I a zombie? How am I supposed to live any kind of life that makes sense?"

Zenobia looked him over carefully. "Mr. Nail..."

"You can call me Rusty."

"...Rusty, I must tell you. I have done this for other people and what I have uncovered in the past has never been pleasant. Especially in the case of someone trying to figure out how they died. Is there anything I can say to make you reconsider?"

Rusty didn't give it a second. "No Ma'am."

Zenobia closed her eyes and pursed her lips. "All right then." As she got up and left the room again, she gave him one last forlorn look. She suspected that digging through Rusty's memories was going to be as hard on her as they would be on her zombie visitor. She left Rusty alone with the dog for a few minutes. Ahy howled as if to say, 'well, if you guys are done talking, can we get back to the music?' Unfortunately for the little music lover, Zenobia returned with a ceramic bowl filled with a very fragrant liquid.

"Rosewater, sage, and a few other things to help me do this," Zenobia explained. "I just hope this doesn't sting too badly, considering you are in a state of decomposition."

"I'll happily suffer the agonies of the damned for the sake of clarity," Rusty declared, his southern drawl making him sound even more resilient in the matter.

Zenobia positioned herself behind the seated Rusty, with the bowl in her hands. "This shouldn't stain your clothes," was the only warning she gave as she poured the rosewater over Rusty's head. Rusty closed his eyes as the liquid spilled over his face and dripped down to his western-styled shirt. Zenobia put the bowl down and placed her hands on Rusty's less than attractive scalp, letting the few hairs on the zombie's head find their way between her fingers.

"Rusty, keep your eyes closed, and try to clear your mind as much as possible."

"Yes, ma'am."

As Ahy watched, neither Zenobia nor Rusty moved an inch. When Zenobia finally opened her eyes, they were white, an indication that her true eyes were elsewhere. Her eyes had fallen upon the woeful times that Rusty had experienced before his first tragic end.

As expected, Zenobia found herself in a vast, white hall of mirrors. She knew that each mirror represented the memories of the person whose mind she was exploring. When in search of a buried memory, she would usually have to look for the mirrors coated with a glistening charcoal grey, dust. She would wipe the dust and expose the lost memory to herself and the subject. The only problem was that almost all of Rusty's mirrors were covered.

The only ones that were clear were the ones at the far end of the hall. Inside the clean mirrors, she could see what looked like short cinemas from his vantage point of his reality TV show audition, the sinister vampire that sent him after Christian Brookwater and how he and the vampire lord finally came to terms. She wanted to know more, but she also knew that's not why she'd entered his mind.

Walking to the dirty mirrors at the far end, she realized that if she cleaned them all, she'd probably cause her zombie 'patient' to have a mental breakdown. Maybe if I get close enough, I can see through the dust without having to expose too much to Rusty.

Skipping the first two mirrors, she peered into the third. There she saw a boy, playing alone in a cornfield with a ball. He appeared bored, but at least he was content. Suddenly, the boy was approached by a woman Zenobia assumed was his mother.

"I could use some help in the house." The boy followed quietly, eventually finding himself sweeping a kitchen while his mother washed dishes. Outwardly, it was the kind of house a sharecropper lived in.

While debating whether she should move on, some of the dust crept up into Zenobia's nose, causing her to sneeze. Even though she was technically not corporeal, her sneeze caused a great deal of the dust covering the mirrors to erupt into an airborne cloud that eventually disappeared. At least three mirrors were way more exposed than they had been. With that, Zenobia saw much of Rusty's childhood laid bare.

From the ages of one to six, Rusty experienced nothing out of the ordinary for the child of a black sharecropper couple in Alabama. Some mischief, a couple of whippings, occasional bouts of hunger, as food was sometimes unavailable. And then, one day, the food scarcity stopped. That day was preceded by a white man visiting the house. His parents greeted the man with what looked to Zenobia a sort of guarded reserve. Unbothered, the man took off his hat and smiled at the three of them.

"Well, this is embarrassing," the white man said.

"Certainly not what we agreed to." Rusty's father, a tall, dark-skinned, middle-aged man in overalls, looked decidedly unhappy.

The white man's hands found his hips. "Look, before you get all bunched up, let's understand a few things. While I won't be spoken to in any ol' manner by a nigger, I realize my error here. And so, Roderick, to make it up to you, I will give you ownership of these here two acres your house is sitting on."

"What?" Roderick's eyes widened. Holding Rusty's six-year-old hand, his wife's jaw dropped.

"Of course, I will still occasionally call on Sybil here. Nothing crazy, maybe once a month we just go for a ride. Just to scratch the itch, you know what I mean. Don't worry, I won't cause you to have another... what you say the boy's name was?"

Roderick moved forward, seemingly ready to harm the white man on his porch. Sybil quickly let go of little Rusty's hand and grabbed her husband.

"I suggest you be passive like your gal there, Roderick. If you were to strike me, I would have no choice but to come back here with Sherriff Willis. And we both know he and his deputies would just hang you on that tree up wonder quicker than you could say the words 'black bastard'."

Sybil restrained her husband with a firm grip on his arm. A grip made hard from decades of manual labor. "Mr. Kelly, as a gentleman, I'm sure you understand we're just not used to talking this sort of thing out in the light of day is all. Roderick and I are very happy to accept the land."

Kelly and Roderick locked eyes briefly, the white man's stare seeming to mock the anger in the black man's eyes. Finally, Roderick broke the eye contact, staring at his shoes as Mr. Johnson walked up the porch stairs and held out the deed. "It's a good deal, Roderick. Pride shouldn't be a part of it. Besides, you're a nigger. You can't afford pride."

Roderick gulped hard as he reached out to take the deed. As he made to pull the paper away, Johnson suddenly increased his hold. "Aren't you going to say, 'thank you'? It's already signed over to you, by the way."

Sybil stepped forward. "We thank you, sir!"

Johnson's eyes narrowed. "I want to hear it from him. Besides, legally speaking, I didn't give you anything. Not any land, anyway."

The world was eerily quiet, as it seemed that even the birds in the nearby trees had fallen silent in this dehumanizing moment. "Thank you," Roderick finally said.

"That's better." Johnson turned his gaze to the boy. "What you say his name is?"

They both answered. "Rusty."

At the time, the confused little boy didn't understand what had happened in front of him. But he did know this white man was not to be trusted. Even as the man smiled at him, and said something about seeing Rusty again, the terror-stricken boy retreated into the house, throwing himself onto parents' bed where he cried until he fell asleep.

Outside, Mr. Johnson tipped his hat and mounted his horse with the demeanor of someone who had just stopped by to borrow a cup of sugar. The horse kicked up dust as it carried its master onward, leaving a broken and humiliated family in its wake.

PRIDING HERSELF AS SOMEONE who didn't normally make mistakes, she was pretty upset at herself for getting too close to the mirrors and sneezing. As she had experienced the revelation of Rusty's true parentage, so had Rusty. No longer shielded by his child-like lack of understanding of the conversation that took place on that porch so long ago, Rusty had relived this recollection as a grown-up zombie. Rusty's head shook in Zenobia's hands as he wept. Still joined together, their collective emotional turmoil was palpable enough for Ahy to whine with concern as he watched them.

And the worst part of me putting him through this is that it has nothing to do with how he died. That assumption would turn out to be Zenobia's second mistake.

RUSTY'S HALL OF MIRRORED Memories shook as if in the throes of an earthquake. As the mirrors shook, more grey dust floated into the air around Zenobia, then disappeared. After thirty seconds, she'd had enough. "Rusty, if you want me to continue, then you need to stop with the shaking."

This prompted an abrupt end to the vibration. Zenobia sighed and looked over the mirrors. The quake rendered them easier to see into, which meant that as fast as she could gather information, she knew Rusty's brain was being flooded with joy and pain. She worried about his sanity and his soul. "Hang on, Rusty. Hang on, baby!"

As she walked, she saw the rest of it. Rusty's sad, lonely childhood living with two parents so caught in their own personal hell that they couldn't be parents. Roderick, having mastered the art of moonshine, went from selling hooch to supplement his sharecropper income, to becoming his own best customer. His liver would kick out by the time Rusty was sixteen. And it was on his sixteenth birthday that Mr. Johnson showed up and gave Rusty his first guitar. But as with any gift Mr. Johnson gave, it was a kindness marred by his racism and ignorance.

"I hear niggers do well in the music biz! If you apply yourself, maybe you can be a somebody. I mean, as much as a nigger musician can be. It'll be like learning a trade. You know, other than this sharecropping shit."

Despite the way the advice was presented, Rusty took to it. He taught himself a little something every day. Whenever he wasn't helping his sad mother in the fields and around the house, he sat in front of a radio trying to figure out how to play songs.

Seeing how playing the guitar seemed to give Rusty a sense of joy, Sybil made a point of going into town and getting Rusty books full of sheet music and other instructions. There wasn't much to choose from in those days, but it would set the foundation for Rusty to be master guitar player in a matter of years. The guitar was not Rusty's only obsession, however. There was also Penelope.

Zenobia had gotten so caught up in the images that told the story of how Rusty started playing the guitar, she almost missed her. It started off so innocently. Rusty couldn't have been more than eight. He spied her one day while working the field with his mother. She sat next to her father in a horse-drawn wagon, both bouncing every couple of seconds as the mares pulled down the country dirt road. They locked eyes; hers filled with girlish curiosity brought on by seeing a boy around her age.

Meanwhile, his eyes literally warmed as something he'd never experienced before overtook him. It was love. But it wasn't the kind of love adults experience, polluted by lust, alcohol, or the bitter aftertaste that comes with a broken heart or several. This was a love so pure and so innocent that it was blinding. It filled every cell in his body with a kind of anxiety that would only find relief in the presence of the one he now adored and would pine over forever.

"That tobacco ain't pickin' itself, Rusty," Sybil shouted at him once she spotted him standing in their field, frozen in place.

Later that night, he mentioned the incident to his mother at dinner. Sybil didn't know the girl very well, but she knew the father. Unlike Rusty, she had noticed the angry look Penelope's father, Mr. Pearl, gave him as he steered his wagon past the house.

"I reckon you keep your mind on your chores and off that Penelope," his mother chided. "I know you're lonely, but there's no telling what that mean ol' Mr. Pearl is liable to say to you if he catches you trying to talk to her."

The funny thing about children is that most of them tend to listen to warnings and treat them more as challenges. Rusty was no different, but it took him a whole three days for him to build up the courage. His other dilemma was age. His mother's concerns regarding Mr. Pearl aside, she would not entertain the idea of Rusty traipsing off down the road to talk to some girl. He had to wait until she took a nap or something, which she eventually did.

It was quite exhilarating, walking past houses he'd only seen in the distance up until now. Only a few people seemed to notice him, as most were too busy working various crops, slaughtering chickens, or engaged in some form of blacksmith work.

"Hey Little Rusty," a woman finally did call out. "A little far away from your house now, ain't cha?"

"Just r-r-running an errand for my mother," he lied nervously.

"All right then! You be careful getting up yonder and back."

"I will."

As Rusty continued his walk, his mind raced. *What if this woman ran into his mother? What if mom had already woken from her nap and was now on her way down the road to find him and whip his tail with a 'switch?'.* Or maybe she woke and after finding him missing, had turned hysterical with the thought that Mr. Johnson, or some other white person had gotten a hold of him. He was just about to turn back around when he saw the house. He knew it was the house because there she was, sitting on the porch, swaying back and forth in an unusually large rocking chair, her feet flying free.

As far as houses go, it was by far the nicest in the town. It was the only house that wasn't a shack. It was the kind of house he imagined Mr. Johnson had lived in, with its white walls and pillars, that made him think of fairy tales his mother told him.

In contrast, Zenobia's thoughts as she watched this memory unfold were that it was a bigger version of her own. But to the eyes of an eight-year-old boy who'd been living in a barely held together shack on a dirt road his whole life, it may as well have been the Taj Mahal or some other wonder of the world.

Equally captivating was Penelope. Sitting on the porch in a rocking back and forth, her legs swaying in the air carelessly, to Zenobia, she was just another black child. Cute and very well kept for the times, which Zenobia assumed was the 1930s. Yet, still just a child.

To Rusty, she might as well have been a siren leading a boat filled with sailors to a watery grave or the goddess Oshun with all the feelings the very sight of her stirred up in that boy. They locked eyes. She smiled. Not love at first sight, by any means. Maybe just happy to see someone her age.

He smiled back, but it was a smile quickly done away with as something sharp hit Rusty on his cheek. He turned to see Mr. Pearl marching towards him. A quick glance on the floor explained the pain. Pearl, from about thirty paces away, had hit poor Rusty with a rock. And while Zenobia certainly disapproved of this, she couldn't help but admire the accuracy.

"You better thank God that was the biggest rock I could find!" Pearl sounded like the preacher his mother sometimes dragged him to see on Sundays. "Now you get your little yellow ass off my property!"

Rusty turned and ran.

"And don't you ever find ya'self here again, you hear me?" Pearl continued. Furnace hot fear filled his belly, urging the boy's legs to find the strength to create distance between himself and Mr. Pearl.

Just as he crossed the property line, he heard something that made things infinitely worse. "You can run. Runnings good. I'm still coming to have a conversation with that mother of yours."

Initially, he was running too fast to cry. But eventually, tears did come.

"WOMAN! I NEED YOU to keep this little yellow boy off my property!"

Rusty had beaten Mr. Pearl back to the house by a few minutes, but only because Mr. Pearl had taken the time to feed and saddle his horse before making the ride to Sybil's. When he'd gotten home, the only thing he could say to his mother was, 'A man is coming, and he's angry with me."

Sybil, a woman grown weary of men and their non-sense, stared coolly at Mr. Pearl as he rode up on a white and brown stallion. Then, as Rusty came to her side, she stared down at her frightened son and gently turned his head to look at the scar left by Mr. Pearl's rock. "Property or no, sir, if you harm my child again, you will find yourself powerful sorry."

Pearl scoffed. "Whatchu gonna do? Get your white man to come after me?" When he saw her eyes widen, he smirked. "What? You don't think everyone living in this godforsaken place don't know about you and that white man. Best thing to happen to that little yellow heathen you got is for ol' cowardly ass Roderick to die."

"Sir, I will thank you to get off my property!"

"You mean Mr. Johnson's property, don't you?" Pearl smiled. "Now that Roderick done drank himself to death, the property reverts back to that ol' white man what been climbing on top of you. The real father that made that little banana-skinned half-breed. That's right! Legally, you can't own no property! Not in these here parts of the US of A, Negress!"

"You have made your point, Mr. Pearl." Her lower lip quivered with rage and embarrassment. Below her, with no idea what else to do, Rusty hugged his mother's waist.

"You know, it's too bad Roderick drank himself to death! He could make some mean hooch! That was the only thing he had going for himself, I guess. Even if Johnson was coming to me, he'd have to do it with civility. I make all the white folks in the neighboring town money, Ms. Sybil. And I police darkies for them so they don't have to come get their white hands dirty. So, if Johnson wants to talk about it, that's fine, because I know you ain't doing shit!"

Tears welled up in Sybil's eyes. He'd called her bluff. There was nothing she could do to Mr. Pearl or any other man in this town without the ending up in a cell or swinging from a tree as white folks ate finger sandwiches under her shoeless feet. "Rusty won't bother you again, Mr. Pearl."

He turned to leave. "You fuckin' see to it!"

The mother and son would stand staring into space, basking in both trauma and humiliation that seemed to come with the sunset. Eventually, they retreated into the house, where they would share a silent dinner. Neither of them would speak a word for nearly two days. They merely existed.

Because Zenobia was experiencing the town through Rusty's memories, her comprehension of things would be limited to Rusty's childhood perceptions, which is to say some information was slow to come. Outside of his ill-fated trip to Mr. Pearl's property, Rusty didn't get to explore the town very much in his early years. Zenobia surmised that there was a neighboring white town that Mr. Johnson lived in, and even heard Johnson reference it during his visits.

As the years pressed on, Johnson's visits became less frequent. By the time sixteen-year-old Rusty had been handed his guitar, the visits had all but ended. It was as if the real thrill in his taking advantage of Sybil was more about emasculating Roderick and less about the sex act itself. He'd sometimes he'd sit down at the kitchen table, stare at Rusty for a few minutes, ask for a cup of coffee and then leave. Thankful for the respite, Sybil could only assume Mr. Johnson found a younger, slimmer lady to take advantage of.

During one of these kitchen table chats, Johnson mentioned something about a school being opened. "Paid for by the white folks, and allowed, so you might as well use it," was the explanation Johnson offered. Unbeknownst to Johnson, Sybil had already received a letter, all but ordering her to enroll Rusty in the school.

Sybil didn't want to send him anywhere and not because she didn't want him to learn to read and write. It had been her experience that nothing from white people was ever free or generated from kindness. She knew the only reason the white people would give the neighboring black town a school would be for the purpose of conditioning them into being docile and obedient. And, of course, while that would seem safer for Rusty to learn not to cross Caucasians, she had secretly hoped Rusty would keep some rebellious fires in his heart.

The school would be built on the same road Rusty had used to get to Mr. Pearl's house. Built equidistant between the two houses, it would take Rusty Nail and Penelope

Pearl a half hour to get to the school, while most of their future classmate a much shorter time.

Zenobia couldn't help but chuckle when she saw little Rusty's face when he saw Penelope walk into the modest classroom. Consumed by his schoolboy crush, he watched her take a seat just one row away. His belly trembled at the thought of being able to eventually speak to her. As his imagination ran wild, he would find himself chastised by the schoolteacher as he seemed incapable of concentrating on anything other than the back of her head.

Thus began a part of the adventure Zenobia only skimmed, as the time she could safely remain immersed in Rusty's psyche needed to be limited if both were to end this exercise with their sanity intact. Most of what she saw of those years were Rusty's pining over his lady love, yet still managing to do enough work to keep his teachers and mother off his back. She watched the boy receiving the guitar again and teaching himself by ear.

As time passed, Sybil's tobacco crop would do well enough that she'd eventually afford a victrola which not only gave her the ability to listen to music, but for Rusty to develop his musical acumen. Zenobia smiled as she watched Rusty grow from an uneasy and insecure child to a daring, invigorated teenager, full of life and open to possibilities, despite being in the clutches of good ol' Jim Crow.

The school taught reading, writing, and arithmetic well enough for Rusty to become more of help around the house. The tobacco was selling more than, so Sybil needed help with chores, inventory, and many other things. But, as Sybil had predicted, the school fell short in one area. The stories of how Black People arrived in this country and suffered immeasurable amounts of tragedy and trauma were replaced by a narrative of how the African was rescued from the jungle to live in a much more civilized place. Sybil would scoff at the notion and give Rusty the truth in small doses every evening at dinner. Zenobia would observe that he seemed to only hear half of her words, as he would continually be distracted by day-dreams of Penelope.

While speeding things up, Zenobia would be treated to a bittersweet montage of Rusty and Penelope slowly falling in love. It started with glances from one side of a classroom to the next. Then it was games with the other children, with many a taunt and jibe as the other children soon picked up on how the two would always pair up or be on the same team. Then, as they both approached an age where their hormones would take over, they discovered a path in the woods. And there in the woods, hidden away from prying eyes, they would share their first kiss.

There was still the wrath of Mr. Pearl to consider. However, no one in the town liked Penelope's father, so no one was willing to snitch on the two young people. Rusty seemed like a good boy who'd eventually marry her, so even the town's biggest Bible-thumpers turned a blind eye to the whole scenario.

As Zenobia and Rusty continued to skim the memories of young Rusty and Penelope exploring each other's bod-ies romantically, Rusty became semi-aroused. "Sorry, Ma'am," a flustered Rusty said sheepishly. She'd never admit it, but her connection to Rusty meant she felt some of his arousal. "It's okay, Rusty. Not my first time. But let's try to fast forward if it's all the same to you."

"Of course!" Speeding up the memories led to a sudden rush of fear for both, as they stumbled upon the distressing moment that Penelope realized something very important.

"Pregnant!"

They were both in their early twenties at this point. School and a few years were behind them, but the world hadn't changed to the point where two young Black kids could just hit the road with no money. And then there was the matter of Rusty not wanting to abandon Sybil.

It had been a few years since the last time Rusty had walked up to the Pearl house, but Rusty was just as nervous as he'd been as a boy. Thankfully, Mr. Pearl was in the house, so there would be no rock throwing. Rusty stood at the door for roughly thirty seconds before finally having the courage to knock. The door whipped open, revealing the grizzled, annoyed black man behind it.

"What the fuck do you want?"

Zenobia heard Rusty say, "I came to talk."

"Ain't you Sybil's boy?" Pearl asked. "I thought I told you to stay off my property. I don't give a fuck if you was six when I told you to stay off my land. Or how long ago! The rule still applies! Now get back to that white man fucking mama of yours and sling some tobacco."

"I was eight." Being annoyed that the old man didn't know how old he was during their first encounter annoyed Rusty just enough for him to make stern eye contact. "I was eight and Penelope is pregnant. I know you forbade her to see me, but we are together now. We're family now, Mr. Pearl, like it or not."

Everything went topsy-turvy as Pearl apparently shoved Rusty so hard that he went tumbling down the porch steps. Stunned, he struggled to his feet. Looking up, he saw that Mr. Pearl was no longer in the doorway. As he steadied himself, Penelope came running out.

"Rusty! What did you say to him?"

Upon seeing this, Zenobia was appalled. "You didn't warn her first?!"

"At the time, I thought only to be brave about the matter," Rusty answered. "I didn't think he'd take things so far."

Dread filled Zenobia as she watched Mr. Pearl reemerge from the house with a pistol in his hands. "Get out of the way, Penelope!"

"Daddy, no!!"

"You're going to shoot me, Mr. Pearl?" Rusty challenged. "You better not miss!"

Zenobia sneered at Rusty's bravado. She'd seen his whole life played out up to this point and knew that all he'd ever experienced were a couple of schoolyard scraps. He'd never fought for his life before.

"I never said I was overly smart," Rusty said after sensing her feelings on the matter.

"Shut up, Rusty!" Penelope, more aware of what her father was capable of, seemed near hysterics. "Run! Rusty, you have to run!"

"Come with me!"

"I can't!" Penelope cried. "I have to stop him from killing you!"

Pearl began walking down the stairs. "Get out of the way, Penelope!"

At the sight of her father approaching, Penelope stood between the two men. "Stop! Please stop!"

Mr. Pearl closed the distance between his daughter and himself. "I'm not going to tell you again! You're going to get out of the way, and I am going to shoot this high yella nigga!"

"No! Daddy, I love him! And we're going to be raising a family!"

He pointed the gun at Rusty's head, fired and missed as Rusty ducked. Penelope screamed.

"Y'all ain't raising shit!"

It was hard for Zenobia to make sense of it, but it looked as if a three-way tussle ensued. Then more gunfire. The last thing she saw was Penelope's blood-splattered, frightened face before everything went black. Zenobia jumped back, breaking her hold on Rusty.

"No! I didn't die here! I didn't! You must go back there's more! I'm sure!"

Seeing the two of them in distress, Ahy yipped. Without an explanation, Zenobia turned and walked to the kitchen and filled her favorite glass with tap water. Seeing Rusty's history had taken a toll on her. Part of her didn't want to go on, not because she didn't want to help Rusty, but because it had all been so emotionally draining. And for Rusty to now say that even after he'd apparently been shot there was more? She drank the water down with three impressive gulps and walked back to the living room, where she found that neither the zombie nor the dog had moved.

"Everything okay, ma'am?" Rusty asked.

For the first time ever after trying one of these, she took a deep breath and, finger by finger, reattached herself to Rusty's messy hair and scalp. Everything was dark at first, and then she was back in Rusty's Hall of Memories. The mirror standing in front of what appeared to be a blurry vision that slowly came back into focus.

"Easy son, you've been out for a while."

As his eyes regained focus, he found himself staring into the stern eyes of a burly, bearded black man dressed in very average overalls and plaid shirt he wore. The man sat him up on what was a bed in a room he'd never been in before, and handed him a glass of water,

"Where am I? Who are you?" he finally asked the man.

The man sighed. "My name is Dr. Arzel Watts. They brought you in here after Mr. Pearl shot you. You are in my house where I treated your wounds as best I could. That said, you should take it easy."

"Where is Penelope?"

"Penelope? The young lady?"

"Yes! Is she all right?"

The doctor shook his head with regret as he placed a hand on Rusty's shoulder. "She's dead, son."

Rusty fell to his knees, slamming his hand on the hardwood floor. "That fucking bastard."

"Yes, that he is."

For several minutes, Rusty wailed and cried. The doctor fell on one knee and put a sympathetic hand on him, but Rusty would remain inconsolable for some time. "I'm going to kill him!" he finally declared.

"You're in no shape to kill anyone, boy," Dr. Watts finally said. "Y'all lost because even though he's much older, Ol' Pearl is an excellent pistoleer."

Rusty finally stood up. "Look here, doctor, I don't care if he gunned down Doc Holliday! I'm going to kill him!"

Dr. Watts pursed his lips. "Ironically, the consumption took Doc Holliday, not a gunbattle. But before you go trying to settle some score with Mr. Pearl, might I suggest you at least try some target practice out back?"

It was then that it seemed that the doctor led Rusty to another part of the house. After observing how vast the place was, Rusty managed a question despite still being grief stricken.

"Do white people live here?"

Dr. Watts seemed to want to chuckle. "No, son. It's a good question, though. And for the record, when you see one of us with a house like this, it means we did something terrible that probably helped white people in some kind of way. In fact, I used to work with your adversary, Mr. Pearl. That's why I agreed with you when you said he was a bastard."

Walking through a dimly lit hall, Rusty eventually found himself in front of an armoire and then stepping back as the doctor opened it. Inside hung an assortment of pistols and rifles.

Zenobia read Rusty's mood. As saddened as he was to be reliving Penelope's death and the loss of the baby, he was also excited upon seeing the doctor. "As you probably guessed, Madam Zenobia, Dr. Arzel Watts taught me how to shoot."

"So, I see," Zenobia answered. Then she caught a glimpse of long–ago Rusty in a mirror. "Why are you so pale?"

Well, truth be told, I think Dr. Watts was some kind of supernatural person. What people might call an alchemist. Hell, I imagine you and he might have had a thing or two in common. Anyway, turns out the way Watts revived me was unnatural by some people's standards. But we had to keep such things quiet, least we both get lynched."

"But Rusty, you were already starting to look like..."

"A zombie," he finished. "Yes, that is probably because I was. That was Dr. Watts' doing. I wasn't in this decomposing state, and I had not developed a taste for human flesh yet, but I was living dead. Not that I knew that right out of the gate, mind you. See, the reason I ended up there in the first place was because after Pearl shot me, my mother had shown up. Somehow, she got me out of there and figured to take me to a doctor who also happened to be the one person Pearl wasn't likely to mess with."

"Wait, so Pearl and Watts were enemies?"

"Yes indeed," Rusty affirmed. "I think the mirror next to the one you are looking at will show you old Arzel telling me what happened between those two."

"It's safe to say that things are starting to come back to you?" Zenobia asked.

"Yes. There is just one thing more I need to see." Rusty sounded alarmed, as if he thought Zenobia was about to pull the plug. "One more dot that I need to connect."

Fortunately for him, Zenobia had no intentions of ending this exploration. Not yet. "No problem, Rusty."

Rusty sighed as Zenobia blew dust away from another mirror, which revealed Rusty and his new host sitting down for dinner. It seemed like some time had passed. Maybe as many as five years.

"Why have you helped me?" Rusty asked as they both slurped their way through their bowls of stew.

"You ever hear the expression, 'the enemy of my enemy is my friend'?"

Rusty shook his head. "No," he said in mid–slurp. "But why are you two enemies?"

Dr. Watts leaned back in his seat, his chair creaking slightly as his weight shifted. "The long and short of it is, we used to work together. Up North, in the Dakotas. We were truant officers."

Watts could see that made no sense to young Rusty, so he continued. "You see, some white people began feeling bad about what they'd done, killing so many Red Men and taking their land. Not bad enough to stop what they were doing to them, but bad enough to consider ways to acclimate them into white society. All over, they started building these schools. The philosophy behind the schools might have sounded okay to white people of the era, but to anyone with a true sense of decency, it was nauseating. 'Kill the Indian, save the man.' That was their godforsaken mantra."

Observing young Rusty and his mentor, Zenobia's emotions nearly overtook her as memories of her dear friend, Indian Chief Qaletaqua and all he suffered under the calloused hands of the US government bubbled to her mind's eye.

Back in the mirror, Rusty's conversation with Watts continued. "My school felt like that," he said. "No slogans, but there was definitely an emphasis on making us palatable to white people."

"I'm sure there was. Pearl helped pay for that school, at least that's my understanding. You see, Pearl didn't care what happened to those little Indian kids and at first, neither did I. But eventually, I caught a glimpse of what would happen when we dragged them boys and girls back to those places. The haircuts. The beatings if they spoke their native tongue. They literally stripped these kids of everything that made them who they were, just like they did our ancestors when they brought us over here. After a while, despite all the money we made, and we made money because we were such great trackers, I couldn't stomach it anymore. When I told Pearl I wanted out, he challenged me to a gunfight. Just like that. He was always so angry..."

"But you're both alive... how did...?"

"Oh, he almost killed me. One thing about Pearl, he had some hand speed. I was laid up recovering from that gunshot for almost a year. Ended up spending so much time in the hospital, I ended up working there, which is why folks around here call me 'doctor'. They don't know that my mother was a healer who passed down so much of what she knew."

"That's how you saved me."

Watts put his hands on his hips. "There may be a day you will not be so happy with me, son. What I did to revive you, some people would call that unnatural. These damn white Protestants are likely to lynch me if they knew what I did."

Rusty nodded sternly. "The secret is safe with me."

The old doctor chuckled. "I should hope so."

With that cleared up, the zombie and the doctor dived back into their stew. "Your mother is a good cook."

For the first time in a while, Rusty found himself smiling. "She sure is."

"YOUR MOTHER WAS STILL around?" Zenobia asked.

"Indeed," Rusty, clearly cheered by the memory, had perked up. "She would drop by every so often and drop off food for me. Some thank you gifts for the doctor as well. Mind you, she couldn't do it all the time, because people would have noticed. Small town folks sure are nosy."

Now it was Zenobia chuckling. "You can say that again."

THE FINAL 'FAST FORWARD' Zenobia conducted with Rusty's memory mirrors turned into a montage of Rusty's firearms training. Watts possessed an assortment of weapons made by either Colt or Smith & Wesson and Rusty handled them all until he settled on a pair of silver handled .45s. When he wasn't shooting at bottles and tin cans Watts had placed on a fence, he was playing that guitar of his. Watts sitting in a rocking chair, smoking a pipe, while Rusty played the blues, would be how most of their nights ended.

The memories and the mirrors went by until Zenobia and Rusty finally happened upon what looked like the vision of a funeral. Sadly, it was Sybil who had finally laid her burden down, succumbing to what appeared to be nothing but old age. For what appeared to be seven years, Rusty had hidden in Watts' secluded house five miles from the heart of town. Five years of training and praying for the day he'd get to stare down Mr. Pearl for one last time.

He probably would have gone after Pearl sooner, but that conversation they'd had about Watts getting lynched if anyone found out he'd turned Rusty into a zombie gave way to patience. At this point, he loved Watts like father and had long decided protecting the doctor was more important than the revenge he could get at any time. But he wasn't missing his mother's funeral.

Despite his pallor, the folks in the church knew it was him. Rusty, with Watts following close behind, had resolved to have his showdown with Mr. Pearl in or outside the church if need be. Pearl had never been a fan of Sybil's and didn't even bother to show up for appearances' sake.

He didn't speak to anyone as he made his way to the coffin, fell to his knees for a quick prayer, and then walked to the back of the church. He could hear the whispers, but he made eye contact with no one. Watts, who had fashioned a dark pair of spectacles for Rusty to wear for the occasion, had cautioned against him looking anyone in the face.

Before the service began, Watts handed the preacher an envelope. After all the beef stew and chicken and other niceties he'd received from Sybil over the years, it only seemed right that Watts pay for the funeral. It had been agreed upon that once the town had finished paying their respects that the body would be brought to the Watts house to be buried on his land.

As people filed out solemnly, a young woman ran to Rusty. It had been years since he'd seen her, but he quickly realized who it was.

"Opal," Rusty said as he tipped his hat. "Been a long time!"

"Rusty," she practically hissed. "Everyone thought you was dead!"

"Well... truth be told..."

Opal's eyes were wide, her breathing panicked. "Mean ol' Mr. Pearl tried telling the town how you was responsible for Penelope's death, but thankfully there were too many witnesses, including your mama!"

"Yes, I heard the stories," Rusty said.

"But he still convinced his sons that you did it. All three of them. If he finds out you're still alive..."

Watts' shadow fell over Rusty and Opal, as if the setting sun itself decided to draw their attention to him. The doctor's face was grim.

"Rusty's been ready for that. Let them come."

As Rusty explained a few things the memories didn't reveal, Zenobia could feel the anxiety growing in him. "When Penelope was killed, her brothers, Ty, Darius, and Tom were ten, eleven and twelve. She talked about them all the time, mostly how they were spoiled useless hellions always making a mess she'd have to clean up. As you might imagine, Mr. Pearl raised his sons to be as mean-spirited as he was. By the time they reached fifteen, sixteen and seventeen, local gossip claimed the goal had been achieved.

It did not take long for word to get to Mr. Pearl that Rusty had made a surprise appearance. "He was there with that coward, Watts? Well, I'll be damned!"

Reflecting on the whole mess, current day Rusty said to Zenobia, "I imagine ol' Pearl must have worked his boys up into quite the lather, because they rode up to the Watts house like they was deputized marshals. Each of 'em had a shotgun in his saddle and a sidearm.

Watts and I stood on the porch, side by side, armed like our approaching foes. We weren't scared, maybe just anxious. I thought we'd win."

As it played out, The Pearls pulled up yards from the house and pointed their pistols at Dr. Watts and Rudy.

"I guess it wouldn't matter to you none if I told you that you're on private property?"

The eldest Pearl ignored that. "You know, the one thing I could never figure out is why you would move to this town in the first place, Watts!"

"That's Dr. Watts to you! And just like you, I just wanted a nice place hidden from prying eyes and white folks who'd be wondering where I got my money from. If it worked for you, it would work for me."

"You got that money because of me!" Pearl shot back. "And how do you repay me? First you flat leave me in The Dakotas and then you take up with this piece of horseshit son of a white man's whore who killed my daughter."

"That's not how I heard it," Watts defended.

"How was I supposed to kill Penelope when you were the one with the gun, you old bastard?" Rusty challenged.

"You shut up!" a quivering Tom shouted.

Daddy Pearl's response was full of angry spittle. "You don't say her name, you piece of shit!"

Watching the vision, Zenobia wasn't looking at Mr. Pearl anymore. She was looking at his sons. Sure, they'd probably all been hunting with their venomous father. They might have been angry as they mounted up on their horses to claim revenge in the name of family honor. But the time it had taken to dismount and listen to the arguing had taken sapped some of their resolve. They looked frightened.

"What you think, Watts? You thinking saving Rusty Nail is going to redeem your supposed sins for turning in them Indian boys? I got news for you, Watts! You're going to the same hell as me!"

"But you and your little bastards are going first! The Watts turned to Rusty. "Do it, boy! Just like I taught you!"

Zenobia said to herself, I must have missed something. Because of the connection, Rusty still heard it.

"In preparation for such an eventuality, Watts also taught me how to use my zombieness to spook animals."

Rusty stepped forward on the porch, took off the shades he'd been wearing to hide his white pupils, and snarled. All four horses bucked their riders off and galloped away. Guns were dropped and multiple clouds of dust filled the yard. And then the shooting started.

Rusty and Watts each put a bullet in Mr. Pearl, while his sons struggled to get up.

As his mouth filled with blood, Pearl screamed. "Watts, what did you turn that boy into?"

Watts shot him again. Mr. Pearl's last words were. "I was wrong. You are going to a different hell." Then, he fell over and expired.

A bullet buzzed past Rusty's head. It was Darius, trying to stand his ground and participate in something he shouldn't have had to. Trained by Watts to defend himself, Rusty raised his Colt and fired. Darius seemed as surprised to be shot between the eyes as Rusty was by his actions.

Zombie or not, this was still Rusty's second kill and at the moment, did not feel as triumphant as he'd imagined. In fact, watching life seep out of Darius' eyes left him aghast. His internal organs may have not been working, but his feelings were. As Darius fell to the ground, Rusty suddenly froze in place.

"I'm sorry, Penelope!" Rusty said just before a bullet hit him in the arm.

In all the excitement, Tom had gotten a shot off.

"Too bad he didn't let me teach y'all to shoot!" Watts cried out as he turned his pistol and gunned down young Tom, placing four bullets in his chest. Then, as another shot rang out, his eyes widened.

While everyone else was preoccupied, Ty managed to catch up to one of the horses, remove a shotgun from its saddle, and take aim at Watts. The doctor was dead before he hit the ground.

Any remorse Rusty may have felt for shooting Darius left him like a runaway slave with a day's head start. He drew both guns and emptied them into Ty, letting the bullets mangle his face to the point where his brain was more visible than his nose. Rusty let out a desperate cry as he rushed to Watts' side.

"No! No! No! No! NOOOO!" But he was gone.

And for Rusty and Zenobia, there was a gap in the mirrors. The next mirror had cracks in it and the few images Zenobia could see were an out-of-control Rusty attacking and eating deer and other forest creatures. There were some other mirrors further down, with similar fragmented images flashing in them.

Real time Rusty became upset to the point where he was making the room shake. "No! This doesn't explain anything. I still don't know how I lost myself. How did I lose my cognizance and become a mindless thing?!"

Zenobia's voice was smooth and calming. "Be at ease, Rusty. I believe I know what happened."

AFTER A FEW GLASSES of water and some deep breathing, Zenobia closed her eyes. She was very tired. Ahy came to her as she sat on the couch across from Rusty. The dog and the zombie both looked worried.

"I'm very sorry," Rusty said.

"No need to apologize. I am actually happy we did this. It leads to something important about you."

"What do you mean?"

"The confusion, your lost years, they all connect to a little-known fact. People like me and your Dr. Watts are practitioners of a certain kind of culture. In fact, I have a sneaky suspicion I knew Dr. Watts' mother."

"Reliving it was not easy." Rusty admitted. "But I still don't know what happened to me."

Zenobia raised her hand. "You lost your anchor. People like me can sometimes reanimate the dead and dying depending on the circumstances. When Dr. Watts brought you back at the behest of your mother, he became your anchor. The problem is when the anchor dies, the zombie, though gifted with a sort of immortality, deteriorates to mindless form. It's the reason we have zombies wandering the world in the first place. Now, thankfully, from what I could tell from the rest of the mirrors, you mostly attacked deer during these many years. There were some people. In fact, I have reason to believe you ate Mr. Pearl."

Rusty chuckled. "Justice, I guess."

Zenobia smiled and nodded. "Hard to tell how long you were wandering, but eventually vampires who were trying to cause problems for our mutual friend created a drug that brought you back, but now you're dependent on the drug in order to maintain your charismatic musical persona."

Rusty looked ashamed. "That is about the size of it."

They sat quietly for a minute. Then Zenobia rose from her seat. There were tears in her eyes.

Rusty raised his arms in protest. "Madam Zenobia, please don't cry!"

"Shut up," she told him. "I'm focusing on your pain." Mystified, Rusty watched as Zenobia continued her approach. Then she was standing over him, her hands gripping his shoulders. "Open your mouth."

"What?"

"Just do it."

When Rusty did as he was told, he suddenly tasted salt in his mouth. As the tears hit his tongue, he began to convulse till he was involuntarily thrown onto the floor. Ahy ran over, clearly concerned for his new friend. Zenobia fell to a knee and placed a hand on Rusty's back.

"Let my medicine do its work. Moving forward, I'll be your anchor."

Now it was Rusty who was crying.

THEY'D SPENT AN HOUR looking into the mirrors that acted as playback monitors for Rusty's memories. Now, they stood together, smiling in a real mirror, the one in Zenobia's parlor, to be exact. Ingesting Zenobia's tears had not only cured Rusty of the need for a drug, but his looks were also restored. An animated rotting, smelly corpse was replaced by a dashing young man in a cowboy hat.

Zenobia admired her handiwork. "All you need now are your guns and your guitar!"

It took Rusty a minute to find his words. "Christian was right. You're amazing!"

"I bet you say that to all the ladies."

They laughed like old friends, which, when considered, they were. In fact, it could be clearly stated that she knew Rusty better than anyone.

An hour or so later, they would have a tearful goodbye. Overwhelmed with gratitude, Rusty would get in the car chauffeured by one very confused vampire driver and shed a few tears of joy as they made their back to the airport.

Zenobia and Ahy watched the car drive until it was out of sight. "Now that's what I call a productive day, Ahy."

Ahy yodeled in agreement as they went back in the house.

10

THE HAINT

BY MARC L ABBOTT

THE SECOND THE DOOR was opened; Smokey knew he and his master were stepping into a dark place.

"What a room, huh buddy," his master, Gabriel Kennedy, said as he entered the hotel room. "I always love the smell of a hotel. Smells like...no, feels like freedom. Like all the weight on your shoulders has been lifted."

Smokey meowed. He didn't sense freedom at all. Whatever had been in this room, left behind a bad signature. When they crossed the threshold, he picked up the smell of rotten eggs coupled with a chill that wasn't coming from the air conditioner. Had he not been in the cat carrier, he would have either stayed in the hall or fled the room immediately. But he decided to stay calm and just answer his master with meows and yowls. He didn't want to frighten his master with his strange behavior. At least not until he was sure what was going on within the room.

Through the slots in the grilled door of the carrier, he could see much of the room. And it indeed looked cozy. A single bed was to his left, a dresser with a tv hung on the wall to his right. Next to that was a desk with a floor lamp against it. At the far end of the room, wall with a sill. Just above the sill was a window, but from where he sat, all he could see was sky.

When the carrier was set down and the door opened, he slipped out and immediately turned to look back at where they came in. That was where the smell had been the strongest. To his now left was a bathroom with a tiled floor. He looked right and there was a closet. He stared at it.

"Well buddy, they say this is a pet friendly place. You have a bed to sleep on and, wow, look at that view."

As Gabriel passed him, Smokey kept his eyes on the door. His tail moving from side to side like a snake. He sensed that was the source of what he was feeling. Of course it was. That's where all evil things like to take cover, the closet.

"Smokey, c'mere."

Smokey slowly turned and looked at the window where his master stood. He trotted over to him, jumped onto the sill, and looked out. Before him, the city of New Orleans was starting to light up in the twilight. The contrast of building lights against the inky blue evening sky that was pushing its way into place above the setting sun was beautiful and calming. And for several seconds, the two of them stood in silence, watching the city come alive below. Then something stirred in the closet. Only Smokey heard it.

He turned his head quickly and looked back at the door. Something was moving inside. It was scratching the walls, followed by heavy breathing. Then the doorknob jostled, not a lot but enough that he saw it. Smokey jumped down off the sill and began approaching the closet slowly.

He heard a low growl. He stopped and yowled. The thing on the other side got quiet.

"He's fine," he heard Gabriel say. "Sure, hold on." There was a deep ringing sound like note being hit over and over quickly followed by a chime. "Go ahead."

"Hey Smokey!" a child's voice called out. Smokey turned to see his master holding out his cellphone and on the screen was his little master, Simon. Smokey made a high-pitched meow and trotted to the phone purring.

"Hey buddy, you like the room? You're keeping dad company?" Simon said, smiling. Smokey meowed and pawed at Simon's image. "I miss you too. Hey, someone one wants to say hi." Simon disappeared as the image began to shake, indicating Simon was on the move. The next image he saw was that of a husky chow mixed dog. "Look, Poohbear, it's Smokey."

Poohbear panted and barked. "So good to see you. How was the trip?"

"Not the most comfortable," Smokey meowed back. "I slept most of the flight."

"How's master's room?"

"Funny you should ask. I think we have another closet monster here."

"What?"

"There's something in the closet, moving around. I don't know what it is yet, but it doesn't sound or feel good."

"Be careful Smokey. Don't try to fight whatever it is alone."

"May not have a choice. It's one room, not many places for me to go. I haven't seen any other cats or dogs here since we arrived."

"I don't know why Master didn't take us both on his trip," Poohbear barked. "You think it will stay in there? Maybe it won't come out."

"It's going to come out. Nothing stays in a closet that doesn't want to. I'll be as careful as I can. But I have to protect Master even if my life..."

"Don't say that. Come home to us."

Smokey touched the screen with his paw. Gabriel raised the phone.

"Okay, I don't pay for you two to have a phone conversation. Crazy cat and dog," Gabriel said it with a sly grin. "Okay Simon, put mom on and you make sure you get to bed on time."

Smokey had walked away and was now back in front of the closet. He could hear the thing inside breathing. After a moment, it stopped. Whatever it was, it knew Smokey was watching.

AFTER A QUICK SHOWER and a change of clothes, Gabriel decided to take a walk to stretch his legs and get some air before meeting up with his college friends for the evening. He was looking forward to the four-day getaway, which would also serve as a mini vacation away from the family. Because his sister-in-law was going to be in town, and she had a fear of cats, he decided to bring Smokey with him. The hotel was pet friendly; they even had an area for cats to play for several hours should people want their pets to get exercise. But Gabriel knew Smokey well. He was happiest in his own space.

In the meantime, he put a collar around him, attached a leash, and took him on the walk. Both felt ridiculous; Gabriel walking a cat and Smokey with a leash, but they dealt with it. They stepped out into the lobby and headed for the front door toward Canal Street. Smokey kept his eyes forward as he thought about the thing in the closet. *What could it possibly be? Would it make itself known when they got back?* He felt a slight resistance on the collar, stopped and looked back to see Gabriel speaking to someone. He sat down and people watched.

A couple of children passing by stopped to pet him. He allowed it only because he liked the gentle way children pet him on the head. He spotted a terrier eyeballing him as it passed in the distance. Neither of them said a bark or meow at one another. He turned to look across the lobby where the concierge desk was and froze. Standing just behind the right shoulder of the concierge was a figure, bone white and thin, with hollowed out eyes and a skeletal mouth, looking at him.

Smokey jumped slightly before getting into a defensive stance and hissing. The figure seemed to glide from around the concierge and move toward him. Smokey looked down and saw it had no legs. It was just a torso moving mere inches by the second. Smokey began hissing, getting the attention of Gabriel, who first looked down, then in the direction Smokey was looking.

"What now? What's up with you? There's nothing there."

Smokey began to pull on the leash, yowling so loud that many people in the lobby stopped to see what the problem was. He tried to scurry for the door just as the apparition was close enough that all it had to do was reach out and touch him. The putrid smell from its gaping mouth made his eyes water.

"Abagail," the apparition cried out. "Abagail."

Smokey turned, claws out, when it stopped just a foot away, then disappeared. Smokey looked all around trying to see where it had gone, fearing it would sneak up on him. But it was gone.

"Okay, let's go. Once around the block and it's back in the room for you," Gabriel said as he picked him up. "I'll catch up with you later."

Smokey continued to look around the lobby for the apparition as they walked through the revolving door. If this was the same thing that was in their room, Smokey now knew there would be no rest for him. He was going to need some help. The problem was finding it.

This wasn't Smokey's first run in with the supernatural. He once had a run in with a demon and a closet monster that tried to harm his little master. He had even seen the spirit of his master's grandfather walking through the house one night. But he had never experienced this. And despite fighting demonic creatures, this entity scared him. It felt wrong. It felt bad and if it was willing to attack him in public, he could only imagine what it would do trapped inside the room.

It took a couple of minutes for Gabriel to get Smokey to cross the threshold when they returned. He sat there, refusing to move no matter how many tugs of the leash Gabriel made. After exhausting his patience, Gabriel picked him up and carried him inside. His only form of protest was to growl.

"I don't get what's going on with you, but you need to cool it," Gabriel said. Once he set him on the floor, Gabriel removed the collar and tapped him on his rear-end to let him know he was good to move. Smokey hurried past the closet, then sat and stared at it. He started to growl again.

Gabriel crossed the room to his carry-on, removed a food and water bowl, placed them on the floor, and then took out a can of food. He pulled the top back, exposing the wet brown food, and dumped it into the bowl.

"Bet you're hungry. Here, before I head out." He took the water bowl to the bathroom, washed it out, then went into the mini fridge and removed a bottled water. He filled the bowl halfway, set it next to the food, then pet Smokey on the head. "I'll be back later. Don't mess up the room." Gabriel looked around to make sure he had everything, then he left.

Smokey cautiously approached the food. He began to eat but kept his eyes on the closet. He stopped only briefly because he thought he heard something. He listened. Nothing. After a moment, Smokey relaxed and buried his face in his food. Gabriel had brought his favorite tuna flavored kind, and it relaxed him. He soon began to purr as he closed his eyes and enjoyed the feast. Once he was at the bottom of the bowl, he lifted his head, licked his mouth, and opened his eyes.

The entity was standing before him. Staring at him with hollow eyes. Smokey screamed, leapt into the air backwards and struck the wall behind him, banging his hind legs on the edge of the sill. He ignored the pain as he tried to go up on the bed to go around, but the entity moved fast and took hold of him. He cried out at the feeling of the icy grip as it brought him to its open maw.

"Abagail," it said. It began to squeeze him. "Abagail."

Smokey cried out from the pressure. He fought to get free and slashed at it. The tips of his claws nicked at something that felt like flesh, but not quite. The entity cried out with an inhuman moan and let him go. There was a smell of almonds in the air. Smokey put distance between them, heading toward the door and realizing that he had no way out. He turned. It was moving toward him.

Smokey arched his back, making his hair stand on end. His ears tucked back as he extended his claws and got ready to attack. He let out a hiss, followed by a low growl. As it inched closer, he let out a series of panicked cries. It moved fast, grabbed hold of him again, and began to squeeze. Smokey let out a terrified screech. A knock came at the door, loud and forceful.

"Hotel management," a voice called from the other side. "We're getting a complaint about your cat."

The entity let out an inhuman howl. There was a brief silence on the other side of the door. Smokey could hear whispering as the grip from the entity started to let him loose. He cried out again.

"We're coming in," the voice called out again. The electronic key lock beeped, and Smokey fell to the floor. The door swung open and in stepped the manager, a tall lanky man with a handlebar mustache. He was accompanied by a security guard and a porter.

"Dear God," the manager said as he stared ahead into the room. Smokey looked back and watched it slip through the door into the closet. He looked back at the manager. "I told them downstairs not to book this room for anyone." He turned to the porter. "Gather up all the luggage and let's get this over to another room right away."

"You want me to come in there, Larry?"

"Christian, it's gone. Grab the bags, bring them out and go get a cart to move them," the manager said. "Davis, you stay with him." He reached down and picked up Smokey. "I have the cat. I'll have him in my office." He turned quickly and headed down the hall with Smokey tucked under his arm.

Smokey sat balled up in the corner of the Larry's office, moving his head like a second hand on a clock as he scanned the room looking for the entity. The manager was busy trying to locate Gabriel to let him know that they were giving him a room change.

"I told everyone in booking that they were not to give that room away. I have said it repeatedly," Larry said to the assistant manager. "We all know the history of that room."

"Sir, it was just clerical error. No one has been hurt. This is an easy fix."

"An easy fix? Now, I've got to find that man a room, not to mention it freaked the cat out. You own cats? I do. They're very sensitive to these things. Once shaken, it's damn near impossible to ease their nerves."

"He seems calm now." They both looked at Smokey, who, sensing their stares, looked at both and meowed. "I mean, he doesn't look shaken up."

"That don't mean anything," a warm woman's voice said from the doorway. "I can tell this one is a fighter, but even fighters can get beat once in a while." She smiled at Smokey. "What's your name, darlin'?"

Smokey froze, wide eyed, when she said this to him. It wasn't so much that she was talking directly to him, but he understood every single word she said, which surprised him. He could understand some human words, mainly the commands or certain phrases that Gabriel spoke to him. But this woman, when she spoke, it was as if he were listening to another cat. Or even his canine partner, Poohbear. But not this level.

"Yes, dear, I am speaking to you," she said. She leaned forward. "It's okay. You can trust me." There was a calmness in her voice. Something soothing and easy going. The way she smiled at him let him know that she was okay to talk to.

"Smokey."

"Hi Smokey, I'm Madam Z."

Smokey looked at the managers, then back at her. "You understand me?"

"I do."

"Are you here to help?"

"I can try."

"There's something upstairs in my master's room."

"Oh, I know all about that. I mean, I know something is up there. Been there for years, but it hasn't shown itself until now."

"Is that why you're here?"

"I just happened to be walking by and–"

"Excuse me," the manager interrupted. "Are you two seriously talking to one another?"

"We are."

"Madam Zenobia, is it? I need—"

"You want to get rid of the haint?"

"The what?"

"You have a haint in this building that's been a thorn in your sides for years. Losing money and not able to rent that room upstairs, right?" she asked, and he slowly nodded. "Well, then, let me speak to Smokey and see how I can help you get rid of your problem." She turned back to Smokey.

"Maybe it's best we go and talk away from here. I know a place. Follow me." Smokey rose to his paws, hesitated for a moment, then trotted to her. Larry tried to protest, but they were out the door and headed through the lobby to Canal Street.

He followed her down a side street off Rue Bourbon Street, where there were colorful shops selling t-shirts, Mardi Gras beads and several bars packed to the brim with revelers. They entered a narrow storefront that looked like it was being crushed by the buildings on either side.

Inside the dimly lit shop, herbs and roots hung from the ceiling. Shelves jammed with mason jars filled with different types of powders and liquids. Towards the back were an array of books that Smokey couldn't read. But there was a distinct smell that hung in the air. Semi-sweet with a calming effect to it.

"That's lavender you're smelling, darlin'," Madam Zenobia said.

"What is that?"

"It's a type of flower. Come back this way."

He followed alongside her to a room in the back of the store that sat beyond a string of beads that covered the doorway. The room was shaped like a half crescent moon. In the center of the room sat a table with two tall back chairs that sat opposite each. other Along the outer wall was a long rectangular table, covered with bowls, glass jars, and roots. Candles in holders on the wall adorned the room.

Smokey could feel the supernatural energy in the room. But it wasn't like the coldness from the hotel. It wasn't warm either. It felt alive and inviting, as though it were a being exuding its aura. He could tell it didn't want to harm him, but he wasn't sure if that was because Madam Zenobia was with him or if it just felt that way towards him.

"You want, you can sit on the table," she said. Smokey trotted to the table and leaped up onto it. He looked around, his eyes adjusting to the dimness around him.

"Where are we?"

"This is a friend's space. A safe place." She reached out and pet him slowly. "You've seen a lot, haven't you? Can feel the energy on you. You've had dealing with the supernatural before."

"I have stopped my share of creatures," Smokey said. "This one, though. This one scares me. The haint. That's what you called it?"

Madam Zenobia sat in the chair. "It's a restless spirit. Sometimes they evil, sometimes they just, well, exist. This one, he been living in that hotel for many years. Doesn't really show himself although some staff people have seen him. He likes moving around the building."

"Have you seen him?"

"I have, but only a few times. He ain't too fond of me," she said with a smile. "I did try to commune with him once, but he got nasty with me. Anytime I set foot in there, he stays in his room." She nodded. "There is one room he is fond of."

"Why is that?"

"It's where he died."

Smokey took two steps back and stared at her. She nodded.

"How did he die?"

"From my understanding, he was killed. It had something to do about a woman he was seein' and her family. I never could get a straight answer on all that it entailed, but what is clear is that the violence he experienced was done out of hatred. His eyes were taken out, and he was found stuffed inside the closet."

"Was her name Abagail?"

"Why do you ask?"

"That's the name he spoke before he grabbed me."

Madam Zenobia's eyes lit up. "Well now, seems you know just a tad bit more than I do." She scratched her chin. "You say he grabbed you? Like physically touched you?"

"He did, only I scratched him, and he let me go."

Madam Zenobia rose from her seat slowly and cupped the side his face. "You were able to harm him?" She began to scratch him under his ear. "Now you would be the first to...Hold on now."

She let go and crossed the room quickly. She removed a candle from its holder, returned to the table, and put the light close to him. She reached out and brushed his fur back in the opposite direction. A smile grew wider on her face.

"Well, isn't that a wonderful surprise?" she laughed. "People really don't know to check these things before they name you."

"What's wrong?"

"They named you Smokey. I reckon they did so because they thought you were grey and black. But your hair is actually blue, darlin'. A very fine shade of it." She pet him gently. "And why that's special is because haints don't like blue. It's a problem for them. And I get the sense that he didn't realize until you scratched him that you could be a problem to you. But the fact that he did communicate to you a name, when he hasn't done that with anyone human, means he's looking for someone and wants you to help."

Smokey jumped down off the table and put some distance between himself and Madam Zenobia. Even cats need a moment sometimes to ponder and consider what is brought forth to them. *Had this haint really try to communicate with him for help?* He thought back to the encounters. At no time did it hurt him. It did have a strong grip on him, but could that have been because it didn't want him to run away? He had become adjusted to dealing with so many malevolent elements that this time it was quite possible he misread its intentions.

"But I felt evil coming off of it," Smokey said. "There wasn't something right about its presence."

"Mm, maybe it's not the haint but the buildin' that you're feeling. Some places will carry negative energy too." She crossed the room and put the candle back, then walked to the table with the roots on it. "And if that's the case, then that also means this haint is trapped in there and could use assistance. Now, this isn't my usual thing, but I know a spell that can aide us."

She began gathering different roots and plants and setting them next to one another. She then excused herself, went back into the store for less than a minute, then returned with two jars filled with powder. She set them down next to the other ingredients, then placed a bowl with a pestle before her. "This will take a moment. But when I'm done, I'm taking you back to that hotel and we're going to save that soul."

It took Madam Zenobia an hour to craft the powder and say the proper spell over it. During that time, Larry had found Gabriel and moved him to another room. He explained to him that the room was scheduled to have work done and should have never been rented to him. When Gabriel went to check on the new room, he noticed Smokey wasn't there. He rushed back to the front desk to confront Larry, who, more than once, asked Gabriel if anything had occurred in the room prior to them moving him.

"Something like what?" Gabriel asked. "And why are you dodging my question? Where is my cat?"

"It doesn't matter; about the room, I mean. And your cat, yes, the cat. Well, we have someone looking after him. A kind of cat sitter."

"What cat sitter? I didn't ask for my cat to be removed. He should be in the room with my things. He better not be lost," Gabriel warned.

"He's not lost." Larry tried to smile, but he looked constipated.

"'Scuse me, Gabriel?" Madam Zenobia said. He turned and looked at her, holding Smokey. "Smokey is with me."

Gabriel looked her up and down. "You're a cat sitter? You look like one of those people that run the local roots store."

"Well, I didn't know that was a style," Madam Zenobia said.

"What?" he asked.

"Smokey's in good hands with me, if that's your concern. I have a good rapport with animals, especially cats. I'd like to take him upstairs, if you don't mind."

Gabriel looked at Smokey, who was tranquil in her arms. "He does seem calmer now than before. I mean, if you're the hotel cat sitter, then I don't have a problem with it. If the manager takes you to the room."

Madam Zenobia looked at Larry. "Do you mind?"

"No. No, not at all. We can do that right now." Larry stepped out from behind the front desk and started for the elevator bay.

"I'll see you later, buddy," Gabriel said as he pet Smokey. "Thanks again."

"No problem." Madam Zenobia said, and then she followed Larry. When they were out of earshot of Gabriel, she leaned forward and said, "Take us to the room. Not the new one. The room."

"I was afraid you were going to say that."

Smokey sat before Madam Zenobia on the floor in front of room 1131. She sat cross-legged, chanting as she sprinkled some of the powder that she had made for him. She did rotation around his head three times, then took a handful of the powder- she had it in a small cloth purse with a silk lined interior- and blew it into his face.

He shook his head and blinked twice. The world before him melted and morphed into a period that was no longer his own. Gone was the electronic keypad for the door, and in its place was a large, round black knob. Even the door itself, once a plain oak, now had an ornate design on it and a gaslight to the right. He looked back at Madam Zenobia.

"It's okay. I'm here. I'm your anchor. Tell me what you see."

The door opened slowly. Smokey walked in. The room was much different, with a four-post bed, beautiful drapes, and an armoire. There was no bathroom, but the closet was still the same. Standing at the window with his back to them was a man in a dark suit. When he turned around and looked in Smokey's direction, he was able to get a good look at him. A handsome African American man with slicked-back black hair and a thin mustache. The man smiled.

"You made it," he said, then he began to advance on him.

Smokey thought the man was going to pick him up, but then he walked through him and toward the door. Smokey turned and saw him approach a young woman holding a baby wrapped in a blanket. She was a beautiful woman with a complexion that resembled coffee with milk. The two kissed, and she stepped further into the room.

"I got us two tickets for the five-o'clock train headed north. I have a cousin in New York who can put us up for a bit. Just until I can get on my feet," he said.

"Lamont, that's a long ride for a baby."

"I know, Jasmine. But it's worth it for all three of us to be together." Lamont looked into the blanket and smiled. "My Abagail."

There is a sudden knock the door. Loud and forceful. Lamont puts Jasmine and Abagail behind him and waits. The door breaks open and standing in the doorway is a large, well-dressed white man with two African American men flanking him.

"Daddy," Jazmine yells out.

"I told you to stay away from this man," her father, Maurice Edison, says as he points at Lamont. "And you, I told you what would happen if I caught you with my daughter again."

"I intend to marry your daughter, Mister Edison," Lamont says. "She is the mother of my child."

"It's bad enough you ruined her reputation now. You want to insult me with talk of marriage?"

"But it's true, daddy. We're goin' up north. Lamont has family there. We can start a brand-new life away from the whispers and finger pointing."

"And have me down here trying to make excuses for why my daughter has run off with a charlatan? No, you're staying here. Your mama has everything fixed up for you. I rather live with the shame of an unwed daughter."

"She is a grown woman," Lamont interrupted. "She has made up her mind. So, with all due respect, you need to leave. This is happening with or without your support, sir."

Maurice smiles, then nods and points at Lamont. The men flanking him rush Lamont and a fight ensues. They begin trying to punch him in the face, but Lamont blocks their advances and counters; one he strikes in the face, the other in the gut. The one who is struck in the face recovers quickly and uses a small blackjack weapon to strike Lamont upside the head.

Lamon staggers toward the wall as the second assailant begins to punch him over and over in the gut. As he goes down on his knees, he is struck again with the blackjack on the back of the head and goes down. Jazmine screams. The baby starts to cry. Maurice shuts the door and moves her to the side.

"Quiet! Shut that child up," he demands. "You two, sit him up. Alabaster, get that sash from that drape over there and tie his hands."

"Yes, sir." Alabaster, the one with the blackjack, helps sit Lamont up, then he hurries to the drapes and removes the sashes from both ends. He gets behind Lamont and ties his hands with one.

"That should do it."

Maurice holds his hand out and Alabaster hands him the second sash.

"OKAY, YOU TWO TAKE my daughter and granddaughter downstairs to the coach. Wait for me across the street. I'll finish this."

Alabaster and the other man move on Jazmine, gently place their hands under her elbows and start to lead her out.

"Daddy, leave him alone, don't hurt him. You proved your point. Daddy, I love him, please. He's your granddaughter's father. Please." She pleads, but Maurice doesn't acknowledge her. She turns to Alabaster. "Take your hand off me. Don't touch me!"

They escort her out of the room. Maurice has his full attention on Lamont. He squats down before him and slaps him in the face multiple times until he wakes up. Smiling, he palms the side of Lamont's face and caresses his cheek with his thumb.

"I gave you an opportunity to leave New Orleans twice. I warned you that if I had to come down here to deal with you, it wasn't going to pretty. Now look where we are."

Lamont coughed. "If you won't let me leave with Jazmine, then let me take Abagail. That would save face for your family."

"And let my granddaughter grow up in New York? Without her mother or a stable home? If I'm not letting my daughter leave with you, you cannot honestly think that I'll give my granddaughter to you. No, my friend, you sir...are expendable."

Like a shot fired from a gun, Maurice wrapped the sash he was holding around Lamont's neck and began to choke him. Lamont kicked and struggled, but with his hands tied behind his back, he didn't have much leverage to fight back. Maurice put all his strength into pulling the sash as tight as he could. Lamont's legs went from kicking to shaking. He gasped for air as the veins in his eyes popped and bled into the whites. He made one final groan, then his head fell to the side.

Maurice let go of the end of the sash and stuffed the rest into his pocket. He rose and looked down at the body. He moved to the closet, opened it, then dragged Lamont's body inside. He set him upright, then backed up.

"You'll never see them again," he whispered.

Lamont's crimson eyes stared back at him. He shivered. He reached into his jacket pocket and drew out a loaded pistol, took aim, and fired two shots, taking out Lamont's eyes. The body jerked and fell to the side, groaning. Maurice turned on his heels and immediately left the room.

THERE WAS AN ODOR Smokey picked up on as Maurice passed. Like that of burned leaves and decay. He turned away and sneezed, clearing his nostrils. Then Smokey walked up to Lamont's body and stared at it. It seemed to be looking right at him. He leaned in, sniffed and it sat up and screamed at him.

"Abagail! Abagail!" Lamont pulled the sash apart with force and started to reach for Smokey, then froze. The entire scene melted away and Smokey found himself in the room he and Gabriel first walked into. The haint was there now, screaming at him. This time, however, Smokey stood his ground. Growling at first, he let out a high-pitched yowl that caused the haint to grow quiet.

"Well, ain't this a show of force," Madam Zenobia said as she entered the room.

"Abagail is his daughter," Smokey said.

Madam Zenobia closed the door and joined him. "Tell me everything you saw."

MADAM ZENOBIA SLIPPED OUT a back way of the hotel with Smokey under her arm. She didn't speak, but Smokey could tell she wanted to respond to what he told her. She was a woman on a mission. Moving through the crowds quickly, she seemed to have a destination in mind. They walked up Canal Street until they reached Claiborne Street. They made two turns until they reached St. Louis Cemetery. They reached the closed gate, and she put him down.

"I need to be sure about this. You said the man who killed Lamont was named Maurice Edison." She pointed to the cemetery. "The spell I put on you should still have enough potency for you to find Maurice's grave, provided he's in there. If you do find it, come back and tell me."

"What more proof do you need than what I saw?"

"There is a very wealthy family here in New Orleans called Edison. They're also involved in a lot of shady practices. If this is the same family, then I know just how to handle the haint. But I must be sure. Let the smell guide you, then come back and let me know."

Smokey looked at the maze before him. He glanced at Madam Zenobia, then slipped through the bars and disappeared through the aisles. She would only have to wait twenty minutes before Smokey reappeared, confirming the location of the grave.

"That's what I smelled when I got close to it. It's the only one that smelled like that."

"Okay, whew, okay." She clasped them together and regained his composure. "So now that we know all that, I know how to get rid of the haint. At least remove it from its current residence."

"We're not going to help it?"

"We're going to help it, but not in the conventional sense. Tell me, how good are you at driving the supernatural out of a place?"

Smokey flexed his claws. "Just tell me what you need me to do. I can handle it."

"You're sure you're okay with handling this haint? You were jittery when this started."

"Now that I know more about it, I don't fear it as much. Getting rid of it won't be a problem. Let's go handle it."

"Well, there's one more thing we must do before we go back to the hotel. One more potion I need to craft for you." She paused to pick him up. "We must take another trip, though. It's a little further out, but it's the best place to prepare you for your journey across the veil. Into the realm of the dead."

Smokey stared at her. "Why would I have to go there?"

"To get the haint. The means by where I need it to go won't work here. But because your kind can see between worlds, traveling will be simple with the right spell, which I know how to do. We have to move now if we're going to get to Honey Island Swamp."

IT TOOK THEM FORTY minutes to get to Honey Island Swamp by bus. The driver wasn't too happy with Smokey not being in a carrier, but he let it slide so long as Madam Zenobia kept him under control.

Upon arrival, she tucked him under her arm again and did her best to keep him close. Tour boats had stopped going out, but Madam Zenobia knew her way around. She had her own boat that she kept hidden under foliage along the bank. Once in the boat, she made her way through the river swamp.

Gnarled cypress trees rose from the water with moss hanging from their branches. The smell of wild azaleas hung in the air. They traveled ten minutes to a small shack that seemed tucked away from the rest of the world. The pier leading up to it was also hidden by tall grass. Madam Zenobia exited the boat and carried Smokey inside. It was dark until she lit a match and got a lantern going. Smokey couldn't help noticing it looked just like the store, with all its jars and hanging roots and herbs.

"We've got to get you prepared, Smokey. This shouldn't take long to conjure up."

"Why did we come here?"

"Two of the ingredients I need grow out here and I also need the swamp water to mix it. And this swamp. Pristine water out there."

She moved around the shack as though she were floating. Getting all her ingredients together before she left with a jar to gather the swamp water. She returned and got to work mixing the concoction. Crushing angelica, boneset and High John the Conqueror root, a pinch of licorice, then combining it with swamp water, she mixed it all together in a pestle and poured a portion of it into a mason jar. Then she went to a small box on a table in the corner and removed a small crystal on a string. She brought it to the pestle, dipped it in the mixture, then tied it around Smokey's neck.

"This protects your outer being. You will have to drink the rest," she said.

"What?"

"It's safe. You'll need it to break the planes of this world to get the haint. Without protection, you could be trapped. I've done this before. Trust me."

Smokey laid down on his side and let his body go limp. It was how he was used to taking medicine when the vet prescribed something for him. He felt more relaxed this way. Madam Zenobia gave him the lip of the jar and gently poured it into his mouth. It didn't taste the way it looked. It had a slightly sweet taste that made it more inviting to swallow.

"Okay, now let's go get that haint."

AN HOUR LATER, THEY were back at the door of the haunted room with Larry. He opened it, stepped back down the hall, and watched them. Madam Zenobia picked Smokey up and whispered to him.

"Remember what I told you, get him out, then follow me. When we get to where we're going, we'll let it go."

Smokey wriggled his way out of her arms and entered the room. Everything around him was devoid of color, moving in waves of black and white. The plane between worlds was often unclear, a grey area. He looked around but there was no sign of the haint. He let out a yowl. Still nothing.

He let out another, longer yowl and that's when the haint walked out of the closet. Only it didn't look like the apparition he'd seen before. He looked like the man he had seen in the vision. Well-dressed but missing his eyes. Despite that, he looked down at Smokey.

"What are you doing in my room? Out you mangy animal," Lamont shouted.

"I'm here to help and to do that, you must leave this room," Smokey said.

"I'm not going anywhere! I am waiting for my Abigail."

"You will not find her here. But I can take you to someone who might." Smokey sat. "You reached out to me for help."

"Help? I wanted you out of here. I only wanted to see my Abagail."

"So, you're not going to leave?"

"No."

Smokey looked out at Madam Zenobia, who shrugged. He then extended his claws and swiped at Lamont's ankle. He felt himself connect with the haint, who screamed and backed up. Smokey circled around behind him and swiped again. Lamont ran for the door, then down the hall, blowing past Larry. He stopped just shy of the stairwell and turned to Smokey.

"I warn you, stay away from me."

"You have no power over me." Smokey arched his back, showing off the strands of blue in his fur. "Move, haint. Leave this place."

Lamont grabbed at him, and his hand began to smolder. He drew his hand back quickly and ran through the door. Smokey looked back and saw Madam Zenobia hurrying toward him.

"Salt that doorway, Larry!" she screamed. She opened the stairwell door, and Smokey saw Lamont running down the stairs. He gave chase down to the first floor, where the door was open.

Lamont turned and kicked Smokey, causing him to tumble back. But he recovered and gave chase, forcing Lamont toward the front door. But he stopped just shy of going through it and turned on Smokey.

"Leave me be. I must stay here and wait," he said.

Smokey swiped at him again and he backed out through the glass door out onto the street. Madam Zenobia caught up and opened the door for Smokey. He turned right and jumped at Lamont, scratching him in the chest. He let out a ghostly cry that caused people to stop and look around, wondering what made the noise.

Madam Zenobia passed them and kept going. Smokey made Lamont follow. The chase continued up Canal Street, around through Rue Bourbon, and the length of the French Quarter to Esplanade where they stopped, then up to Rampart. They ran two more blocks until she stopped at a large house behind a tall fence.

"In there, Smokey!"

Smokey chased him through the fence and halfway up the walkway before he stopped. Lamont turned and looked back at him.

"Why? Why would you chase me...here?" Lamont looked back at the house. "Of course."

"Lamont?" Madam Zenobia called to him. "You know this place."

"The home of Maurice Edison."

"If you're looking for answers, it would be in there, not where you died."

"Will they know where my Abigail is?" he asked.

"It's possible. It has been a long time. But if there is a place where you should reside until you get answers, it's here. When you have gotten your answer, you will be at peace."

Lamont looked at her, then at Smokey. He let out a wail that was a cross between a cry of sorrow and a scream of rage, then moved fast down the walkway and through the front door. Smokey turned and trotted back to Madam Zenobia, slipped through the fence, and looked at her.

"What now?" he asked.

From inside the house came a blood-curdling scream.

"Let Maurice's descendants deal with him. For the crimes of that family should not go unpunished. He will find the answers in due time." She bent down and took the crystal from around his neck. "The potion will wear off by sunrise."

Smokey cleaned himself, put his paw down, and stared down the street.

"I hope he finds what he's looking for."

"I do too."

"Madam Zenobia?"

"Yes, Smokey?"

"You're going to take me back to the hotel, right?"

Madam Zenobia laughed and picked him up. She tucked him safely under her arm and headed back to the hotel.

11

THE LESSON

BY ROBIN REED

RUFUS SKANT BRAKED HIS Mercedes GLS63 to a halt and looked up the road. The pavement had disappeared several miles before and now a cliff face loomed ahead of the big car. Rocks had fallen and were scattered on the remaining stretch of road.

"What now?" Skant growled.

"Now we hike," his assistant Kamal said. "I did say we would need to cover the last part on foot."

"I still think I should have rented a helicopter."

Kamal opened his door and stepped down onto the road. "The terrain is much too rugged from here."

Skant glared at the cliff as if his will alone could make it move. Then he got out of the luxury SUV and went to where Kamal stood. Rufus Skant was not a tall man, but he was bulky from an addiction to his personal gym. He was vain about his appearance, but would not change his hairstyle, saying it was practical. Millions on the internet made fun of it with memes and jokes about Moe of the Three Stooges. He wore brand new hiking clothes and boots. Kamal had difficulty convincing him he couldn't wear his usual khakis, sport jacket and tie, and Gucci loafers.

Skant set out toward the cliff with an energetic stride. "Where are we going?"

Kamal caught up with his employer. "There's supposed to be a path to the left."

As they got closer, they saw a level area that led upward.

"You'd better be right about this place." Skant started up the path.

"You saw what I discovered," Kamal said. "Almost two miles of a canyon that doesn't show on Google maps or any satellite view."

"Still don't know how that's possible."

"You're the billionaire electronics mogul, sir. If you don't know, I certainly don't. But you saw all the information I was able to find, and the canyon here in the Rockies does not register anywhere. The physical distance is there, but the numbers and GPS signals skip right over it."

The path grew steeper, and both men had to put more effort into walking. Skant stopped and breathed hard. Kamal waited behind him. An amazing view of the mountains had opened up as they got higher.

"How am I supposed to get construction equipment and personnel up here?" Skant asked.

"Surely a man who can send people to space, build robots, and upend the electronics industry can build a shelter in the mountains. You have told me many times how important an emergency bunker will soon become."

"More than a bunker." Skant gestured to the mountains that surrounded him. "A home for the best and the brightest to wait out the cataclysm to come."

"A cataclysm that is fast approaching, sir. My grand-mother lives in the Louisiana bayou and is deeply worried about rising waters and ultra-powerful hurricanes."

"Can she cook?" Skant asked. "My robots will do most of the work, but I haven't been able to teach one to cook."

"Well, yes sir, but..."

"Then she's welcome. I've already told you that you can come. We will need a few human servants." Skant turned and continued up the path. Kamal followed, with an angry expression. After a short time, the path split. One side followed along the cliff; another went down. Towering walls on each side made it very narrow.

"Which way?" Skant asked. "Let me check." He took out his phone, then swore.

"There's no connection here, sir." Kamal gestured toward the narrow way.

"You better be right about all this," the billionaire said, putting his phone back in his pocket. "I want to start building as soon as I can."

"I'm sure, sir." The assistant didn't say how he knew. Ahead of them, the path split several more times. Each time, Kamal was sure of the correct turn to make. The slot canyon they were in grew darker as the sun moved away and the light was blocked by the high walls. They came to a place where a large boulder was embedded in the ground. Going on would mean a little bit of climbing to get over it.

Kamal easily got to the top. "Are you coming, sir?" he asked. Skant looked up at him.

"This better be legit." Skant put his hands on the stone and looked for footholds. "If I find out this is a ploy to get a raise or something, I will not be happy."

"No, sir. I would never."

Doubled over, both feet and hands on the boulder, Skant found his way up. He stood and breathed heavily.

"I told you that you could do it."

"Are we almost there?"

"Yes, but I want to tell you more about my grandmother." Kamal turned and led the way.

"I don't care about your grandmother."

"You should. You will meet her soon."

Skant grunted as he walked over the rough ground.

"She's not really my grandmother, you see. I was a poor child who found her cabin in the bayou. She doesn't like people to come to her door, but I didn't know. I asked for some food."

"I said I don't care."

"I won't say she took me in, but she allowed me to stay sometimes when I had nowhere else to go. I was quite surprised when I got a full scholarship to college. I had not applied for one."

"Shut up, Kamal. That's an order."

"As you wish. You will be interested in a few minutes."

Skant rolled his eyes and kept walking. Soon the air around them seemed to thicken. Fog spilled down from the cliffs above.

"What the hell?" Skant said.

"Step carefully, sir."

The fog filled the canyon until they couldn't see anything. Kamal ran his hand along one wall to keep himself steady.

"Hello?" Skant's voice trembled a little. "Are you there?" Kamal had never heard his boss scared. He didn't answer. The education of Rufus Skant had begun. After a good five minutes of not being able to see anything, the fog began to turn to shreds and reveal that they were entering a more open area.

It completely let up and showed a valley between high rock walls. Grass and low flowering plants covered the ground. A spring gurgled out between two boulders and formed a pool. A frog jumped from the side into the water. Skant looked around.

"This is perfect."

"Hello, Mr. Skant." A woman's voice filled the valley.

"What? Hello?" He turned and saw the source of the voice. A tall, imposing figure wearing a purple head wrap, a copper ankh on her chest, white blouse and black skirt. A medium-sized, all-white dog with big ears and a tail that curled over his back sat at her feet.

"This is Grandmother Zenobia," Kamal said.

"You're the cook?" Skant asked. "I didn't expect you to be here already. And I must say you don't look old enough to be a grandmother."

"Your aura is dark, Mr. Skant. You are blocked from the blessings of love and light."

"My what now?"

"You will spend some time with us," Zenobia said.

Hands grabbed Skant's arms from behind. He jerked to get away, but the grips were strong. He turned to see who held him. The one on his right was a human figure, but the head had to be a mask. It looked like some African animal that runs around being chased by lions. It had two long horns rising near its large ears.

The one on his left was even more of a nightmare. A turtle perched on the man's shoulders. A big one. The little head came out from the shell, and Skant could tell it was looking at him. The two pulled him away, making him stumble as he walked. "Wait!" he shouted. "What is going on? You can't do this to me!"

The two creatures pulled him toward one wall of the canyon. He soon saw a dark opening. There was a cave there. They entered it, dragging him with them. Kamal followed. Inside, a single bulb on a stand filled the space with harsh light. A pile of dirt filled one side of the cave. A shovel had been stuck into it, with the handle sticking up.

"You've been hired, Mr. Skant," Kamal said.

"What is going on here? Tell them to let me go!"

"You are now a first level shoveler. Your job is to move that dirt from where it is to the other side of the cave. Your wage is one dollar per hour."

"You work for me, Kamal!"

"Not anymore. I am your supervisor."

"This is insane! Let me out of here!"

"You have a half hour unpaid lunch break after four hours. Your shift starts now." Kamal signaled to the creatures, who let Skant go.

"Screw this." Rufus ran out of the cave. The light was dimming as the sun set. He ran to the far wall and looked up. There was no way to climb it. Looking wildly around, he saw no help. The strange woman, grandmother whatever, was gone. He started to walk all around the valley. After a complete circuit, he found no way out. There had to be one. *How had they entered?*

The last of the daylight played on the top of one rock wall, then vanished. The glow of the light bulb in the cave led him back to the pile of dirt and the shovel. Kamal was no longer there. Skant looked around, then shouted, "I'm not shoveling dirt! I am a billionaire!"

From behind him came Kamal's voice. "Your pay is docked for every minute you don't work." Skant whirled around but didn't see anyone.

"I'm hungry." In fact, he was very hungry. He couldn't remember when he last ate.

"Lunch is two dollars. You will have to work to earn enough to buy one." Skant saw Kamal this time and lunged at him. Kamal vanished.

"Lunch costs two hours of work?" There was no answer. The cave grew chilly. The only light came from the bulb on the stand. The dirt stayed in its original pile, taunting him.

"I want to go home!" Skant howled. He was cold and starving. He couldn't believe this was happening to him. He should be in his king-sized bed with silk sheets in the master bedroom of his thirty-room mansion. "Shit," he said. He grabbed the shovel and scooped some of the dirt. He walked a few steps to the other side of the cave and dropped it. He did that again and again until about half the dirt had been moved.

"You happy now?" Skant screamed.

"Do you want to sleep?" Kamal said. He stood near the new pile of dirt.

Skant realized how tired he was. "Yes." He was led deeper into the cave, the light fading behind him. Kamal produced a flashlight and shined it on a sleeping bag on the floor.

"This room is available for rent," Kamal said.

"You have to be kidding."

"You can sleep out in the open valley, with no covers."

"This is insane. The whole thing. Let me go or I will press charges for kidnapping."

"Really? You have no way to call anyone. You don't know where you are. You may never see your home again."

"I am Rufus Skant, damnit. I can buy or sell you, that woman, this whole mountain a hundred times over."

Kamal looked at him for a second, then said, "There is a deposit of first and last month's rent, and a cleaning deposit."

"I'll pay you a million dollars to let me go."

"You've only worked for forty-five minutes. You have earned seventy-five cents."

"Then I can't pay anything you just said!"

"You could apply for credit."

"Credit?"

"Yes, we can open a credit line for you."

"All right. Do that. I use credit all the time."

"Very well. You have rented this room and the sleeping bag."

"And some food."

The horned demon or whatever came in with a tray that had a sandwich and a glass of water on it. Skant took it carefully, avoiding the strange gaze of the creature. Kamal and the demon left, leaving him in the dark. He ate the food and drank the water. He got in the sleeping bag. It wasn't easy to sleep without a pillow. He decided to put one on his credit the next day.

He didn't sleep long before the turtle demon came in holding a gong. He struck it and the deep sound filled the little room. Skant sat up. He didn't feel rested. He was hungry again.

"Back to work," Kamal said. Skant hadn't even seen him come into the little room.

"No."

"Very well, you are being evicted due to lack of payment."

"What happened to my credit?"

"Your account has a negative balance. There is a daily overdraft fee."

Skant stood up and advanced on the shorter man. "My staff must be looking for me. When I am out of here, I will sue you for everything you have!"

Kamal said nothing and walked away. Furious, Skant followed and found himself in the room with the pile of dirt. He ignored that and left the cave. Dawn was beginning to fill the little valley with light. It was still dark at the bottom, but the sun reflected off the top of the rock walls. Skant still saw no way out.

He walked toward the center and saw the spring. The water gurgled pleasantly. He hadn't noticed before, but the woman sat on a rock next to a small pool. He could see fish in it, and a frog nearby. The dog he had seen before sat next to the woman, with its head in her lap. He walked up to her.

"Get me out of here."

"Please sit." She gestured to another, smaller rock. Skant was sure it wasn't there a moment before.

"Is this a kidnapping? I can pay whatever you want."

"Not at all. Sit."

He gave up and sat. "When I get out of here, I will find you and make your life miserable."

"You are not enjoying yourself?" the woman asked.

"LET ME GO!"

The dog raised his head and growled a little. The woman put her hand on its head. "Shh, Ahy. He doesn't mean it."

"Of course I mean it!" Skant shouted. "You are holding me against my will! Who the hell are you, and why are you doing this?"

"I told you before, call me Grandmother Zenobia. I am old and I have seen human beings behave foolishly in many ways. They slaughter each other, they make animal species extinct. They hate for no reason. But now they threaten the world itself."

"I don't do any of that."

"You mine material with slave labor in Africa. You build products with low-paid workers in China. You use enormous amounts of fossil fuel to move them around the world. When you saw all the damage that you do, the rising water, the extinctions, the storms, your reaction was to plan a bunker, to hide until it's over. With the same resources, you can prevent much of the cataclysm that is coming."

"Even I can't fix it all."

"Do what you can." Zenobia smiled kindly.

"You're insane." Skant stood up. "There is nothing I can do. I don't want to! Humanity stinks! Good riddance!"

Zenobia was no longer there. Wind began to blow. His feet felt wet. He looked down. The pool of water was overflowing. It quickly rose to his calves. Then higher. He saw a wave coming toward him. It knocked him backward and washed him down the valley.

He struggled but there was no way to fight it. His head hit a rock, and that was the last he knew. After an unknown period of darkness, he woke up standing over the pile of dirt with the shovel in his hand.

ZENOBIA TOOK HER HAND from Skant's forehead. He lay in his king-sized bed in the master bedroom of his thirty-room mansion, dreaming of a valley he couldn't escape.

"Is it done?" Kamal stood on the other side of the bed.

Zenobia nodded. "He will repeat the lesson many times until he truly learns it. When he wakes, he will be a changed man."

"I hope so. The world needs these guys to put everything they have into saving it. Who's next?"

"Someone who sells everything but cannot buy happiness."

Kamal smiled. "I'm looking forward to that one."

12

THE PRICE OF SALVATION

BY DENISE TAPSCOTT

Carrefour Parish, Louisiana: Present Day

I WAS RAISED IN the deep, depressing part of the South; God help me, I never wanted to go back there, to those people. Passing skeletal, abandoned homes brought up memories of where I grew up, far away from the glittering lights of Los Angeles, my adopted home and beloved sanctuary. I knew the ride to Carrefour Parish would be arduous.

Having to stop every so often to puke my guts out didn't help, either. The trip better be worth it. After receiving the sweetest kiss I've ever had in my entire life, on my wedding day, everything changed for me. I'd been sick for over two weeks.

First, I thought holistic medicine would help. My appointment with my acupuncturist was horrific. The moment she saw my black tongue, she screamed at me in Cantonese and immediately kicked me out of her office.

After a barrage of tests at Cedar Sinai in Beverly Hills, while wearing those ridiculous paper gowns, doctors didn't have a clue about what was wrong with me. My husband thought it was all in my head. I love him, but he's an idiot. He's my handsome Prince Charming, but an idiot.

I had my monthly visit with Oceania, "Psychic to the Stars," sporting her turquoise highlights and matching nail polish. She insisted that I travel to New Orleans and see some Hoodoo Voodoo person. Luckily, I thanked her for my "something blue" garter she gave me for my wedding before I vomited in her turquoise trash can.

In between dry heaves and sips of water she offered me, she told me that I'd been cursed, and it was a doozy. Oceania swore the Voodoo High Priestess worked miracles. The little old lady better be good. I immediately packed my Louis Vuitton travel bag and told my husband I was going on a trip to review a new boutique in New Orleans. He had no idea what I was really up to.

"Visit my parents. Spend a little time with them in that big old house of theirs," he said. "If we want to stay in their good graces, it would be best if you made an appearance. Besides, you need to return my mother's antique pearl earrings you borrowed for the wedding."

He came from old southern money, and I came from old southern trash. He made a good point, so I couldn't really refuse. His parents hated that I made him escape to California after high school, but he continued to keep the family business successful, so they couldn't argue too loudly.

IT WASN'T TOO LONG before I found myself standing at the front door of my in-laws' mansion. The tall white pillars reminded me of a similar home I visited often as a teenager; a girlfriend I grew up with lived in a smaller mansion with the same typical hanging gas lamps. Her parents didn't like me very much; she didn't care, and neither did I.

George, the family butler, greeted me. I'm fairly certain he is almost as old as the house. His knees cracked when escorting me to the parlor, where I met up with Mr. and Mrs. Jurel. Although their personalities were lackluster at best, they always wore high-end, custom-tailored clothing. Mrs. Jurel wore a light tan colored linen dress, and her husband wore a button-up shirt and matching tan linen slacks.

I couldn't tear my eyes away from her freshwater peach pearl earrings with matching pendant and bracelet that her husband brought her from his last trip to China. They had enough money to spend on anything they wanted for three lifetimes.

Spending the night in their creaky old mansion was better than I thought. After exchanging pleasantries, we were ushered into the formal dining room where we would be served a five-course meal. Sadly, after drinking a glass of filtered water, most of my time was spent on my hands and knees in the guest bathroom. It was decorated with flowers and cherubs, right down to the trash basket next to the toilet.

Once I returned her earrings that I borrowed for my wedding, my mother-in-law was unexpectedly polite to me. It was the first time I can remember that we didn't fire off condescending remarks at one another. When they die, it would be unfortunate, but I will have a wonderful time redecorating that huge house. I'd be true southern royalty then.

THE NEXT MORNING, I finally arrived in Carrefour Parish. I parked on the side of a dusty, two-lane road, a few feet away from the Voodoo woman's house. I had wanted a shiny silver Rolls Royce, but the rental company only had black, which showed dirt and scratches. I'd be sure to make a note of their service (or lack thereof) in my article 'The Do's and Don'ts of New Orleans'. My work gave new meaning to the old saying, "the pen is mightier than the sword." My reviews could make or break any business.

As I managed to shove open the car door, the southern humidity smacked me in the face. Back in Los Angeles, I never dealt with this kind of weather. I was desperate for ocean breezes. This sticky, heavy air was ridiculous. After I managed to stand, my stomach gurgled so loudly I swore I scared off a flock of blackbirds. A nasty, sour belch climbed its way up, escaping through my mouth. At least it wasn't from my ass.

The house seemed miles away. I should have stopped right at the door, but Oceana's instructions were clear. No parking in front of the house. I trudged along toward the small wooden home. It was actually almost charming, in a southern sort of way. It was odd, though, that it was all alone, in the middle of nowhere.

Driving here, I had seen a few shacks and broken down, rusty mobile homes, similar to what I grew up in, and miles and miles of dark green grass. I might have seen an occasional patch of swampland in between my dry heaves. With the right amount of publicity, I bet I could make New Orleans the newest hot spot around. It's already called Hollywood South.

I was light-headed, but it was probably because I hadn't eaten anything since my honeymoon. I could barely keep down chicken broth. There was a strange buzzing sound in my ears; hopefully, it was those pesky June bugs. Without any warning, my stomach balled up like an angry fist. I fell to my knees as bile rushed up through my raw throat. Gravel bit into my knees and the palms of my hands as I retched hot, sticky fluid.

After choking a few times, my stomach relaxed. I was tired of continually grabbing tissue to wipe my face. I was tired of reapplying my favorite lipstick to sore, swollen lips. I was tired of groveling to a porcelain god every day. I would have given anything to feel normal again.

After backing away from a puddle of frothy bile, I crawled through dry grass, over to a wooden post. I pulled myself up, barely able to stand. I noticed a sparkly ruby red, high-heeled shoe perched on top of the latch of a wooden gate. The instructions said it was a sign that visitors were welcome onto the property. My own Italian brown leather heels were scuffed and dusty. They'd have to be replaced when I got back home.

Pieces of grass and small bits of gravel were still embedded in my knees. Once I was back to being myself, I would meet with my personal shopper. My clothes didn't fit from all the weight I'd lost. Too bad I wasn't sick before my wedding. Six months ago, shedding pounds was almost impossible without a personal trainer. Here I was, not even a month after the ceremony, and my brand-new custom-made Vera Wang wedding dress fit like a muumuu. The seamstress in the cute bridal shop worked a miracle. She mentioned she was from New Orleans. I should look her up once all of this is over.

I glanced at my watch and noticed it was 3 o'clock in the afternoon. Somehow, I managed to be on time for my appointment. Mustering up as much energy as I could, I pressed through the heavy wooden gate. It squeaked, announcing my presence. The vibrant purple front door of the one-story home caught my eye.

"That's Tyrian purple," I heard myself say out loud to no one. The first time I learned about it was in Ancient History class, in the 10thth grade. We'd learned random trivia about the Phoenicians. I was popular with lots of people back then, too. I don't remember much else I supposedly learned in high school.

I also knew that tidbit from my piece 'Which Museums are Hot or Not'. I discovered an exquisite display of items in London at an out-of-the-way nautical museum. The purple dye came from snails. The Tyrian color is a symbol of royalty, dating back to the Phoenicians and other ancient civilizations. The Romans couldn't get enough of it. Too bad that little museum was on the "not" list. The drab old curator rambled endlessly. No real food, no adult drinks. Wonderful treasures, but barely even a gift shop. My readers would hate it.

I flirted with the idea of getting a closer look at the color of the Voodoo woman's front door. I was drawn to it. Images of luxury, regalness, crème de la crème opulence flitted through my mind. The instructions I clung to so fiercely in my sweaty, sticky hand were clear.

DO NOT APPROACH THE FRONT DOOR UNDER ANY CIRCUMSTANCES.

As if on cue, another wooden door squeaked from the side of the house.

I GLANCED UP AND made a small wish. Let this be over. Large fluffy clouds floated in a blue sky, offering no solace from the punishing sunlight. Sweat rolled down my back. My head wouldn't stop pounding. As I drew near the wooden stairs that lead to the side porch, my stomach spasmed. My legs, too shaky to stand, forced me to crumble, causing 'leakage' from my butt. I couldn't bear the thought of soiling myself again.

I cursed as I crawled on achy hands and bruised knees. I wiped my hair from my face. When I got back to LA, I'd have my assistant arrange an emergency appointment for me at the salon. My hair was thin. The blonde highlights needed a boost, too. I missed my witty stylist Michel, the only person that I could talk to about anything. Honestly, though, I couldn't consider how I looked. I knew I was hideous. I wanted to curl up in a ball and cry my eyes out.

I dragged myself through the open doorway, and when I entered, the humidity vanished. Cool air caressed my face. Somehow, I stood up straight and sighed. When was the last time I took an honest, deep breath without coughing or puking? The aroma of freshly baked cinnamon rolls filled the air. My escape from the southern heat was so glorious that I might never leave.

"Settle down," a voice said while my eyes searched in the darkness.

"Close the door, and have a seat, Mrs. Jurel."

The voice of the Voodoo woman was clear and melodic, only slightly tainted with a New Orleans drawl.

After blinking a few times, I saw a small metal folding chair. My eyes still hadn't adjusted to the darkness, so I fumbled around until I could sit obediently. The chair was more comfortable than I expected. Resting in the darkness was wonderful. Once I regained my focus, I noticed I was sitting at a small table covered in soft black velvet. I wanted to brush my fingers across it, but my hands were dirty, accented with ragged nails, so I opted instead to fold my hands in my lap.

Sitting on a large purple and gold throne across from me was a pleasant-looking-dark skinned woman. Her hair was covered with a purple turban, matching the royal purple on her front door. She wore a black gauze tunic blouse. Around her neck, a shiny copper Ankh glowed against her skin. She didn't wear any other jewelry, except a large black and gold fleur-de-lis ring that adorned well-manicured fingers. Was she wearing a skirt or pants? I probably shouldn't care what kind of shoes she was wearing, either.

She was not the toothless, gray-haired woman I expected. If I were to guess, she looked like she was in her 40s? My assistant Tasha joked, "Black don't crack". I could never say that, but I think she's right. This woman didn't look old enough to be a grandmother. She reminded me of that lady with the popular television talk show. Everyone in her studio audience went home with expensive vacations and new cars.

Three fresh, tapered candles, one black, one blue and one white, formed a triangle on the table to my right. A thicker, taller, purple candle sat close to the Voodoo Woman. From my research, I knew the black one warded off negative energies and promoted healing. Royal blue was for seeking wisdom and truth. White was for protection and purification. Lastly, the purple one was for spiritual protection. All the candles on this table represented protection, but the purple one supposedly canceled the negative effects of bad karma. The Voodoo woman made interesting choices.

Reluctantly, I lifted my head to take in my surroundings. My neck was sore from my head being tossed back and forth every time I vomited. When I glanced around the room, I saw shelves of books, crosses, various kinds of statues and other religious-looking artifacts. If I was not mistaken, there was a shrunken head in the corner. To my left, there was a jade dragon perched on a shiny black surface. Was that a human skull staring down at me? Heavy red velvet curtains with gold trim covered windows, presumably protecting us from the sun. In another corner, there were large, dusty trunks. Simply being in this spooky room was worth my $500 dollars.

"Mrs. Jurel, you look like you could use some water." She said. Grandmother Zenobia handed me a chilled plastic bottle of water. I was scared to drink it; when I vomited all over the luxurious black velvet table, I would be mortified. "Go on, drink." She said.

I swirled the cool water in my mouth a few times before swallowing. I braced for the burn. Instead, the liquid was sweet and went down smoothly. It was an ordinary bottle of water, but it felt like I was drinking tears from heaven. I paused, waiting for my stomach to betray me. It rumbled for a moment, but then, silence. Carelessly, I chugged the water as fast as I could.

Panicked, I looked around for a trash can, for when my body-double crossed me and the water forced its way back out. There was no trash can. There was no vomit. There was peace while sitting in a cool room. I was so grateful that I cried.

"Do you need a moment to collect yourself?" She asked, while passing me a tissue. It was softer than the ones I've religiously kept at my side. Wiping my tears away, I noticed my eyes didn't sting when I blinked. I cried even more. It would take centuries to stop sobbing and catch my breath.

Attempting to compose myself, I noticed that I sat taller. My fever faded away. "Thank you, Zenobia."

"Feeling better?" She asked.

"Yes," I can't believe that I actually do feel better. Thank you so much for seeing me."

"I prefer to be called Grandmother Zenobia." She said. The black candle, the one for healing, flared brighter than the others, illuminating the room. The voodoo woman mumbled to herself; the flame obeyed her muttered commands and returned to its regular state.

I re-adjusted in my seat and for the first time in months, I was almost my old self. I took another deep breath and appreciated the smell of cinnamon again. Aware I was on the clock, I got down to business.

"You know, you should change your name. You'd get more customers and followers, if you were on social media. You don't look old enough to be a grandmother. Try something like 'Lady Z' or 'Madame Zenobia'. Those names are easier to sell. It's about your brand, know what I mean?" Words poured from my lips faster than I guzzled the water. The Voodoo woman stared at me with one eyebrow raised. The floorboard behind me creaked like a cue for me to stop rambling.

"Apologies. I always look for business opportunities for people."

The pesky black candle sparked a few times and then continued to shine with the others. Grandmother broke her cold stare. She looked to my right for a moment and then shrugged.

"It's your session. We can chat about whatever you like."

SHE PULLED OUT A worn deck of tarot cards and shuffled. The edges were black, slightly curled. The deck was ivory colored and had black swirls with tiny roses.

"As you saw when I first came in, I'm not well. I haven't been able to eat or drink anything for a while. A psychic back in Los Angeles sent me."

"Ah yes, Oceania. She's sweet." She said.

"She is, but eccentric with the crazy hair and nails, don't you think? Anyway, I did my research. You are a bona fide Voodoo High Priestess, highly recommended by her and a few others." She nodded, as if I were chatting about the weather. She seemed too casual, and I needed her to know I meant business.

"Before we continue, Zenobia, I'm laying down a few ground rules. First, I ask most of the questions, not you. Second, I expect you to keep my dealings private. If I choose to let people know I was here, it's because I decide, not you. If all goes well, I could make it possible for you to have a line of people waiting outside your door. Third, if you shake a rattle at me and then make a snake burst through an egg, I will walk right out of that door and demand my money back. I refuse to pay for parlor tricks. For what it's worth, I like the candles. They're a nice touch."

The Voodoo woman smiled to herself and continued to shuffle the cards. All three candles close to me flickered. The purple one was undisturbed.

"Settle down." She said.

"Excuse me?"

"Is there anything else, Mrs. Jurel?" she asked as she studied my face.

"No, I guess that's about it, Lady Z." I'm not sure why, but I had a hard time looking directly at her.

"How about we start with a general reading from the Tarot cards?" She suggested.

"No. Do a seven-card spread. I want details."

"Sure thing." She said. She set the deck before me. I noticed it was cooler in the room than before. I didn't mind it too much, but if it continued, I would ask for a window to be cracked open or the A/C to be turned down.

"Shuffle the cards for as long as you'd like. Clear your thoughts and when you are ready, create three smaller separate stacks."

The cards were soft. As I shuffled, I swore I smelled roses. I looked closely at the back of one card to examine the details. It was just paper, with little black lines and drawings of red roses. It was a weird trick, but I liked it.

The obvious question I wanted to ask was, "why was this happening to me?" It was always so hard to clear your mind when someone told you to do it. I took stupid yoga classes. At the end, you lie around and focus on breathing. "Sink into the earth" the vegan tree-hugging yogi said. I only went because they were the latest craze around town. *Clear my mind? Yeah, right.*

I needed to get on with this. I growled and made three small stacks. Lady Z (as I've decided to call her) collected the cards, then methodically placed a total of seven cards before me, face up. As each card was revealed, she studied them and nodded her head. The feisty black candle, the one for negative energies and healing, sputtered and extinguished by itself.

"Are you going to re-light that one?"

"No, that's not how it works." She said.

"I see. All right then, Lady Z, go for it."

"The first card is the Princess of Swords. Some call it the Page of Swords. This card is reversed. It represents a woman in your life, or a feminine energy. She is jealous and represents a difficult lesson you need to learn."

The folding chair I was sitting on wasn't as comfortable as when I first sat down.

"The second card is the Wheel of Fortune. It represents the universe as it spins its wheel over people's lives. If you pass tests placed before you by God, good things will come to you." She said.

So far, I was not enjoying this reading.

Lady Z continued to go over the cards. There was the reversed Hanged Man, Death, the Tower, and the Page of Cups, reversed. The last card was the reversed Empress. The cards all looked and sounded miserable. She rambled on and on about lessons to be learned, transformation, blah blah blah. The reversed Empress represented a blockage of feminine energy, the loss of a loved one, and something about vanity.

None of this was new. When Oceania did my reading, she insisted that the reversed Empress card represented my mother. My mother was dead to me, literally and figuratively. Before she died, she begged for me to come home to the trailer park and help out with the family. Going back there would never be an option for me. It was her fault she and the Catholic Church didn't believe in birth control. It was her fault that half of her 13 kids came out retarded.

She told me she had a chance, once, to leave my father. She stayed for my sake. For my sake? I didn't ask her to make that sacrifice for me. She was too stupid to get government assistance. She always said the family had "too much honor. Welfare was for colored folk". It was her fault they were poor white trash and stayed white trash. I was lucky to escape when I did. I realized that I was lost in thought while Zenobia went on with my reading.

"Zee, where did you get that turban? Is it a scarf? I simply must have one like it." It was rude to interrupt someone, but I didn't care. I pretended that I was bored, but actually I was scared shitless. I didn't like where this reading was going.

She stopped and shook her head. "I've had this thing for so long, I honestly don't remember." She said.

"I noticed it's the same color as your front door and the candle on your left. That's a hard color to get, if it's the real deal. Not that you would have real Tyrian purple paint or dye. The dye is from snails. It goes back to..."

"Mrs. Jurel, let me stop you."

I put on my best poker face for whatever she was going to say. If this was about my mother, I was running out the door.

"The overall picture is that you have a communication problem." She said.

"I have a communication problem?" I thought she'd go a different way. "I'm a great communicator. Have you read any of my magazine articles? They're everywhere. I have thousands of fans and followers on social media. Did you see my wedding announcement in the New York Times? It's impossible to get a spot, but we did."

Surely this woman had heard of me, even if I hadn't heard of her. People loved me.

"The problem is that you talk too much and most of it is deceptive. You manipulate people and their words." She said.

"Are you calling me a liar?" Clearly, she was going on my 'not to do list' of New Orleans. The Voodoo woman mumbled something and collected the tarot cards. The royal blue candle, the one for wisdom and truth, did the same flicker trick as the black one. It sparked a few times and kept shining.

"Why are you here, really?" she asked me point-blank. "I know that this was the exact same spread you've received from Oceania and a handful of other spiritual people. If you don't want the truth, then say so. We can sit and be social. You have some time left in your session." She said.

A cold chill ran down my spine. There were no open windows. There was no fan. Yet a cold breeze passed right by me. How does she know that it's the exact same spread? The information was supposed to be private. The pictures of the cards from other readings looked different, but she was right. I knew it was the exact same spread again. I couldn't escape it.

"Girlfriend, I'll be honest. I'm here because someone cursed me. I need to know who did it, and why."

"Why didn't you say so, instead of wasting my time? That's easy." She said.

Why did I test this woman? If she had the answer I needed, I could be rid of the curse and get back to being me. Maybe I could help her get more business or whatever it is she wanted. She was back on my 'do list of New Orleans'.

"Rhoda Jurel, I am the one who cursed you."

THE BLUE CANDLE GLOWED. Its flame changed from yellow to dark green to blue. I practically fell out of my seat.
"YOU CURSED ME?"

"Settle down," she said simply.

"Oh, no. How dare you tell me to settle down!"

The flame of the blue candle exploded, leaving only the white candle active on my side of the table. It was the most important anyway, representing protection and purification. It was strange that the purple one still burned steadily. I stood up, knocking the chair away. I looked for something I could use to hurt this woman. Something snatched the back of my head and scratched my scalp. What kind of trick was this?

"I wasn't talking to you, Mrs. Jurel," the Voodoo woman said. She looked to my right and waved her hand dismissively. "Pick up the chair and have a seat." She pointed at me, indicating that now she was talking to me.

I realized that I hadn't vomited in the past half hour. I was weak and smelly, but I was all right. Or at least I was. We were alone, but I had that creepy feeling someone was watching when no one was there. I didn't want to sit, but if I left, I might never know what it was like to feel normal again. I had to be rid of the curse once and for all. Like a child following orders, I picked up the folding chair and returned to my place at the table.

"Why are you doing this to me?" My words weren't clipped and polished. My stupid southern twang wormed its way back into my life. How was that possible? I paid good money for diction classes.

"Sally Mae Ramelle," she said, like it had a grandiose meaning.

"What in the hell does..." No matter how hard I tried, the drawl was still there.

"Watch your language in my presence." She said. The black velvet card table rattled. "You're safe," she said, looking over my head. I turned around and saw nothing but a small sliver of light coming from the door I came in.

"She died because of you."
The table stopped shaking.
"I hardly think..."
"That is another problem, for another day." She said.
"What?"
The Voodoo woman kept talking, not skipping a beat.
"Sally Mae tells me you are a bully. The way you run your mouth, I see it's true."

The room was freezing. My teeth chattered. I wished I could stand in the Southern sun, to warm up. The white candle for healing and purification burned boldly. Smoke slowly swirled over the flame. Then the name clicked for me.

"What do you mean, Sally Mae told ya?"

"Now's your chance. Take your time, like we discussed," Grandmother Zenobia said. She was not looking at me while she spoke. It appeared she was having a conversation with someone else.

"I understand," she said. She turned her full attention back to me. "Sally Mae wants an apology. She says you used to be best friends. Her parents didn't like you, but she didn't care."

Little Sally Mae. That bitch. She had the same beautiful, thick straight hair as my ma. I've spent a fortune at the salon to wrangle my hair.

"The day she told you that she lost her virginity to Cedric Jurel, you decided you hated her."

Hot wax dripping from the white candle turned blood red as it ran down the sides into the candleholder. I ain't never seen nothing like it.

"What in the hell kind of trick candle is that?"

"Language! This candle is for Sally's protection and your purification. It's melting red wax because red stimulates personal power. Sally is regaining courage and her power to stand up to her enemy."

"My purification?"

"This is your last chance to come clean. You humiliated that girl in front of other people whenever you had a chance. You insisted that everyone hated her. You tormented her for quite some time. I've seen the letters you thought were destroyed. The bible says, "Thou shall not bear false witness, Exodus 20:16.""

I wanted the Voodoo woman to shut her ugly mouth.

"OBVIOUSLY, SALLY GAVE UP. She was too weak to fight against your intimidation. The rest is history. Personally, I suspect she reminds you of your mother. I had a nice chat with her too. You didn't get along with her either. By the way, don't bother returning her old pin you wore at your wedding." Grandmother Zenobia winked at something near me.

"Sally Mae's spirit was awakened the day you married her boyfriend, Cedric. You were wed on the anniversary of her death, not that you paid any mind to that. Sally's distraught mother asked for my assistance. After talking to her, talking to your mother—may she now rest in peace—and Sally, I agreed to hex you. The request was justified. Something old, something new, something borrowed, and something blue did the trick." She said.

I could only sit speechless at the stupid table. Sally was really here? That was impossible. Yet, no one knew what I did to her. She was the teacher's pet in every class we had together. Always Miss Goodie Two Shoes, so pretty and so smart. Everyone liked her. When we were supposed to graduate high school, she could go anywhere she wanted, be whoever she wanted to be with perfect, rich Cedric. I couldn't stand her. She had to die.

Another chill passed by me. The white candle flared six inches high, and I swear I saw a shadow to my right.

"I cursed you because you hurt Sally and other people around you. You are jealous and insecure. You make others feel worse, to make yourself feel better.

"You win, Zee. What now?

"My name is Grandmother Zenobia," she corrected me. "To remove my curse, you must pay me $500,000 by sundown tomorrow and say a prayer of forgiveness with Sally. I accept cash, cashier's check, or wire transfer to this account." She slid a white piece of paper with a bank account number across the black velvet table over to me. "I'm sure you can understand why I don't take personal checks over $500."

"$500,000 and a prayer?"

"Sally wants me to charge you an additional $25,000 for adultery, but she never married Cedric. He's such a nice man. Anyway, I'm going off track. You can try to get someone else to lift my curse. Won't work. If Papa Lou and the Broken Army catch wind of you, you'll be in far worse trouble than you were when you came through my door. Psychics and shamans say the curse is karma. Fortune tellers will laugh at you. Santeria specialist and Wicca people won't touch you with a ten-foot pole. Neither the neighborhood Catholic priest down the street, nor your fancy pastor in that mega church in Los Angeles will bother sniffing in my direction. We spiritual people have a large, tight-knit community." She said proudly.

The Voodoo woman pulled out a gold pocket watch.

"If it matters at all to you, and it probably doesn't, the money goes to good causes. Aside from my personal fee, some of the funds will go to Sally's family. They've suffered a lot. The rest will go to the National Suicide Prevention Lifeline, a few groups that fight against bullying in schools, and programs to assist and educate people fighting depression."

"If I don't pay and pray?"

"As soon as you walk out that door, the curse will return. You'll be dead in three days. Maybe sooner, judging by how you crawled your way here in the first place. Sally Mae says she's excited to escort you to hell herself."

A cold, gray mist shimmered right next to me. I rubbed my eyes in disbelief. Sally Mae Ramelle stood before me. Her face was pale, her eyes dark as the black stones found in my koi pond. Dark red tracks ran down her arms, where she slit them lengthwise with a razor. Her lips were blue from all the pills she swallowed. She was damp head to toe from the bath she died in. She followed my suicide instructions perfectly.

The white candle sparked a few times and died. My stomach quivered and spasmed. The ghost of Sally Mae rushed at me, howling in my face. I closed my eyes, but her screams blasted in my ears. Hot scratches burned my face.

I should have been lounging at a spa, not cowering in a prayer room. My husband would have me committed if I told him I needed $500,000. Or worse, my wicked, old-money mother-in-law would insist he file for divorce. Their pack of lawyers would make sure I didn't have a cent to my name. I couldn't have that. I'd rather die than be poor again.

"Your time is up," Grandmother Zenobia said as she blew out her purple Karma candle. I bet she had the audacity to smile at me in the darkness. I could barely hear her voice over Sally's screaming.

Denise Tapscott

Denise N. Tapscott was born and raised in California. She left her heart in San Francisco, but somehow managed to leave her soul in New Orleans. When she's not creating and cultivating her characters, she enjoys dining on spicy tuna rolls, sharing a bottle of red wine with friends, and watching the latest monster flick. From time to time, this radiant left-handed vampire-pirate will even challenge others to a fencing match or two.

But watch out. This Gemini is determined to win! You can hear her laugh and cry with fellow horror authors on the podcast Beef, Wine and Shenanigans. As an actress, playing a sassy vampire is one of her most favorite roles. She can be seen as "Tasha" on the YouTube web series *The Vamps Next Door.*

One of her greatest joys was publishing her first novel *"Gypsy Kisses and Voodoo Wishes"* and the sequel novel, *"Enlightening of the Damned"*. As a member of the HWA, there is much more to come.

Denise's website is www.denisetapscott.com

Kirk A. Johnson

Born in Trinidad in 1971, he credits his love for Sci-Fi Adventure, Sword & Sorcery and Heroic Fantasy from watching old movies with his dad. He began writing his own fantasy adventure short stories in 2005, and in 2014, he sold his first short story to MV media, LLC for its first anthology *Griots: A Sword and Soul Anthology.*

In 2022 he released his first independently published book, *The Obanaax: and Other Tales of Heroes and Horrors*, which is a collection of short stories that mixed Sahel cultures with the pulp ascetics of western literature. In 2023, his short story, *Carnivora*, was published in the Issue 1 of New Edge Sword and Sorcery. In 2024, his second short story, *The Concord of the Outhar*, published in Issue 4 of New Edge Sword and Sorcery, made the coveted cover by Bebeto Daroz with interior illustrations by Trevor Ngwenya.

The Big, the Bad, and the Miserable, debuts in sci-fi anthology, Spacefunk!, edited by Milton J. Davis.

Robin Reed

Robin Reed was born in the Midwest but has travelled all over the United States looking for stability and happiness. So far, no luck. She washed up in California early in the twenty first century and is glad to be far away from cold winters. She has worked many low-paying jobs and has never succeeded at much of anything.

She writes science fiction, humor, and humor mixed with horror. She also writes horror and thrillers under the name Robin Morris. Titles include *"Vampzompocalypse,"* *"Twas the NIght,"* and a series based on the "Silo" universe, called *"Worldquake."* Her horror novel *"Mama"* and thriller trilogy starting with *"Play the Game"* are from Robin Morris.

Steven Van Patten

Brooklyn native Steven Van Patten is the author of the critically acclaimed *Brookwater's Curse* trilogy that features an 1860s Georgia plantation slave who becomes law enforcement within the vampire community. In contrast, the titular character in his *Killer Genius* series is a modern day hyper-intelligent black woman who uses high-end technology as a socially conscious serial killer.

SVP's well reviewed short fiction includes contributions to nearly a dozen horror anthologies, including the Bram Stoker Award nominated *Under Twin Suns* as well as *Even in The Grave* and *Tales from The Canyons of The Damned*. A collection of short horror and dark fiction stories entitled "*Hell at The Way Station*", published by his company Laughing Black Vampire Productions, and co-authored by celebrated storyteller, Marc Abbott. The sequel, "*Hell at Brooklyn Tea*", which introduces sword and sorcery writer Kirk Johnson, was released in early 2021.

When he's not writing, he can be found stage managing television shows in New York City. His website is https://brookwaterscurse.com/

Marc L Abbott

Marc L Abbott is a Brooklyn native horror author. He is the author of the horror novel, *"Sinister Ascension"* from Mocha Memoirs Press, co-author of Hell at Brooklyn Tea and the two-time African American Literary Award-winning horror anthology, *Hell at the Way Station.*

His horror short stories are featured in the anthologies *Blackened Roots, The Chaos Clock, A Woman Unbecoming, Soul Scream, Even in the Grave,* and the Bram Stoker Nominated horror anthologies *New York State of Fright & Under Twin Suns: Alternate Histories of the Yellow Sign.*

John Palisano

John Palisano's writing has won the Bram Stoker Award®, the Yog Soggoth Award, been nominated for the Rondo Hatton Award and the Imajinn Award and has been published and appeared in such notable venues as Vanity Fair, The Log Angeles Times, Blumhouse Online, Cemetery Dance, Fangoria, and more.

His screenplays have won acclaim as finalists in Shriekfest, Project Greenlight, Latent Image, and more. His professional career started with an internship and work with Ridley Scott & Associates, then with director Marcus Nispel, Tony Bon Jovi, and more.

He recently served as President of the Horror Writers Association. www.johnpalisano.com

Linda D. Addison

Linda D. Addison is the first African–American recipient of the HWA Bram Stoker Award® and has received five awards for collections of prose and poetry, including *How to Recognize a Demon Has Become Your Friend.* She has been honored with the HWA Lifetime Achievement Award®, HWA Mentor of the Year and SFPA Grand Master of Fantastic Poetry. She is a member of CITH, HWA, SFWA, SFPA and IAMTW.

Find her in anthologies: *Bestiary of Blood, Spacefunk, Blood Games, Enter Boogeyman, Playlist of the Damned, Weird Tales: The Bram Stoker Awards issue #369,* and *Where the Silent Ones Watch, You.* Work out in 2025: *Everything Endless,* a cosmic poetry collaboration with Jamal Hodge; *An Illegal Feast* poetry collaboration with Consuelo G. Flores, Andrea Goyan, Elizabeth Eve King & Elizabeth Wong.

Addison's site: https://www.lindaaddisonwriter.com/
Headshot courtesy of Courtney Hartley